Lightning Attraction:

A year to remember

TESS M GARFIELD

First Published 2015

ISBN: 1517231140
ISBN-13: 978-1517231149

DEDICATION

To Ian, my lightning attraction, or should I say distraction?
He loves it, I hate it. Thank you for protecting me from
all the thunderstorms over the years, except for the one
when I stayed up to comfort the dogs, the very one that
inspired me to write this book!

CONTENTS

ACKNOWLEDGMENTS

I would like to say an enormous thank you to all the people who bought my first book; Virtually Strangers, and another one to those who have sent me feedback or left reviews. Your support has given me endless motivation and focus whilst writing this book.

Being a new author is daunting, but I have been lucky enough to meet some incredibly supportive authors who are always willing to share their knowledge and experience. So I want to take this opportunity to thank them for welcoming me into their community.

Finally, I want to say an extra special thank you to my family for their ongoing encouragement, especially my mum for her sales and distribution skills, and my children, aka The Marketing Committee.

1 PICKING UP THE PIECES

Jessie picked up her phone, looked at the screen, sighed and threw it on the bed. Lisa had been trying to call for two weeks but she couldn't face anybody. Tears began to flood down her cheeks again.

It all started when Mike told her it was over, then took the hand of another woman and walked out of the bar. The feeling of rejection lingered, filling her with a fresh wave of pain every day. Even worse, knowing he had already picked up another woman shrouded her in embarrassment. People must have known. They must have been talking about her.

Lisa had been her best friend since infant school, so although she would understand, her dominating protectiveness would be overwhelming. She would try to force her to move on, but she didn't feel ready. Mike had been her first boyfriend, and although their relationship had been far from perfect, their breakup left her swamped with grief and emptiness.

If it wasn't for the usual clatter of slamming doors and the dull thud of bass music in the student accommodation block around her, Jessie would have been completely isolated and deafened by silence. She walked into the shower-room and gazed at the mirror for a few minutes. The sight staring back wasn't someone she knew. Her normally golden blonde hair hung around her shoulders, dull and messy, limp with no volume. Her crystal blue eyes were reddened, swimming in stagnant tears.

Another door slammed below and footsteps echoed from the staircase on the other side of the wall. She sighed and returned to lay on her bed.

"Jessica Samantha Williamson, open this door

immediately before I kick it open."

She sat up, looking at the door hesitantly. Lisa was serious. Whether or not the door could be kicked open didn't matter. Lisa would certainly try. She was just about to get up to let her in when Lisa knocked loudly. The sound of her knuckles on the solid wooden door echoed through the room.

"I gave you time, but now you need to pull yourself together and pass your exams because that parasite is not worth wasting your—"

She got up and turned the lock. The door swung open and she threw herself back on the bed. Lisa appeared in the doorway, disappointment in her eyes.

The room was compact and clinical, but Jessie had made it feel comfy with fluffy purple cushions, lilac curtains and a purple rug to hide the grubby carpet.

Lisa opened the curtains and opened the window to let some air in, dispersing the stench of grief. She looked at Jessie and shook her head before sitting down beside her on the ruffled duvet.

"Please don't let him ruin your life. The next few weeks are so important and could mean the difference between passing and failing." She rubbed her shoulder softly.

She sniffled and sat up. Lisa fetched some tissue from the shower-room.

"I've covered for you in lectures. I said you're getting over a virus. I also collected handouts and photocopied my notes because you *are* going to pass your exams. It'll be 1st June next week, so you must go back on Monday. You've two weeks to catch up."

"Thank you." She lowered her head and sighed. "But I can't face him. I can't sit there in lectures looking at his smug face."

Lisa knelt down on the soft rug in front of her, making eye contact. She held her hands, and spoke in a lower voice, empathetic and straight from the heart.

"I will be with you every moment, and as soon as exams are over, we'll be going off to Webber Online Media Corporation for a year." She squeezed her hands. "Come on, try to tell me that's not exciting."

Jessie shrugged.

"He just landed himself a placement at a newspaper publisher near his father – 200 miles away."

It surprised her and she felt some relief, but she still had to get through two weeks of lectures and a week of exams. She sniffled into her tissue once more.

"Just focus on July and Webber OMC."

She had been looking forward to her placement and had worked extremely hard for two years to make the grade and secure the position. Webber OMC Ltd produces online and digital media for a vast array of clients. She had wanted to work there for as long as she could remember, so realistically, giving that up wasn't an option. That job was the whole reason behind her studying for a degree in media studies. Lisa was right, allowing Mike to ruin her life would be stupid. She had to accept her help and get through her exams.

Lisa dropped by again on Sunday afternoon. "You're looking brighter. Ready for tomorrow?"

"I guess."

She pulled a pile of paperwork out of her bag and placed them on Jessie's desk. "I've brought the notes I promised. How about I stay over tonight and walk in with you in the morning?"

"Are your brothers getting on your nerves again?"

"Always, but I want to be here to support you, not to avoid them."

She walked over to the bookshelf and picked up a DVD. "One condition. Jim Carey and pizza."

Lisa smiled. "That's more like it."

— ❦ —

Jessie paced the floor, her nerves on edge. She hated Monday mornings at the best of times, but she had to face the world with a smile and show Mike he didn't bother her. Lisa didn't take long to get ready, but looked as stunning as ever with her chestnut brown hair all silky and smooth, and her hazel eyes bright.

In the shower-room, Jessie stared at her reflection in the mirror, desperate to look the best she could. Her eyes looked clearer than they had, and her hair was wavy and golden once more. She looked at her tummy, thighs and bottom, lumpy and round, just as they had always been. She sighed and walked out to join Lisa, putting on a long cardigan.

"It's far too warm for that, you'll melt in the lecture theatre."

"I'm not going to let him gawp at my fat bits. I'll take it off when I sit down." She felt incredibly uncomfortable talking about it. "Let's go before I change my mind."

They set off. Her room in the new north campus accommodation block was only a few minutes walk from the main lecture theatres, but on this occasion it felt much further as she prepared herself for the inevitable reunion with Mike.

Lisa coached her as they walked. "Don't make eye contact with him unless you intend to speak with him. Look confident, smile, laugh even, just don't let it look like he bothers you."

Jessie nodded, her heart pounding. She was a woman on a mission. She had exams to pass. They walked along the path in front of the building and she gasped. Mike stood leaning against the wall, smoking.

"Slow down, but keep walking. Hopefully he'll go inside before we get there." Lisa tugged Jessie's arm lightly. "We can use the back door, then we don't have to walk past his seat."

Mike threw his cigarette end into the bushes, glanced at the girls, snorted and spat on the floor before strolling through the side door. They followed him in slowly and walked up the back staircase. Jessie took a deep breath and followed Lisa in. They sat in their normal seats – near the back – on the opposite side of the curved lecture theatre to Mike. They could see him clearly, sprawled out with his ego radiating around him. His black hair – short on top, shaved at the sides – looked carefully manicured almost daily.

Lisa leaned over. "Are you okay?"

Jessie nodded. Still fixated on Mike. He wore a sleeveless vest, exposing a dirty looking tan and a large snake tattoo, apt for him. Suddenly he turned, burning into her with his dark brown eyes full of hatred and anger. She looked away, returning focus to Martyn, the lecturer who had just arrived.

She didn't want to think about it at all, but she had to wonder why Mike looked so vile. He behaved as though she had dumped him, not the other way around. Martyn soon took her mind off him with his fun and eccentric, teaching style. As a lecturer in his thirties, he always tried to be cool, wearing bright polo shirts with jeans and a stylish flick in his mousy hair. She had carried a flame for him since the very first time she saw him, but he was completely out-of-bounds. She glanced back at Mike before returning her focus to Martyn.

Opposite ends of the spectrum!

After an enthralling hour of Martyn's lecture on the difference between typefaces for print and visual display, they went for a break-time sugar fix.

Lisa leaned against the side of the vending machine. "How are you feeling now?"

"Glad to be back and definitely seeing him in a different light. I used to think he looked cool, but she's obviously massaged his ego because he's coming across as so arrogant. Such a snake."

Lisa nodded. "He's definitely changed. I suspect they hooked up around the time he got his tattoo last month. Plus he's recently taken up smoking just because she does. Talk about putty in her hands."

Mike drifted in from the side door, wreaking of smoke. The ladies turned around and headed back to the lecture theatre, luckily getting through the rest of the lecture without any confrontation.

Lisa chaperoned her for the whole week, and they avoided coming face to face with him, so apart from him glaring in their direction from time to time, they had an uneventful week. She felt much better, even grateful for, her breakup. She had definitely had a lucky escape. The aggression in his eyes made her skin crawl. He had always been quite aggressive and dominant, but every bad thing about him suddenly felt massively amplified. Absence had definitely not made the heart grow fonder on this occasion.

— 🐦 —

Another week neared the end. On Friday afternoon, Jessie lay on a picnic bench outside waiting for Lisa.

A group of students poured out of the building, escaping the sweltering heat inside. Mike wandered past, completely ignoring her. Good riddance.

Lisa peeled off from the back of the group. She shoved Jessie, forcing her to sit up. "You seem more confident around him now. How are you feeling?"

"Grateful for your support the last two weeks. I couldn't have imagined being ready to face exams."

Lisa punched her arm. "There's the spirit. I think we should have a pre-exam night out."

She froze. "I don't think I can. I mean, this is okay, but we'd be more likely to bump into him on a night out, and he's not nice after a few drinks."

"How about a compromise. I could bring the night out to you? We can listen to music, make our own cocktails and order in a curry."

No hesitation. "Go on then, I can manage that."

"Good. I'll come over for around 8pm."

They trooped back into their lecture and joined the rest of the class in yawning a lot.

Martin switched the display off. "Nobody will learn anything this afternoon. Spend the time revising or relaxing, as you wish." He opened the door. "Good luck for next week. I'll see you all in the exam room."

Everybody shuffled their books, laptops and bags, and left. Martyn had always been a soft touch. The rest of the class headed off to the bar, a common occurrence for a Friday afternoon, but Jessie walked to her room while Lisa drove home to get changed.

She got dressed up as she normally would to go out because it made her feel like she was socialising rather than just having a friend over. Good practice for their next big night out. Soon after 7pm the doorbell rang, and as most people were either out or visiting family for the weekend, there was nobody around to open the main door as they had done two weeks earlier. The doorbell rang again.

She's almost an hour early, new for her. She sprinted down the stairs and opened the door.

It wasn't Lisa. It was Mike, and he was drunk. She tried to close the door between them, but he managed to overpower her and get in the way, stopping her from locking him out. He was unsteady, lurching. She retched at the smell of beer and cigarettes on his breath. He tried to grab her but she moved out of the way, leaving him to fall in the doorway. In a moment of panic – while he lay in a heap – she ran outside and took her phone out to call Lisa.

Her hands trembled in time with the pounding of her heart. "He's here, come quick."

He scrambled to his feet and stumbled towards her, reaching for the phone, but she dodged out of his way. His reaction times were slow because of his drunken state, giving her time to fumble with her key and unlock the main door. She closed it between them and ran back upstairs. She could hardly breathe, but he wouldn't give up easily, so she locked her bedroom door and called campus security.

He continued to shout outside her window. "It's over with her, it was a mistake. I want you back."

She waited in hope for help to arrive. It could have been so much worse if somebody else had opened the door. She shuddered at the thought. He continued to shout and began to throw stones at the window. She paced the floor, terrified, but felt secure behind two locked doors, as long as he remained outside.

It seemed like an age had passed, but it was only a

quarter of an hour. Mike suddenly went quiet, and assuming security might be there, she peeped through the window. Lisa had arrived and she faced up to him, showing no fear. Their quiet dispute filled Jessie with dread because he knew no boundaries. Their exchange got physical and Jessie observed as he kept reaching out to her, grabbing and stumbling. Just as the security patrol car pulled up nearby, he pushed her. She retaliated by slapping him.

Good for her.

She ran down the stairs and out onto the path, meeting a very angry Lisa. Two security guards escorted Mike to the main gate, returning to reassure the girls they had warned him not to come back.

Lisa threw her arms around Jessie. "I'm so glad you're ok."

"Thank you for coming to my rescue."

Lisa gave her a shove. "I only came for the drama."

Jessie rolled her eyes.

They wouldn't let Mike ruin their evening, so they continued as planned and made a jug of fruity vodka punch, lined up two glasses and drank to girl power. Jessie didn't really feel powerful, but the sentiment still counted. By the time they reached the bottom of the jug, they were both quite tipsy and Jessie expressed her thanks for the umpteenth time.

Lisa shook her head. "You don't have to keep saying that, I couldn't just let that idiot hurt you." She wrapped her arms around Jessie.

"I do because you're my hero and I love you."

Lisa lifted her head from Jessie's shoulder, making eye contact, then in the blink of an eye they kissed, a real lingering, full-on passionate kiss. As their lips parted, Jessie realised what had just happened, but before she had time to think or say anything, Lisa grabbed her bag and headed for the door.

"Lisa, where—"

"That shouldn't have happened." She opened the door and left at speed.

The door slammed shut behind her. Jessie couldn't think straight because she had drunk too much. She couldn't even begin to comprehend what had just happened. Who kissed who? She loved Lisa, but it wasn't *that* sort of love.

Maybe I gave her the wrong idea when I said I loved her.

She lay on her bed while the world spun around her, unable to do anything. Her thoughts spiralled along with the room, from Mike to Lisa, then to the ultimately trendy lecturer Martyn who she had secretly fancied for such a long time.

The room soon stopped swirling and she found herself fighting with Mike and Lisa over who loved who. It became quite confusing, and nothing made much sense, but her vodka fuelled dreams rarely did.

She woke with the hangover from hell and looked through the window, remembering what had happened the previous evening. She wasn't sure if it had all been part of her dream, but seeing Lisa's silver Mini outside confirmed her fears. Among her mixed feelings, relief washed over her. Driving after so many drinks would have been dumb, though how she had got home would be anybody's guess.

As the morning went on, she kept checking to see if the Mini had been collected, then started to worry. Mike might have got her. She rushed to the window to see if Lisa's bag was visible in the car, but this time found it gone. A feeling of relief was soon replaced by sadness. She had collected the car without dropping in. Then she remembered the kiss. Lisa must have been extremely upset. She felt awful

Torn apart by confusion, she couldn't bring herself to contact Lisa because she didn't know how to explain her feelings. She just didn't feel *that* way. She felt embarrassed about allowing herself to cross the line. They had always been close, and spent many weekends together, but nothing like this had ever happened before, not even almost. She decided to wait and allow Lisa to come to her, after all, she was the one who left in a hurry.

She spent the rest of the weekend revising so didn't have much time to think about Lisa or Mike. They would no doubt be doing exactly the same thing.

On Monday morning Lisa arrived just in time, not even looking in Jessie's direction. A tense atmosphere lingered like an invisible brick wall. It was too late to apologise, so she decided to focus on her exams and wait for Lisa to approach her.

—  —

Exam week was difficult, but the whole week had gone by and while Mike keeping his distance pleased her, she felt saddened by Lisa's avoidance. She had nobody to celebrate the end of exams with, and she had ruined her friendship with her best friend. The devastation left her feeling dreadful. The week ahead should have been a fun-filled week, making the most of their time before starting work. Instead, it would be a lonely week of waiting, not knowing how she would cope when Lisa snubs her on their first day at work. She spent the week toying with the idea of calling or texting Lisa, but she was in a tailspin, the excruciating fear of rejection held her back.

2 STARTING WORK

It was Monday morning and Jessie felt nervous. Desperate to make a good impression on her first day, she planned to arrive early. Her excitement had been overshadowed by her worry over Lisa, but with a two week induction ahead of them, she hoped it would give her time to clear the air and make a fresh start. The last thing she needed was to enter this new chapter of her life with a lingering fear of controversy.

"Good morning. My name is Jessica Williamson. It's my first day. I'm due to meet George Wong."

The receptionist tapped away at her computer. "It's nice to meet you. I'm Jane. George should be down soon. Would you like to take a seat?"

"Thank you, Jane."

She sat down, assuming she was first to arrive. The large glass atrium felt light and airy, and from where she sat, the staff canteen looked like a hive of activity. People wandered in, collected coffee and made their way up the large spiral staircase.

"Good morning, Jessica." George offered his hand.

She stood and shook his hand. "Nice to see you again."

He led the way to the training suite. "How did your exams go?"

"I survived!" She giggled. "I don't like exams."

George opened the door for her and smirked. "Good job we just make you do the fun stuff then."

She smiled.

His phone rang. "I'll get some drinks for everybody when I get back. I have some more people to collect."

Her heart was in her mouth. She psyched herself

up, expecting Lisa to walk through the door at any moment. It was a false alarm. He arrived back with two young men. She felt partially relieved, but it was only delaying the inevitable. She wanted the reunion with Lisa over with.

"Jessica, this is Max and Ethan, also on the student placement scheme." He ran his fingers over his tablet. "We're expecting two more, then we can start."

Max slouched. "Did you have exams last week?"

"The week before last. You?"

Ethan sat beside Max, fiddling with his phone. "We finished on Thursday."

"You two go to the same university?"

Ethan nodded. "We share a house too."

"Cool." She kept half an eye on George.

He tapped his tablet, then looked up. "We've just got one person to wait for now."

One? I thought he said two. He must have been confused.

The phone rang again. Lisa had obviously arrived.

"Thank you Jane, I'll collect her now." George stood and made his way to the door.

This is it then. The moment of truth. She took a few deep breaths and braced herself, but when George returned, he was accompanied by a young lady called Claire.

What had happened with Lisa. Maybe she requested a transfer. She had other placement options and didn't care where she went. She choose Webber OMC to be with Jessie.

George began but Jessie didn't concentrate. She couldn't help but wonder about Lisa, hoping she was just running late, but as the morning went on, that became much less likely.

The whole day went by, but Lisa didn't arrive. Jessie

resigned herself to reality. Lisa had obviously changed her plans, and they wouldn't be spending the year together after all. Although mildly relieved at not having to face her, she felt extremely disappointed and worried, hoping she was okay.

— 🐝 —

After a restless night, Jessie returned to work on Tuesday ready to focus. She would face her issues with Lisa another time. Entering the training suite, the last thing she expected was to find Lisa sitting there. She gasped. All her inhibitions fizzled away.

"I was so worried about you when you weren't here yesterday. Is everything okay?"

"My youngest brother was in hospital. He fell off the garage roof on Sunday. We were all extremely worried about him because my dad found him unconscious with a cut on his head."

She sat beside Lisa. "Oh my, is he okay now?"

"He's on the mend. Still in hospital for observation, but the doctors are reassured by his test results. He certainly won't be climbing on the garage roof any time soon."

George walked in with Ethan and Max. Claire followed a moment later.

She greeted them with a nod, lowered her voice and seized the moment. "Look, can we have lunch together today? We should talk."

"Yes, please, I was going to ask you the same thing."

— 🐝 —

At lunchtime, they walked to the park opposite their building. A tense atmosphere lingered. They avoided heavy conversation by commenting on the trees and flowerbeds, but they needed to clear the air if they had any hope of moving on. A curve in the path took them to a large duck pond, and at the side, a chunky wooden bench.

Jessie stopped. "Should we sit here to eat?"

"Sure. It's a nice sunny spot."

They sat, not too close. Lisa placed her bag between them, like a physical barrier.

"Look, Lisa. I'm so sorry for kissing you." Jessie struggled to look her in the eye. "I didn't mean to, it must have been the cocktails." She couldn't bear the tension and looked away, pretending to stare at a baby duck nearby. "I love you, but not in *that* way. I really hope you can forgive me for—"

"I thought I did it. I really don't remember."

Jessie looked back suddenly, feeling less guilty, but it still seemed awkward.

"I'm sorry I ran off. I was embarrassed."

Jessie sighed. "I don't remember how it happened either."

"Well whatever happened, can we just take joint responsibility and move on?" Lisa shrugged. "Like you said, I love you, just not like *that*. Besides, I really miss you."

The air felt much clearer. It was a relief to have got it out in the open.

"I couldn't agree more, I felt so embarrassed because I thought I had upset you."

Lisa nodded. "Snap, great minds, eh!"

They finished their sandwiches while they watched people passing by, mostly individuals, smartly dressed, clearly on their lunch breaks, doing exactly the same as them.

Several minutes had passed when Lisa broke the silence. "Have you had any more contact from Mike?"

"No. Absolutely nothing. I assume he travelled to his dad's as soon as exams finished. Besides, I think the security guards really spooked him, or at least I hope so."

Lisa held up her hands widening her eyes. "Oh, yes. I almost forgot. I heard somebody in the bar talking about that Tracy girl he went off with, and if I heard it correctly, they said she had to get an injunction out against him."

Jessie suddenly turned her whole body towards her. "Seriously, who said that?"

"One of those first year lads on the football team, he's on the same course as her. And look. While we're clearing the air, I need to admit something. I should have told you sooner. Mike tried it on with me three or four times while you were together, he didn't get anywhere, but I was stupid not to tell you."

"Nothing surprises me where he's concerned, truly, but I won't hold it against you." Jessie gave her a reassuring wink and smile.

She was momentarily distracted. A young man with blonde hair walked past, he smiled at her and she smiled back. He was in his mid 20s and exceptionally smart in black trousers and a crisp white shirt.

Lisa nudged her. "Eyes back in your head please."

She craned her neck to watch the passerby. "Sorry but he's a real sexy boy!"

"Jessie!" She furrowed her brow. "He's hardly a boy."

"Minor detail. Let's head back."

Sadly, the sexy boy had vanished from sight on the path where it weaved between the trees and bushes. She was disappointed, but if he visited the park regularly, she may bump into him again at some stage.

At the end of a tiring two week induction, the five students arranged to go for drinks. George recommended The Red Lion at the end of the road, so that was ideal. Jessie looked forward to having a night out without the danger of running into Mike. Avoiding social situations had been a necessary sacrifice. She had been keeping a careful eye out in the park for the sexy boy every lunchtime, but it must have been a one-off.

Claire arrived at The Red Lion first, closely followed by Jessie and Lisa. Claire was stunningly attractive with a gothic-like appearance. She wore quite a lot of makeup, especially thick black eyeliner that overpowered her big brown eyes. Jessie studied her quietly, observing. Her finest feature was definitely her long black hair with a glossy cherry tint, trailing over her short, petite figure. The three ladies pushed together two small tables, making space for Max and Ethan, and ordered a round of drinks.

"What do you think of the boys then?" Claire raised her eyebrows.

This was Lisa's sort of conversation, her favourite subject, boys.

"I've never been too keen on guys with blonde hair, so Ethan is definitely not my type, but Max is rather cute." Lisa puckered her lips. "She's off men though, so her opinion definitely doesn't count."

Jessie rolled her eyes and started giggling. "More trouble than they're worth, I'm off to join a convent next year to get away from them."

"She got dumped recently by the *bad boy* on our course. But she knows she's better off without him."

Jessie laughed. She slapped Lisa's arm. Claire

laughed at them as they slapped each other playfully.

Jessie held her arm out to shield herself. "So what do *you* think?"

Claire smiled, her cheeks turning pink. "I think…"

Max and Ethan walked in. They replaced their chatter with laughter, and while the guys stood at the bar, Lisa quickly probed for a response.

"Go on, quick, what do you think? Do I have competition?"

"No. I prefer Ethan's Scandinavian attributes." She peered over at the blonde guy. "Just look at him."

Jessie looked over to see what Claire meant because she hadn't really paid much attention to their looks. Ethan was short with light blonde hair, blue eyes and a very pale complexion. She was just thinking about how young he looked, then realised he was smiling back at them. She looked away quickly, hoping he didn't see her staring.

They were just getting over the awkwardness of their giggling when a man approached to ask if they wanted to take part in the quiz, and after a short discussion, they agreed to participate. While they disputed a suitable team name, Jessie studied Max. He had broad shoulders, dark hair, brown eyes, and a very masculine stubbly jaw line. She could see how Lisa would find him attractive. Rough and ready, but definitely not something she was looking for.

"University Challengers." Ethan slapped his hands on the table.

They all just looked at him and shook their heads.

Claire bounced up and down. "Flaming Five?"

Lisa giggled. "You can tell we're strangers, still to find something we have in common."

They all started laughing.

Max waved his arms in front of the group, grabbing their attention. "Absolute Strangers!"

It wasn't great, but it fitted, so they went for it, after all, the quiz was starting soon. They argued and laughed all the way through, coming up with some hilariously wrong answers because they couldn't agree on anything. Still it wasn't about winning, it was about taking part, or so Ethan claimed. As they all drank more and more, Claire and Ethan started becoming more physical, putting their arms around each other giggling for no reason, leaving Jessie and Lisa to entertain Max, who took it on himself to try and entertain them instead. He was funny, but Jessie and Lisa excused themselves to visit the ladies.

"Did you want to come back to mine tonight?"

Lisa was washing her hands. She didn't even look up. "No, I can't. Sorry."

"I won't kiss you, I promise!" Jessie smiled.

"Oh no, sorry, please don't get me wrong, I plan to leave soon because I don't have a key, and I don't want to wake the family."

Jessie shrugged. She didn't push the subject, but wondered if it was just an to save her feelings.

When Lisa left, she started to feel extremely uncomfortable. Ethan and Claire were all over each other, leaving her with Max, with whom she had absolutely nothing in common. She certainly had no interest in pairing up with him. She tried to keep the other two involved in their conversation, but as soon as they ended up attached at the lips, Max started digging out his worst chat up lines. Jessie felt under pressure. She definitely didn't want to give him the wrong impression. She just had to leave.

She downed the rest of her drink. "I best be getting

home. I'm expecting a phone call from Australia."

"That's the worst escape line ever." Max laughed.

"Seriously. My parents live down under, so I can only talk to them late at night!" It wasn't all a lie, but it was enough. She felt bad for leaving him, but she didn't want to be forced into a position where she had to reject any alcohol induced advances. She had enough experience from Mike.

— 🐦 —

She woke up on Saturday feeling quite guilty for leaving Max on his own with the lovebirds, but she knew she had made the best decision for herself. She hadn't thought about Lisa, and how she fitted into it, until she landed on the doorstep.

"I hope you didn't get the wrong idea last night. I really did have to get home early, but I can see how you might have interpreted it."

"I did initially think you were avoiding being alone with me, but if I didn't believe you, I wouldn't be a very good friend, so I didn't think about it. Besides, I had much more to think about after you left."

Lisa looked intrigued. She fetched them both a drink, and sat down ready for Jessie to fill her in on the gossip.

"Claire and Ethan were full on, and I'd be surprised if they haven't woken up together this morning. Being left with Max was, well, kind of interesting." Jessie gave her a side look.

Lisa looked slightly shocked. "Did you move in on my man?"

She looked at her in amazement, eyes wide open, bottom lip falling. "No, oh no, I didn't feel comfortable so I left soon after you did! Anyway, when did you officially stake your claim on him?"

Lisa just laughed. "You looked so worried then. Anyway, look. How about I make up for last night. We can have a cinema night followed by drinks."

"Of course. I—"

"On one condition." Lisa cleared her throat. "As long as I can stay over."

Jessie couldn't help but wonder if she was trying to prove a point, but as she was pleased to have her friend back.

"That's hardly a condition. More like a given if we're having drinks."

The morning after the night before. Luckily much less eventful than their previous night alone together. There was no repeat of the kissing incident, and Jessie felt relieved because she had worried about whether the kiss would change the dynamics of their friendship. They sat and discussed work over breakfast on Sunday, excited about being allocated to their departments on Monday.

Lisa leaned over and took a slice of Jessie's toast. "It's going to be strange splitting up and mixing with the regular staff, don't you think?"

"Yes, I just hope we fit in." Jessie snatched her toast back. "Get your own toast."

Lisa put another slice in the toaster. "I'm sure it'll be fine. Just different."

When Lisa left, Jessie tried to imagine what the office would be like and whether she would be sitting near the window so she could see the park. She imagined the people, expecting the worst. At least then things could only get better.

3 A PERFECT VIEW

Jessie arrived at work feeling terrified. Being allocated to a department and having to face real people was far more daunting than their induction. They all met at the training suite in the comfy sofa area, and awaited their fate.

George thundered into the room. "Good morning. I trust you all rested up at the weekend ready for a hard week." He perched on the edge of the table. "Now, Ethan, Max, Claire, your manager is on leave, so Kathy will look after you today. She'll be along soon to show you to your office on the second floor."

Jessie and Lisa looked at each other. He handed them both a laminated sheet and headed to the door.

"If you two would like to follow me, we're destined for the fifth floor." He led the way.

Jessie scoured the seating plan as they stood in the cramped lift, wondering what the point of the plan was if he could just show them their desks. There were rows and rows of names she had never heard of before, they didn't mean a thing to her. She spotted her own name and searched for Lisa's. They were to be seated near each other, only separated diagonally by an aisle and one other seat, so it wasn't too bad.

The lift came to a halt and they stepped out. To their left, the long spiral staircase led back to where they came from, and to their right, a set of double doors. They followed George and were immediately shocked by how big the office was. All open plan with vertical rows of desks as illustrated on the laminated seating plan. They walked nervously through the office, a hundred or so eyes following them. George stopped and waved his hand at an empty desk at the aisle end.

"There you go Jessica, this is your desk. Lisa will be just over here." He took a step forward, turned to the right and stopped at the second desk along.

Jessie blinked, looked away, blinked again and looked back. Lisa was only sitting right next to sexy boy from the park. She mouthed at Lisa, indicating discreetly with her eyes. It took Lisa a moment, but her open mouth confirmed she recognised him. Talk about wanting a nice view, diagonally opposite him, she couldn't have got a more perfect view.

She worked through a short tick list, checking that her workstation had all the software she needed, setting up passwords and mapping network drives, nothing too taxing. She kept glancing over at Lisa, and every time, she was met with a nice smile from sexy boy himself. She smiled back, losing herself in his dreamy eyes.

She checked her seating plan discreetly and identified him as Dean Whittle.

He must be an Online Content Developer too.

She tried to focus on her screen, but every time he moved from his seat, she studied him, admiring his ash blonde hair and swimming in his bright greenish blue eyes. They were like an ocean of pure pleasure. He wore dark trousers and a white shirt, just as he had in the park two weeks ago. Smart, but relaxed, no tie. His smile gave her goose bumps and little tingles, and the spicy wood fragrance of his aftershave made her mouth water.

Lunchtime couldn't come soon enough. She was bursting to talk to Lisa.

"I don't understand the fascination you and Claire have with blonde men." Lisa shrugged. "Dark and handsome all the way for me."

"It's not purely a blonde thing. Ethan is far too blonde for me, and Mike certainly isn't blonde. Okay, bad example. Mike was an arse."

They were looking for somewhere to sit with their sandwiches

"We could go back to the bench by the pond."

Lisa raised her eyebrows. "Just in case he walks past again? You've been drooling over him all morning."

"No, it's just nice there." She tried to sound convincing, but a smile tried to squeeze out, giving away her true intent.

"Oh come on then. We need to get you back in the saddle again."

They walked to the park and sat on the same bench next to the pond. They were eating their sandwiches and chatting about what they had been doing all morning, but Jessie kept an eye open for Dean, just in case. He didn't walk past this time, even though she watched all the paths, willing him to turn up. It had been two weeks since that chance meeting, so she resigned herself to the fact it must have been a one off last time.

She cleared her throat, grinning. "His name's Dean."

"Oh, my God. You're like the total stalker. What colour underpants is he wearing?"

"I've no idea. How am—"

"I'll give you until the end of the week to find out."

Jessie frowned. She felt like she was being mocked.

Back in the office, George introduced them to individual members of the department to help them

settle in. "Now, the people you will be working most closely with are the Online Project Managers." He headed towards Dean's desk.

Lisa nudged her. Her heart pounded. She was about to speak to the sexy boy for the very first time. They had shared endless shy smiles during the morning, but she had yet to hear his voice.

"Hi, Dean. I expect you've spoken with Lisa already, since she has been sitting beside you, but this is Jessica. They'll be working on some of your projects during their placement with us this next year."

"Hi. I'm pleased to meet you both." He blushed. "My name is Dean Whittle and I'm one of the Online Project Managers. I predominantly look after the short to mid-term projects for corporate clients, so I expect we'll be spending quite a lot of time together in the coming months."

Jessie could feel herself melting, not just because of the heat, but because Dean sounded so sweet. He showed them some of the work he was pulling together ready for a client review meeting. It was very impressive. She suddenly felt totally justified in her career plans. The variety of work and scope for creativity in digital media had no boundaries. There was a certain hot blonde too, but she tried not to focus on him too much.

She just about felt brave enough to speak up. "I can imagine it to be massively fulfilling to take a few paper-based scribbles like that." She pointed at his project folder. "And turn them into something like that." She diverted her finger towards his screen.

"It is. Nothing motivates me more than anticipating the end result. If George can spare you for a few hours, you'll have to join me at a client review."

She had to make a conscious effort to stop her mouth from falling open. Lisa widened her eyes.

"I think that would be great experience for them. We can compare calendars later." George poked at the tablet that may as well have been surgically attached to his hand.

Jessie walked away feeling like she was walking on air. His gentle voice still as fresh as the spicy smell of his alluring aftershave. They moved on to meet Colin and Janet, two more Online Project Managers, but they weren't as interesting. She wanted to get back to organising her calendar when Dean. She had just arrived back at her desk with George approached.

"I would like you to start working on a short task for Colin. It should only take a few hours. Lisa is going to join Dean in his client review meeting."

She gasped. "Oh sorry." She coughed. "Of course. That'll be great." It didn't feel great though. It felt like Lisa had bagged her man.

Colin gave her a dull spreadsheet to crosscheck copyrights. That certainly wasn't very inspiring. Lisa looked over and gave her an apologetic look, but she understood it wasn't her fault.

Green with envy, she sat in front of her screen and watched Lisa and Dean leave the office together. Lisa glanced in her direction and gave her another apologetic smile and shrug, clearly knowing Jessie would have preferred to go instead.

The spreadsheet exercise was tiresome and unfulfilling, and she kept looking at the time, wondering what was going on in the meeting.

Almost two hours later, they returned laughing and smiling, but when Lisa caught her eye, she obviously remembered the man she was laughing with was the same man Jessie had been lusting after. She excused herself to visit the ladies. Dean made his way towards his desk, blushing in response to Jessie's gaze.

"How did the meeting go?"

He sat in his chair and leaned towards her. "They were really pleased and approved most of what we presented." He sighed. "I wish you could've been there. I think you would have got a lot out of it."

One thing she would have got out of it is two hours with him, but putting that image aside, she managed to formulate a more professional response. "I was disappointed to miss the meeting because having seen you preparing the presentation, I would've liked to have seen their reactions. I was impressed, and I'm not the one who requested the project."

"I've got another one soon for another project, so I'll get George to pencil you. You can help with the preparation, then accompany me to the meeting." He sounded upbeat and enthusiastic.

She felt happy enough with that. "That sounds perfect. I can't wait."

He smiled and returned to his work.

— 🍎 —

The ladies spent the rest of the week working on an education project for Colin. They were surprised when he revealed he used to lecture in the media department at their university. It was before their time, but he knew some of their lecturers, including Edward Jameson.

"Is he still known as Dead Ed?"

Lisa started laughing. "Yes, has he always been stone-faced and monotone then?"

Colin smiled. "Yes, that's a first class description. He's a nice guy though, definitely knows his subject."

It was very surreal to know he could have been one of their lecturers, but they didn't hold it against him. They refocused on their work, pleased to finally get round to some creative work, populating a website with diagrams. They were more than pleased to know it was for the science faculty of their own university, you can't get more fulfilling than that.

After a productive week, Lisa had Friday afternoon off for a dentist appointment, so Jessie walked her to her car at lunchtime before wandering to the park. She sat quietly on the bench near the duck pond, ate her sandwich and pulled out her phone. She was startled by a familiar voice beside her.

"Hi, do you come here often then?"

She looked up to find Dean sitting beside her. She almost choked because having looked out for him all week, without any luck, she didn't expect him to just turn up as soon as she was alone.

"Most days, you?" She smiled, her cheeks warming.

"Occasionally. How's your week going so far?"

She tried not to look too happy to be in his company, but her pulse raced. His proximity made her nervous. She clamped her shaking hands between her knees. "Very good. It's been nice to put theory into practice at last. It probably sounds crazy, but I'm motivated by results."

"You and me both. It's a sign of your true passion. I see it in your eyes."

She swallowed hard. That's not the only passion in her eyes, but she played it cool and changed the subject. She fanned herself with a flailing hand. "I can't believe the temperature is set to hit 32 by the end of next week, last week was so mild."

"Another muggy heatwave. Just what we need."

He glanced at his watch. "Do you want to walk back with me?"

She looked at her watch. "Of course, I didn't notice the time."

"Time flies when you're having fun."

I'd like to have a little more fun with him!

"Here's the plan. I'll drive over to yours, we'll take a taxi to Purple Passion. Max, Ethan and Claire will meet us there. We can get hammered, and I can stay at yours."

Jessie yawned, glad Lisa couldn't see down the phone. "Okay. I'm only doing it for you though."

"Live a little. You stay in too much. Let your hair down and party. You'll thank me one day."

"I said okay. Don't push it. I'll see you later." She threw the phone on the bed and slumped.

Promising to visit the new cocktail bar on Saturday night had been a dumb idea. Lisa would always hold her to it, and being a fancy place, on opening night, she had to dress up to fit in. She scoured the wardrobe and found a sparkly black top. *I can wear that with black jeans. No-one will notice because it'll be dark.*

Lisa arrived, walked in and shook her head. "You so can't wear that to go to a cocktail bar."

"Why not? It's not like I'm on a mission to pull. Who cares what I wear? Just be glad I'm going."

She sighed. "As you wish. I'll call a taxi."

The Purple Passion looked very modern and trendy. The mirrored walls made it look much bigger than it actually was. They weaved in and out of people and made their way to the bar, where Lisa ordered two Purple Cosmos - whatever they where. Jessie stared at the rows and rows of brightly coloured bottles to avoid making eye contact with anybody. So much for it being dark, the neon lights in the window and around the edge of the bar illuminated everything. She normally tried to avoid busy places, but once again, gave in to peer pressure.

Lisa nudged her. "There they are, near the window."

She spotted Claire waving an arm in the air and they battled to get through the crowd. They had a great table except for the bight lighting. The glowing drink looked toxic, but Lisa assured her it was just vodka with extra colour. The hum of background chatter meant everybody had to shout, so Jessie didn't bother. It only added to her misery. Ethan and Claire were as close as they had been at The Red Lion, and Lisa was all over Max like a rash.

Jessie didn't know where to look. The kissing couples made her feel invisible. Wrapping around each other shamelessly. Hands, flesh and tongues. Oh, get a room. She downed her drink imagining it was a love potion. If she couldn't be invisible, she wanted a little bit of what they had. Looking over at the bar, she met the gaze of Dean.

Oh, my...

Maybe she was imagining it. She blinked a few times and looked back, but there he was, real as ever. He stood near the bar with two other men. Not wanting to appear ignorant, she raised her hand in a nervous wave, which he returned with a gorgeous smile. She suddenly wished she had made more of an effort. She swallowed hard. He had started to make his way over to their table.

She looked at her empty glass. *Love potion indeed.*

Being the only singleton in a group of five had been

the worst feeling in the world, but being approached by sexy Dean took the edge off her agony.

"Do you mind if we join you?"

She shuffled over, allowing him to squeeze onto the bench beside her. His friends perched on tall stools behind. Lisa didn't even appear to notice. Claire stood up, clinging to Ethan, waving goodbye.

Lisa looked up at the back of Claire and Ethan as they drifted onto the street outside. She leaned close to Jessie and said something, but the combination of music and chatter made it difficult to understand.

"You wanted to do what?"

"No. Max wants me to go home with him."

Jessie pouted. Abandoned again. An all too familiar event.

"You're in safe hands, so do you mind if I go?"

How could she refuse? It wasn't her place to give or deny permission. She looked at her male company, then back at Lisa where she clung to Max. She wasn't happy at being the only one left, especially when she was the one who hadn't wanted to go to a noisy cocktail bar in the first place, but her compensation was the sexy boy at her side.

"No, you go, I'll be fine."

Lisa and Max practically fell through the door and onto the pavement outside. Laughing the whole time. Jessie shuddered, grateful to be almost sober. Although slightly uncomfortable at being abandoned by her best friend. She felt very safe in Dean's hands.

She turned to him, leaning in to make herself heard. "Looks like I'm stuck with you guys if you don't mind."

"Stuck is a strong word. We're planning to move on to our regular haunt, so if you don't mind being stuck with us, you're more than welcome to tag along."

"Where is this place?" She leaned close enough to get a brief whiff of his aftershave. The fresh woody fragrance had spicy overtones and took her breath away. Wandering hands, flesh and tongues seemed much more appealing all of a sudden.

"A little place down by the river. The Old English. If not, we can drop you home in a taxi?" He lowered his chin, smiling gently. His eyes fixed firmly on hers.

She could almost hear him telepathically willing her to say yes. "Will I like The Old English?"

"Yes. I think you'll fit right in. Do you play pool?"

"I love pool, but I'm not very good." She started chuckling. "Actually, I'm awful, but it's fun and beats this upmarket, overpriced and crowded hellhole."

It didn't matter where they were going. If she had a personal invite from him, she couldn't refuse.

They piled into a taxi and set off.

"Sorry. I should have done this earlier. Jessie, this is Dan, and this is Rob."

They offered a polite nod, nonplused by her presence. Dan was short, black, with short dark hair and huge brown eyes. Rob was tall, lightly tanned with light brown hair and brown eyes.

The taxi pulled up outside The Old English. She had never been inside, but she vaguely knew the area.

Inside, the pub was quite old and had a lot of character, low ceilings with beams and a big open fireplace, which luckily wasn't lit on such a warm summer evening. They made their way through the bar to the pool table near the back.

Dan flashed his wallet at her. "What would you like to drink?"

"Brandy and coke please."

He headed to the bar while Rob set up the pool table. Dean passed her a cue and flipped a coin.

Rob rubbed his stubbly chin. "Heads"

The coin spun, dropped and bounced on the green table before landing tail side up.

Dean looked at her with a smile. "It looks like you're playing me first."

He played well. Her lack of skill came as no surprise, but she hit a couple of balls in. Rob wandered off to fetch another round of drinks and completely missed Dean's absolute classic shot on the black. A nicely lined up shot. No way could he ever miss. She put her cue on the rack and sat down, looking back just in time to see the black drop into the far corner pocket, right on target, followed smoothly by the white. He hung his head in shame.

Dan cheered loudly.

She couldn't believe her luck. Dean sat down beside her and shrugged. Could he be skilled enough to do that on purpose? Would he?

Rob set up ready to play her, but she had no chance. Her coordination was way off, probably due to the brandy and coke topping up her cocktail, so she sat aside with Dean while his friends played each other. The end of the game coincided with last orders.

Dean pointed to the bar. "Another drink?"

Jessie passed. "Not for me, I've definitely had enough, but can I buy a round before I call a taxi?"

"No thank you. Me an' Rob are off for a take away." Dan sounded like he'd had enough too.

She looked at Dean.

"Not for me. You can buy next time. I can drop you off in a taxi if you like because I'll rest better if I know you're home safe."

She couldn't refuse when he put it like that, but feeling uncoordinated, she needed a steady hand to support her. He took her all the way to her bedroom door, ensuring she got up the stairs okay. She opened the door and stumbled inside.

He stood in the doorway. "Sleep well and I'll see you on Monday. Oh, but don't tell anyone you beat me at pool."

"I didn't really beat you, you just messed it up." She broke into a drunken giggle.

He smiled and left.

She watched from the window with a mix of relief and disappointment as he climbed into the waiting taxi. He looked very sexy, but if they had hooked up, work might have been a little awkward. She threw herself on the bed, in no state to make such an important decision.

I'll save him for another day.

4 PROFESSIONAL DISTANCE

Jessie woke on Sunday morning to birds singing and the summer sun glaring through a gap in her curtains. She had a sudden recollection of Dean in her doorway, just before she fell asleep. She got up and paced the floor, talking to herself.

What if he thinks I'm rude for not inviting him in.

Her guilt played on her mind. She started to imagine inviting him in, then remembered work.

I couldn't do that, it'd make things awkward. I just hope he doesn't hold it against me.

She doubted herself. She had let a seriously hot guy walk away. It might have been her one, single opportunity of a lifetime.

He might never... no, he's sensible, he should understand.

Things could have turned out so differently. So much better. Waking up next to him would be a real treat, but she had always thought drunken desire lacked meaning, so through her emotional turbulence, she felt relieved. She hadn't allowed her lustful thoughts to corrupt her.

She continued to pace. It would only have spoilt their evening and made working with him difficult. Soon, her thoughts drifted to Lisa and Max, a clear justification for her own actions. She had spent many hours picking up the pieces from Lisa's mistakes.

She had a mouthful of toothpaste when her phone rang. She spat out and rushed to see who it was. Lisa's picture flashed on her screen. She answered.

"Are you on your own?"

She almost choked. "On my own?"

Lisa elaborated. "Do you have a certain hot blonde male in your bedroom?"

She tried not to sound outraged. "No, it's just me, where are you?"

"On my way to see you."

The line went dead.

A few minutes later, the doorbell rang. She briefly hoped Dean had returned to give her another chance, but that wouldn't happen in the real world. She ran down the stairs and opened the door. Lisa looked radiant, especially considering the state she was in when she left Purple Passion with Max.

"Sorry about last night, I had to seize the moment." She poked Jessie in the arm. "Besides, you were rather comfortable with three handsome gentlemen. Lucky girl."

Jessie avoided the subject, still unsure how she felt about passing up such an opportunity. "So you went home with Max?"

"I had planned to but he passed out in the taxi. I got the driver to drop me at home before taking him to his place." She sighed. "It's a shame. Dean's friends were cute."

Jessie chuckled. "You're crazy. You think everyone's cute!"

It wasn't long before Lisa began her interrogation about what happened after she left, but the details of Jessie's evening at The Old English only made her regret running off with Max.

"So he brought you all the way back here, right to this door, but you didn't invite him in?" Lisa sounded shocked and extremely disappointed.

Jessie nodded, still unsure how she felt about it. "He had a taxi waiting. That's not a man expecting an overnight stay."

Lisa looked slightly bemused. "Opportunities like

that don't happen often. You must be mad."

She felt mad, but she couldn't tell Lisa that.

"I wouldn't want to make things awkward at work. It wasn't an easy decision."

Lisa sat on the rug cross legged. "I didn't think of that. I can understand your reasoning to an extent."

Not that she had made a conscious decision, but Lisa doesn't need to know that. She sat twiddling her fingers, thinking about what Lisa had said, combined with her own feelings.

"I can see you're struggling with your decision."

Jessie shrugged. "I need to get to know him better, then maybe see what happens."

"If you really like him, don't let him slip through your fingers. Even the fact he walked away from here last night without trying to come in proves he's much too good to walk away from."

"Or he doesn't actually like me."

Lisa shook her head. "I don't believe that."

"Whatever will be will be, but until then, can we just have a girlie weekend next week? No dodgy cocktail bars or men who pass out in taxis."

"As long as it doesn't interrupt your love life."

Jessie sighed and looked heavenwards. She didn't even have a love life.

— 🍂 —

After a quiet evening by herself, Jessie felt refreshed and excited about returning to work on Monday morning. She arrived nice and early to get a good parking space, and after reversing her little blue Ka into a nice shady space under a tree, she sat for a few moments planning how she would approach talking to Dean after Saturday.

What if he wanted something more? He might feel let down.

She ran through different scenarios, not denying how much she liked him, but worried she may have missed her only chance. She pictured his smiles and the way he blushes. Maybe he does that to everybody.

Men are so damn confusing.

She sighed, shook her head and pulled together her bag and lunchbox. She reached for the door lever, but hesitated. A black car had just driven into the space beside her, so she waited for it to straighten up and stop. She turned her head ready to get out and there she discovered Dean's greenish-blue eyes looking straight at her. Her heart skipped a beat. They sat staring at each other for a few seconds, smiling. His cheeks flushed, his eyes warm and welcoming, definitely not offended or rejected.

"You first!" He mouthed with a smile.

They were parked door to door and would clash if they opened at the same time. She giggled and got out carefully, desperate not to scratch his flashy car.

He jumped out of his Mazda RX8 and flipped open the back to collect a small grey rucksack. "Good morning. You're keen." He joined her to walk towards the main path.

"Only for a decent parking space. Obviously." She laughed.

He looked at her straight faced. "It's okay, I know you can't resist me."

"Oh, I didn't know you would be here this early." An air of panic crossed her mind.

He started laughing. "Only joking. The look on your face was funny though."

She slapped his arm and joined in with his laughter. He wasn't wrong though. Saturday night flashed into her mind, but she didn't dare to mention it. Luckily he didn't bring it up either.

They continued to walk slowly towards the building and she had a sudden vision. They were going to end up alone in the lift together. How would she keep her hands off him in such a confined space, especially if he gave off the same fresh woody scent as he had on Saturday? She needed some serious self restraint. She took a deep breath and walked through the main door towards the lift. They were met with a laminated sign.

`Lift undergoing maintenance, please use the stairs.`

Fate!

He led the way to the spiral staircase. "This is a common occurrence. No fun for us on the top floor."

She looked up. "Well I wont need to go to the gym after this."

"Me neither." He took the steps two at a time, pausing at each level to let her catch up.

She felt so unfit. He looked so relaxed as they entered the office, but she slumped in her chair to catch her breath.

"It gets easier. They usually have it up and running within a couple of hours."

She gave him thumbs up and he disappeared down the office, returning with two cups of water.

"Thank you." She should treasure the cup forever.

By the time George arrived fifteen minutes later, she felt much better. He looked even more unfit than she felt. It reassured her, especially as others drifted in breathlessly. She caught Dean's eye and exchanged a cheeky smile. Their eyes locked and she wanted to stride over and kiss him. He looked so fresh and clean. Extremely sexy.

"Sorry Jessica, erm, Jessie." George disturbed her lustful thoughts.

She jumped, tearing her eyes away from Dean.

"Janet has an urgent task for you. Lisa will be updating some images this morning, but I need you to prepare the templates ready for final editing and completion. I will send you the details, but this takes priority over all other tasks this week."

Her heart sank. What if Dean's client review had been scheduled while she was busy and unable to participate. There would be other opportunities, but she missed out by a whisker last time, and didn't want to lose out again.

— 🐦 —

She concentrated hard on her project, desperate to get it perfect. She was on schedule to complete it by the end of the week, but on Wednesday afternoon she looked up to find Janet's tall thin structure standing over her. She jumped at least a foot off her seat. Lisa and Dean sat diagonally opposite, falling off their chairs, laughing hysterically. She glanced out of the corner of her eye, wanting to wave a fist at them, but held off while Janet spoke with her.

"I need you to pause what you're doing, Mr Muhara at Jameson's has just sent through another change of spec for the images Lisa has been working on, so she needs to change them all again." Janet sighed. "Hold off on doing anything else until the images are ready. In the meantime, Dean has a task for you.

Her disappointment turned to excitement. She tried hard not to gasp at the mention of his name, but inside, she started leaping up and down, cheering. She kept her face straight, nodded and agreed. Janet walked away, and Jessie diverted her attention to Lisa and Dean. They were still grinning in her direction, so she raised a hand and waved a fist at them.

They laughed even more.

She stood up and walked over frowning sternly. They looked away.

She stopped just beside Dean's desk, crouched and gave him a cheeky smile. "Janet said you'd like me to do something for you."

Her mind raced, imagining what she would like to do for him, but she kept calm. Lisa's gaze burned into her, but she ignored it and focused on him.

"Yes, I'll email you the details, it's quite easy but if you need any help, wave at me and I'll come over."

It *was* a simple task, just making some minor changes to a questionnaire. As she worked through it, she noticed a couple of parts of the layout that would benefit from being repositioned and a heading that would stand out better in bold, so she waved at him.

He shuffled his chair over to sit with her, his fresh woody scent invading her space, pulling her closer.

She maintained her composure. "I've made the required amendments, but I was wondering how much scope we have to change the layout."

"It's just an old template. It's been converted from a PDF and reworked over and over, so if you have any suggestions, fire away." He looked around and leaned lower, dropping his voice. "We have an awful lot of templates like this, and I do mean awful. They could all do with a fresh set of eyes if you fancy taking that on."

She nodded. "I think I can manage that in exchange for coffee."

Yikes. I said that out loud. Idiot. Stupid stupid—

"White, no sugar, right?"

"Right!"

He got up and vanished through the double doors. Lisa looked over with a furrowed brow. Jessie shrugged. Within a few minutes he returned with a large coffee from the canteen. Her cheeks flushed. Luckily he hadn't quite got her meaning.

"Thank you. I was—"

"Next time we should go together and have mugs instead of paper cups." He sidled over to his desk with his chair.

Had he really said they could have coffee together? Excitement flooded through her. She made the changes and moved on to the full set of templates he had emailed to her. The finished questionnaire and forms looked fresh and impressive. She forwarded them to him and twenty minutes later an email arrived from HR. He had recommended her for an initiative reward. Not bad for her second week.

— 🍎 —

At the end of the day, Jessie set off with Lisa.

"Where did you park?"

Lisa pointed to the right. "The overflow car park. Where are you?"

"I'm here, but my car is in the main car park." She pointed to the left. "See you tomorrow then."

Jessie made her way to the main car park. She was startled by hurried footsteps behind her and turned around. Dean was jogging to catch up.

He slowed to walk at her side. "I didn't want to ask in the office, but will you be going to Purple Passion again on Saturday?"

She played it cool. "No, I think Lisa is coming over to mine for a quiet night in. It's not my sort of night out, so I wasn't exactly impressed with it."

"I know what you mean, that's why we ended up moving to The Old English last week. I'm not really into the big night out scene, but I promised the lads I would go with them."

It surprised her, but she understood what he meant. She often did things like that because Lisa wanted to. She could take it or leave it herself. It felt great to have something in common with him.

"The Old English was certainly more my sort of venue." She started blushing. "I didn't really get the right opportunity to say thank you for last Saturday. I had a really good night in the end."

"Me too. We should do it again sometime."

She nodded. "See you tomorrow."

They smiled at each other, got into their respective cars and waved. She set off, her mind drifting back to what he said. She looked in her rearview mirror and saw him two cars behind. He followed for half of her journey, turning off towards the river. She had grown up on a housing estate on the other side of that river, so she knew the area quite well.

I can't imagine him living on that side of town.

She couldn't help but wonder. There's very little more than derelict factories and warehouses between the turnoff and where Jessie used to live. She couldn't imagine him living on a rough estate with such a flashy car.

Her thoughts drifted to their conversation, and she started to feel bad. What if the question about going out on Saturday was a shy attempt at asking her on a date?

There's no harm in playing hard to get if that's how he reads it.

5 A MAN FREE WEEKEND

Jessie had just got out of the shower on Saturday evening when Lisa arrived with her overnight bag. She had almost finished drying her hair, so Lisa headed out to the grotty shared kitchen to prepare drinks and popcorn. She put the hairdryer away and slipped out of her bathrobe ready to put her favourite shortie pyjamas on.

The door swung open, and Lisa stepped in. "Oh sorry, I should have knocked." She quickly turned to face the door.

Jessie felt embarrassed but giggled it off. Lisa was her very best friend, and she had seen her naked plenty of times, but probably not since puberty.

"It's safe now."

"I'm so sorry. I couldn't find the popcorn."

"It's okay, I should have locked the door." Jessie opened the wardrobe and pulled out a box of food. She searched through and found the popcorn. "My fault, I had to move the food because someone kept stealing it. It's the hazard of living with a bunch of first years."

They walked out to the kitchen together and Lisa put the popcorn in the microwave.

"I'd accept having to hide food over being at home any day, my brothers are so annoying. Mum thinks I'm a slave and I can't *even* take boys home. I've got no privacy at all. I certainly couldn't keep a diary like you do, they'd have my deepest feelings printed in The Gazette."

Jessie didn't understand her situation. As an only child, her home life had been very different. As for boys, she had never had a boyfriend before Mike, so she had never been in the position to *want* to take anyone home.

"I miss my Mum and Dad, it was a tough decision to stay here when they went off to Australia, but I sometimes wish I had gone with them." She dropped her head and sighed.

Lisa put her arms around her and gave her a big squeeze. The microwave dinged and the popping sound stopped.

"I'm glad you stayed because who else could I watch movies and eat popcorn with?"

Jessie smiled, tears still in her eyes, then followed Lisa back along the hallway to her room. She loaded up the DVD player and pressed play. They propped themselves up on the floor with fluffy purple cushions, and sat back to watch *Bed of Roses*.

"I love Christian Slater in this. He's so gentle, affectionate and handsome."

Lisa raised her eyebrows. "Like someone else we know, maybe?"

"Maybe."

She could see the likeness. Dean seemed gentle and kind, but she didn't *really* know him. Lisa grinned at her. She clearly knew what was going on in her head. They sat silently watching the film, glued, whilst sipping several rosé spritzers and eating popcorn.

Jessie had never been any good at watching romantic movies because – as an old romantic – she always ended up in tears. This was no exception. Lisa put her arm around her and cuddled her. The movie continued to play, but Lisa suddenly leaned over and kissed her. Caught in the moment, Jessie responded. She suddenly thought of Dean, the mystery man from over the river, and pulled away.

"Lisa! No, I'm sorry. I just don't feel like that. Please don't run away like last time. I think you're great, but just lacking a hot man in your life."

Lisa didn't respond. Her face was blank. Jessie sat looking at her, wondering how to fix it for her.

She had an idea. "We can go over to Purple Passion tomorrow and look for Max, give it another shot with him." She didn't think that would solve anything, but it's all she could think to say.

In truth, it's not what she wanted to do herself. Her heart was longing for a trip to The Old English, but she had to put Lisa first, as she always had.

"Sorry, I just got carried away. Sometimes I feel like you're the only person who will ever love me. I try so hard but men just don't want me."

How could Jessie respond to that without sounding patronising? She couldn't just leave it at that though. Why Lisa was so obsessed with needing people to love her was a mystery.

"Come on Lisa. It can't just be any man. You try too hard, and that makes it harder. Relax, and don't take things so seriously. Mr Perfect is out there."

Lisa began to cry. The drink didn't help, but Jessie wanted to help because Lisa had a problem. She would stand by her because that's what friends do.

— ❦ —

Lisa seemed much better with a sober mind on Saturday morning.

She sat up on the fold-up bed and poked Jessie. "I am so sorry about last night. I don't want to fall out over it again."

"It's okay. You're my dearest friend, and I don't want to lose you. We have to make sure we don't let it happen again. I have feelings for someone else."

Lisa sniffled.

Jessie handed her a tissue. "You need to come shopping with me this morning. Refresh my summer wardrobe, then maybe we can go over to Purple Passion this evening to see if there's anyone interesting there."

"Like Dean?"

Jessie snapped. "No. Like Max."

Lisa gasped. "You have feelings for Max?"

"No. We can go looking for Max. I have feelings for Dean."

They both began to laugh.

Jessie threw the tissue box to Lisa. "Clear yourself up. Before we can sort your love life out, I need a different sort of help. I need some cool clothes, suitable for work, but must hide my fat bits."

"Fat bits indeed. You always say that but…" She cleared her throat. "I've seen your self-proclaimed fat bits and it's nonsense. You're curvy and beautiful."

"Oh stop it, please just help me. Curvy and beautiful, fat, flabby, whatever, it's ok for you sitting there in your perfect smaller than average. I could only dream of getting close to average."

"You're not fat." Lisa always got the last word.

Jessie glared at her and walked into the shower-room.

Shopping trip done. Jessie got dressed up in one of her new summer dresses. If they didn't find Max at Purple Passion, there would be no reason not to go over to The Old English. Lisa enjoys a game of pool sometimes. No ulterior motive, obviously.

They walked into the cocktail bar. Jessie's nerves were on edge. She didn't expect to see Dean there, but still hoped, just in case. There were nowhere near as many people there, but it still didn't suit her taste.

"No Max. No Dean. No hope." Lisa crossed her arms and frowned.

Jessie smiled. Plan B could come into play. "How about we drop over to The Old English?"

"The old what?" Lisa scowled.

"You thought Dean's friends were cute right? That's where I went last week." Jessie pursed her lips, hoping to have given enough incentive.

"Oh. We could have just gone straight there. Max had his chance and blew it."

Jessie shook her head. She'll never understand Lisa's thought process.

A taxi had just pulled up when they stepped outside, so they hopped in and headed to the other side of town. Jessie's heart thumped hard at the thought of seeing Dean. It would go one of two ways. Either he would be pleased to see them, or he would think she was stalking him.

They walked through the old wooden door and skirted around the edge of the bar. Rob and Dan stood beside the pool table, jeering at each other.

Rob spotted them straight away. "Hey, Jessie and friend. Join us. Can I get you some drinks?"

Jessie's eyes darted around the room, desperate to see Dean. "Thanks. Let me buy a round. I owe you after last week."

"Arm-wrestle. Winner buys the drinks." Rob sat and rested his elbow on the table.

Lisa looked bemused. Jessie sat, flexed her fingers and joined hands with him. She had no chance. Her arm was flat out in seconds.

Rob headed to bar. "Brandy and coke, two of?"

The girls looked at each other, smiled and nodded.

Dean was nowhere to be seen. Jessie didn't want to ask where he was in case it made it obvious she was only there looking for him, but it left her feeling disappointed. She didn't let it spoil their fun because there was always a chance he would turn up.

Within half an hour, Lisa had latched onto Rob, sitting on his lap, giggling, running her fingers though his hair and whispering to him. Dan kept rolling his eyes and touching Jessie's hand. She felt awkward. The pressure to entertain him was too much. She couldn't do it.

She looked at Lisa and frowned. Dan shuffled his seat closer to her. She stood up. It wasn't her style to pick up a man for the sake of it, but more importantly, she felt like she would be cheating on Dean, even though they were little more than friends. She didn't want to upset Lisa by suggesting they leave, so she visited the ladies to gain time. It didn't help. On return, she found Lisa smooching in the corner with Rob. Jessie couldn't stay.

She fiddled with her phone. "I need to go home and make a call."

Dan looked disappointed, but it wasn't her problem.

Lisa raised her head for a moment. "I'll be fine here, but I'll catch up with you later."

She knew Lisa well enough to know that wouldn't happen. On her way out, she stopped at the bar, paid for a round of drinks, and beckoned Dan to collect them.

"Sorry I can't stay, but it was my turn to buy."

"You didn't need to, but thanks."

She stepped outside and filled her lungs with the evening air. Her selfish plan had caused the situation, so she couldn't be angry with Lisa. She headed home in a taxi. Once there, she thought about Dean, then Lisa and their most recent kiss. A vision of Lisa with Rob popped into her head and she couldn't help thinking Lisa was out of control, a sexual predator in training. It left her feeling unsettled. It was none of her business, but she couldn't help but worry. Nobody knew Lisa like she did, but it was plain for anybody to see how she hopped from one man to the next at the drop of a hat.

— 🐾 —

The ghostly silence of the virtually empty student accommodation block allowed Jessie time to think, and over think. Most students had gone home for summer. Sunday afternoon already and still no contact from Lisa. She'd normally turn up early on the morning after the night before, and what happened to Dean? Where had he been on Saturday night? Something was wrong.

The silence continued. She'd never get to know about Dean. He wasn't accountable to her. Neither was Lisa, but she's different. Who knew it would be so boring to have no essays to complete? Jessie fiddled with her phone, planning a way to bump into Dean.

The doorbell disturbed her thoughts. *Lisa!* She ran down stairs to let her in. The silence was broken. They made their way back upstairs.

Lisa flopped on the bed. "You missed one hell of a night." She beamed from ear to ear. "You're loss my gain. I ended up going home with them both."

"Them both as in—"

"Yeah, as in double the fun is twice as nice."

Jessie raise her hand to her eyes and shook her head.

"Please tell me you're joking."

Lisa shook her head, still beaming, eyes twinkling.

"You realise how other people see... Oh, Lisa. I'm so disappointed in you."

Her face dropped. "You're just jealous, either of me having men tripping over themselves to be with me." Her voice grew louder. "Or of them for bedding the woman you keep rejecting."

How dare she drop her emotional baggage at her feet.

"They can't help but trip over you when you lay yourself out with a great big sign saying '*Screw me, I'm easy*'" Jessie's face reddened as she raised her voice to match Lisa's. "And as for me rejecting you, it's not about rejection at all. It's about self respect. You've got to a stage where you'll snog anything that moves."

Lisa glared. She didn't say another word, picked up her bag and left. Jessie's heart pounded. She held a hand out in front of her. It trembled. She had never shouted at Lisa before, and it felt bad. The truth hurts, but Lisa needed to hear what she thought. If her own best friend felt like that, others must have thought and said much worse.

Monday morning brought extreme trepidation. Being in the office with Lisa was bound to be horrendously difficult after such an awful weekend. Dean hadn't even crossed Jessie's mind until she arrived in the office and saw his smile, and those cute little dimples. Lisa didn't as much as look at her. The atmosphere was frosty enough to freeze the balls off a brass monkey, but Jessie held her head high. She couldn't allow it to affect her work.

Half way through the morning, Dean strolled past

Jessie's desk, threw her a quick smile and vanished through the double doors towards the staircase. Jessie sighed and tried to focus on her work. A few moments later, a hand appeared over her shoulder, placing a paper cup on her desk.

"Coffee, white, no sugar." Dean's breath felt warm on her neck. His aftershave overwhelmingly alluring. "You look like you need something stronger, but that's the best I can manage from the canteen."

She took a deep breath in, fighting the urge to turn, fearful of her need to kiss him. Whatever did he mean? Before she had chance to reply, he was gone. He shuffled papers on his desk, met her eyes for long enough to accept a silent thanks, and set off to his next meeting. He returned briefly just before lunch, barely meeting her gaze before hurrying off to yet another meeting. There's nothing more lonely than being in a room full of people, alone.

The days began to merge. Days filled with icy cold reception from Lisa and warm smiles from Dean dragged. Jessie was heading for a very long and frustrating year. She tried to keep her mind off the hurt of Lisa's ignorance. Dean was another matter. She couldn't keep her mind off him because despite him hurrying off to meetings, then back, then off again, every time he passed her desk, he cast her an inviting smile. The waft of his aftershave engulfed her every time he brushed past her desk, leaving her unable to resist falling deeper and deeper in love with him. Her belief in fate had always been strong, but love at first sight had never felt possible before.

Returning to work after a long and lonely weekend, she longed to feel his presence, but heavy traffic prolonged the agony and forced her to park in the overflow car park. The thought of bumping into Lisa filled her with dread because the last thing she needed was to start her day in Arctic conditions. Arriving to find Lisa's car already there negated her fears and put her back on course to be reunited with the love of her life.

She walked through the double doors, cast a gaze at Dean's empty desk and frowned. It was unlike him to be running late. Lisa turned and cut through her with the usual cold stare. How long would she keep up the ice queen act? Jessie considered having a word, but thought better of it. The mystery was solved in an email from Dean himself. A selection of tasks for the two weeks ahead. He was on annual leave. She felt lost without him.

—  —

Another very long two weeks had passed, and Jessie burst into the office. She had to restrain herself. There he sat, sexier than ever. He looked up suddenly, his eyes glowing. She barely reached her desk before he made a beeline for her.

"How have you been getting on?"

She nodded, focusing hard to control her breathing. "It's been good." He took her breath away. She switched her computer on and sat down.

He perched on the edge of her desk. "How about I buy you that coffee I promised?"

"You already did."

"I mean…" He twiddled his fingers. "No. I promised coffee in a mug, together. If you want."

Her hands trembled as she typed her password and sat back. "I want, I mean yes. I think I can squeeze you into my busy schedule." Her heart pounded.

His nerves appeared to fizzle away behind a fresh smile. "Is 10am okay for you?"

"That's good for me."

He drifted back to his disk, a triumphant smile fixed as he sat down and glanced over. How should she take that? Two colleagues having a coffee break together or a strange sort of date? However it could be classed, she didn't care. Coffee with Dean was more than she could have dreamed of for the day ahead.

He wandered over and paused. "Ready?"

Unsure what she needed to be ready for, except coffee, she nodded. "Sure."

Lisa's glare burned into her as she stood, but it was different. The look in her eyes asked far more than it told. She wouldn't like being in the dark, but that was her doing. Just as they reached the double doors, Dean's phone rang. He pulled it out and answered.

"Oh right... they're an hour early." He rolled his eyes. "When?... No, you've got to be joking." He stopped, leaned on the wall and mouthed sorry to Jessie. "Okay. It would have been nice to have had some warning. I'll be there in five."

"Problem?" She felt her moment being snatched away, tearing her heart out.

"Apparently my 11am meeting had to be rescheduled while I was away. It's now at 10am." He sighed. "I'm so sorry. I'll buy you another coffee on the way, but I promise we'll get to have a proper coffee break soon."

The disappointment hurt, but it wasn't his fault. Some things are clearly just too good to be true. She returned to her desk with another paper cup coffee and avoided making eye contact with Lisa. She'd love to know what had happened. If she could have planned it, she would have.

—  —

Later in the day, still feeling sensitive about the abandoned coffee break, Jessie spied a new meeting request on her calendar. It had come from Dean, scheduling her to work with him on the Dixon & Newton project. A moment later, another request arrived for the client presentation on 27th August. It cheered her up no end, and she accepted each invite in turn.

Working with him on the project felt great, but outside of work, she had nothing. Without Lisa, she didn't socialise, and even when she felt like turning up at The Old English, she didn't think she had a good enough excuse. Her lack of self confidence held her back, but Dean's behaviour left her confused. He had been flirting with her. At least that's how it felt. But he hadn't made any attempt to ask her to go out.

Their coffee break became entwined with one of their planning meetings, and he seemed to think that was okay. It felt unsettling, and she started to wonder what it all meant; his smiles, cheeky grins, the day he chased after her on the way to the car park, even little things he said. She couldn't have been wrong about all those things, they couldn't have been completely meaningless. Thinking back to the night when he took her to The Old English, then delivered her safely home, why did he do any of those things?

6 RUNNING FROM THE STORM

Lunchtimes felt lonely without Lisa, but after almost a month since their argument, she had become used to going for walks in the park alone. The fresh air afforded her space to relax away from the tense atmosphere, and the warmth of the summer sun melted through the chills left by Lisa's cold stare.

On Wednesday, the humidity – lingering below the blanket of cloud covering the sky – made Jessie reconsider her walk. The refreshing air-conditioned building offered a sanctuary from the heat outside, so she succumbed to the lure of the canteen. Having taken no more than two steps through the doorway, she spotted Lisa with Claire. Unable to face the humiliation of sitting alone, she doubled back.

With no other option, she walked slowly through the lobby towards the main entrance, destined for her usual walk in the park. Just as she neared the doors to the lift, they opened, and there stood Dean.

His face lit up. "Are you heading for the park?"

She screamed inside, delighted, but maintained her composure. "Yes, what about you?" She had fate on her side, but tried to look as natural as possible.

"Yes, would you mind if I join you?"

Did she mind, was he joking? She felt her cheeks flushing and smiled. Surely that could only happen in a dream. "Of course, you're always welcome to join me." Her vocal tone a notch higher than normal. "I won't be going far today though because it's much too warm."

"That's fine by me."

They walked along the footpath together, exchanging smiles.

"Are you looking forward to our presentation next week?" He looked blank, clearly looking for a topic of conversation. "You've been waiting far too long."

"Six days to go, not that I'm counting." She gave him a big grin. "Does that indicate excitement?"

He smiled and nodded. They continued to walk, crossing the road, entering the rusted iron archway. An air of quiet awkwardness built up around them. They had nothing in common to talk about.

After a few minutes, he finally spoke. "I notice you and Lisa aren't talking."

Wrong subject. "Slight disagreement." She didn't want to talk about Lisa. "She'll come round eventually, maybe."

"Can I ask what happened?" He obviously didn't know anything about that awful weekend, but it wasn't her place to say.

"I offered her some advice, but she didn't like it." She considered opening up. She owed nothing to Lisa. "But I'll leave it there, out of loyalty for her privacy."

"It's sad, you're clearly a very good friend, even now wanting to protect her privacy." His face full of sympathy, or was it appreciation? "Whatever it was, I'm sure you had the best intentions. If I had a friend like you, I'd consider myself very lucky indeed."

They arrived at the bench near the duck pond, and he sat down, beckoning her to sit beside him.

She sat, discreetly patting the perspiration from her forehead with the back of her hand. "You *have* got a friend like me."

He furrowed his brow. "Who?"

"Me!" She cocked her head. "I'd like to consider you a friend. As long as that's okay with you?"

A friend yes, but all they had in common was Lisa. Such an interesting friendship.

"Well I suppose I *did* take you home when you were drunk!" A beaming smile broke through his serious face.

"Don't!" She cringed. "You'll embarrass me!"

Memories of that unforgettable night – him standing in her doorway – were still fresh in her mind. She could have snapped him up right then, but didn't.

"That's just what friends do." He shrugged. "Though I did worry it might have given you the wrong impression. I mean, normally when a guy delivers a girl to her bedroom, he's angling for something more."

Her chest tightened and she had a lump in her throat. She *had* got the wrong impression. It felt like she was being dumped from an imaginary relationship. She had to fight to stop her bottom lip from trembling.

"Friends do things like that, so it's fine." She gave him half a smile, not entirely sure she was fine.

She sat, almost frozen, beside him. She felt cold and numb despite the searing warmth in the air. She was screaming inside, her ego had taken a nosedive and she wasn't sure what else to say. Her eye's threatened tears, and it took all her effort to control them.

The sky above them suddenly became dull. Quite apt given how she had just had her dreams of romance – with the most perfect man – shattered. He wasn't interested in her as anything more than a friend. She swallowed hard, still battling with her inner despair.

The worse she felt, the more the darkness washed over them like a dark shadow of grief. Suddenly, the sky blinked as a flash of lightning danced along the horizon, followed by an almighty rumble of thunder. She almost jumped out of her skin, then tensed up, the reality of her fear difficult to hide.

"Hey, are you okay?" He looked quite concerned.

"Thunderstorms." She took a deep breath and exhaled slowly. "They kind of scare me." Her honesty shocked her, but if she couldn't be honest with her only friend, who could she be honest with?

He hadn't laughed yet, so she had nothing to lose. "They have been my biggest fear ever since I got locked out during a storm when I was fourteen. I wasn't keen on them back then either, but when lightning struck the chimney on a house just a few metres away from me, it left me kinda terrified." Fear radiated from her trembling body as another flash and crash threatened to spoilt their moment together.

"I can imagine something like that would stay with you for a long time." He rubbed her arm.

"I've suffered with nightmares about it for many years. Night-time storms are definitely the worst." Another series of flashes followed, then a long rumble. She shuddered.

Dean put his arm around her and gave her a gentle squeeze. "Looking at that sky, we should probably make a break for it before the heavens open."

She nodded. They got up and began to walk, slowly at first, then slightly faster. Another flash of lightning introduced a lingering rumble and a sudden downpour. They began to run. Dean ran faster, so he hesitated, took hold of her hand and pulled her along. The rain came down in sheets, soaking them both to the skin. Her fear turned to laughter until the next flash of lightning struck with an almighty bang.

"I've got a towel in my locker, you can share it if you like." He led her into the building, traipsing through the main entrance towards the gym block.

"I didn't realise there was a gym here."

"Yes. I've never been in it though. I brought a gym kit in a few months ago, full of good intentions, but as yet, haven't managed to use it."

They held a side each of the towel and wiped themselves down, tugging and wrestling, giggling like teenagers.

"Thank you, I would've been lost without you out there."

He rubbed her arm. "I'm pleased to be of service!"

Something came over her and she hugged him, pausing as his washed out aftershave invaded her nostrils. She released her grip, his hands resting firmly on her hips. He looked her in the eyes, almost longingly, as she moved away slowly. If it hadn't been for their conversation, she would have said they had a moment, but she kept her feet firmly on the ground to save herself from further heartache.

They returned to the office, attracting some funny looks because nobody else had been silly enough to venture out in the storm. Lisa almost forgot herself when she saw them and smirked, then remembered she their fight and quickly looked away.

Despite the continuing heat outside, she continued to enjoy her daily walks in the park, though sadly without her new best friend. He was busy collecting everything they needed for their presentation next week, so he didn't have time to socialise. He invaded her thoughts constantly, but she was extremely pleased to have him as a friend. Having had time to think about what he said about not wanting to give her the wrong impression, she had to change her mindset and accept they would never be anything more than friends. He would always be a treasured friend though, anybody who helped her run from a storm was well worth having as a friend.

Having had yet another quiet night at home on Friday, Jessie felt brave and considered a trip to The Old English on Saturday. Her friendship with Dean, nothing more, affirmed. Uncertainty lingered, she didn't want to set herself up for a fall, but imagined he would be there to play pool and brighten her day.

She psyched herself up, preparing, then saw the weather forecast and realised she had no hope of going anywhere. A thunderstorm was coming, and despite her fond memories of Wednesday, her nerves got the better of her. She had a difficult night ahead. She couldn't go and get caught in a storm again.

She sat down at her desk, turned her diary to 24th August, and began to write, pouring her heart out about her one-sided feelings. Just as she put the diary in her drawer, the first flash of lightning struck. She was in for a long night. It was almost 9pm, and the sky was pitch black. She closed the curtains and hid under her duvet, dulling the effect, but it had no affect on her fear. Rain lashed at the window like the storm knocking to come in. Suddenly the doorbell rang. She looked at the clock. It was 9:15pm. She hadn't been expecting anybody, so hesitantly, she looked through the window, wondering if Lisa had come over to apologise. She couldn't have been more wrong. Dean stood there looking lost. She definitely hadn't expected that and ran downstairs, eager to let him in. He was soaked.

She opened the door. "What are you doing out in this?"

"I was at home when it started." He rubbed his wet feet on the weather rug, though he needed something more like a human tumble dryer. "I immediately thought of you and couldn't stand the thought of you alone, scared and tormented by your nightmares."

She took in a huge breath. "That's the sweetest thing anybody has ever done for me, thank you." It warmed her heart, but she kept in mind what he had said about not wanting to give her the wrong impression. *He's here as a friend, nothing more.*

She led him up the stairs and welcomed him in. "It's not much, but it's home."

The bed was still ruffled from her hiding under the duvet, so she quickly straightened it out, allowing him somewhere to sit.

"I was a student not so long ago, so I understand the trendy student lifestyle." He stood and examined the collection of colourful postcards from Australia. "Mind you, my student room wasn't as stylish as this, you've made it feel very comfortable."

Returning the favour from Wednesday, she gave him a towel and a change of clothes. Just joggers and t-shirt, quite girly and way too big, but it served the purpose. As much as she would have liked to have got him out of his clothes, that's not something he would have wanted, not when doing so would *definitely* have given her the wrong impression.

He stepped out of the shower room, beaming from ear to ear and gave her a twirl.

"You look, erm, different." She giggled

He smirked. "I feel dry, and that suits me fine."

Getting him into her clothes wasn't quite the fantasy

she had in mind, but it was better than nothing. It had certainly taken her mind off the storm for a short time, but another rumble of thunder provided an unwelcome reminder of why he turned up. They sat on the side of her bed while flashes and crashes shook the building. She shook with fear, so Dean put his arms around her, providing comfort, holding her firmly against his chest. She suddenly felt safe, it felt like magic. His aftershave was barely noticeable after his soaking in the rain, but it remained fresh in her mind. Typical. The only two times she had got close enough to get a good sniff, were the only two times she had seen him soaked to the skin.

At almost midnight she noticed the storm had calmed, she had been asleep in his arms. His heart beat in her ear as she rested her head on him. He stroked her hair, adding to the feeling of calm. As she moved her focus back into the room, she heard the rain gently bouncing off the window ledge and couldn't help but wonder what his plans were.

"How long are you staying for?"

He leaned in, looking into her eyes. "Are you planning to throw me out in the rain?"

She shook her head. "No, I wouldn't like you to get wet again."

"It looks like I'm staying all night then."

She almost gasped. Not only did he have her safely snuggled in his arms, but he also sounded content with staying all night. She felt overjoyed, but slightly confused. *Why is he doing this?* Having a man stay all night felt odd, but if any man was welcome in her room, it was definitely the very sexy Dean Whittle.

They curled up together with him still holding her in his arms, obviously falling asleep at some stage. She had no nightmares, only vivid dreams about him laying on her bed with her, kissing her forehead and stroking her hair. She was woken by a loud noise.

"Lightning."

He rubbed her shoulder softly. "It's okay. It was only a door." He was so gentle and caring, and made no attempt to make a move, just cuddling and comforting her.

The next morning, at breakfast, She thanked him over and over for being there for her.

He smiled. "Do you have a pen and paper?"

She passed him a notepad and pen, unsure why he wanted it. She watched intently as he scribbled something.

"That's my number." He passed her the notepad. "You're welcome to call me any time, storm or no storm, day or night."

She almost choked. *Dean's number!* It left her almost speechless, he was so sweet. She hesitated, worried it might be slightly presumptuous, then proceeded to rip a page from the notebook. She scribbled, just has he had, then passed to him. "There's my number, if ever you feel scared of anything, any time, or you just want to say hi, call me."

She couldn't imagine him being scared of anything, but it was all she could think to say. His eyes lit up, and cute dimples appeared at each end of his smile.

7 CONSEQUENCES

No storm had ever been so refreshing. It left her walking on air. Although nothing had actually happened, Dean's warmth and companionship meant everything. She lay back on her bed and programmed his number into her phone. She kept looking at it, missing him, longing to hear his voice. Less than an hour had passed since he left and she fought the temptation to call, mostly because she had no idea what she would say.

Thunderstorms will always have a new precious meaning. She lazed about all day and thought about her night in his arms and the fear she had struggled with for seven years. Had it not been for that, she wouldn't have spent a night in his arms. A sudden thought drained the warmth from her body, forcing her to keep her feet firmly on the ground. He had been very clear on Wednesday. He didn't want her to get the wrong impression.

"Men can be so confusing sometimes." She groaned and snuggled into her fluffy purple cushion.

The week ahead looked brighter than the previous week, but she couldn't get carried away. Nothing happened. She crawled along on Monday morning traffic on her way to work, wondering what she should say to him. Maybe like last time – when he delivered her home drunk – she would be better saying nothing. He clearly liked professional distance, having avoided the subject in the office.

Stepping through the double doors made her heart race. She had one chance to do the right thing. His eyes met hers in an instant, and his dimple framed smile melted her fears. All he needed was a smile. She managed that. Neither said a word about it, both far too busy. The best way to thank him was to put her heart and soul into making their presentation materials absolutely perfect. Her feelings for him drove her to some extent, but a successful client review was the ultimate motivation.

Lisa cast suspicious looks in her direction, not the same icy cold stares she had done for weeks. Lisa had a sixth sense for things, so she knew. She wouldn't approach her though, she was far too stubborn and Jessie was more than content to let her stew. Setting off for a walk at lunchtime on Monday, with Dean, Jessie noticed Lisa staring. She ignored her. Lisa had burned all her bridges, so it was up to her to take steps towards a reconciliation. If, a very big if, she even wanted to.

They had a pleasant walk, uneventful compared to the day of the storm, but relaxing and getting to know him felt right. His warmth radiated. It felt like more than purely friendship, but she had to fight her feelings. Good friends are hard to come by. Hot ones even harder, but she had to protect what they had rather than dwell on what they didn't have. Look what happened with Lisa.

— 🦋 —

After working with Dean all morning finalising their presentation, Jessie went for lunch alone on Tuesday. She hadn't had time to prepare a packed lunch in the morning, so she dropped into the canteen to collect a sandwich, almost coming face to face with Lisa.

Lisa didn't see her as she slipped into a seat beside Claire, at a table opposite Max and Ethan. Jessie just about managed to overhear Claire mention her name, she listened more closely, filtering out the buzz of chatter in the busy canteen.

"No chance. Jessie's far too busy with her *boyfriend*." The sarcasm in Lisa's voice made Jessie clench her teeth.

She saw red, and couldn't help herself. She stomped over. Her thumping heart echoing in her ears. Max and Ethan watched, open mouthed. The girls had their backs to her. She cleared her throat, making them jump. Their shock evident by their wide eyes and silent gasp.

"Just to clarify." She stared straight at Lisa. "I've been busy with my friend who just *happens* to be male. There's a difference, but clearly a mindless gossip like you wouldn't see that. Some of us have the ability to see more in men than sex."

Filled with fury, she collected her sandwich, paid and left. Her short walk in the park allowed her time to calm down ahead of her meeting, but she worried that if Dean knew, their friendship would be in jeopardy. He wouldn't want to be the subject of canteen gossip.

On returning to the office, she made eye contact with Lisa, expressing no emotion at all. Lisa blinked, curled one side of her lip and turned away, eyes full of regret. Jessie found it reassuring. Her point had been made, and there would be no repeat. Dean looked up, surprised. He had been focussed on final preparations for their meeting.

He moved his lips without making a sound. "Ready?" He made his way towards her, papers and laptop tucked under his arm.

"As ready as I'll ever be." She looked pointedly at Lisa as she stood to join him.

They left he office together, heading for the meeting rooms. She had opted to wear a long black skirt with her new white scallop bottomed blouse, looking quite the part beside Dean in his usual smart attire. Quite the double act. They reached the door, cast each other a smile and walked inside to meet their visitors.

A few handshakes and familiar smiles made Jessie feel like an outsider. She was out of her depth.

"I'm pleased to be joined this afternoon by Jessica Williamson." He waved a hand in her direction. "She's with us for a twelve month placement as part of her degree in media studies. She has a special interest in digital and online innovations within the media sector, so this project is right up her street."

Astounding. She hadn't told him any of that, but it was all absolutely true. She found his eyes briefly and smiled.

"This is Arnold, Jennifer and Carol from Dixon & Newton Leisure."

They each shook her hand before relaxing back around the table. Dean docked his laptop and loaded their presentation.

Trying to put Lisa out of her mind didn't work. She couldn't help but think she had benefitted greatly by waiting for this opportunity, because unlike Lisa, she had been involved in the work, the preparation and now, presenting part of the project herself, supported by Dean. Lisa had presumably just tagged along and looked pretty, as Lisa does.

It had been almost two hours since they had walked into the meeting room when their visitors finally left. For a first presentation, it actually went quite well. Jessie felt extremely pleased with herself.

He gave her a high five. "You were amazing, not

just the presentation, but answering questions and suggesting ways of making the impossible possible was very impressive."

"I was only able to do it because you gave me the opportunity and kept me involved throughout. Without that, I would have been way out of my depth."

"Quit with the modesty. You were confident and they loved you. You spoke their language, made them feel in control and we came out of it with half the amendments I had expected." He lowered his voice. "They're normally very difficult to please, but you nailed it."

Her cheeks flushed.

"If you're not busy, how would you like to join me for a celebratory drink at The Red Lion after work?"

It took her by surprise. "Oh, erm… Yes. That'd be great."

"Don't let me force you."

She giggled. "You're definitely not forcing me at all. Just don't make me drink brandy and coke or you'll have to carry me home."

He flashed his eyes at her and opened the meeting room door. She followed, catching up with him. He grinned and raised a finger to his lips. His desire to stay private reminded her of Lisa's comment earlier. He can't find out.

The Red Lion was quieter than the last time she went there with her fellow students, but that was expected for a Tuesday evening. They had both left their cars at work so they could drink.

Dean brought the drinks to the table. "It'd be silly to pay for two taxis each way because you practically go past my place. You could drop me off and pick me up in your taxi. I'll pay for it obviously."

Intriguing. Having seen him turn off towards the river, wondering where he lived, but was still none the wiser. "That sounds like a cost effective approach, I'll pay for the one home, and you can pay for the one back."

He shook his head. "I love your good ideas, but on this occasion I have to overrule you. It was my suggestion to do this so I'll pay for both journeys."

"But—"

"But nothing, give in to my stubborn side and make me a happy man."

She was all for making him a happy man, and equally for allowing him to make her a happy woman. A sudden recollection reminded her not to get carried away. Wrong impressions were not allowed.

They enjoyed a few drinks, chatting about their presentation, then she remembered how he introduced her in the meeting.

"When you introduced me in the meeting." She cocked her head. "You gave them a very accurate description. How did you know so much about me?"

"When you were allocated to our department – during your induction – we were given a brief profile of you to help us plan how best to utilise your skills and provide you with an educationally enhanced experience." He switched off his mobile phone and slipped it into his pocket. "I remembered it yesterday and checked back to ensure I introduced you in the best possible way."

They chatted – mostly about work – and shared a few more drinks. The room began to fill up, increasing the volume around them so they could no longer hear themselves think.

He leaned in, almost shouting. "Ready to go?"

She nodded. They made a break for it and hailed a taxi.

"North Campus accommodation via The Moorings please." He directed the taxi driver,

She knew the area well, but had never heard of The Moorings. It had to be a houseboat down on the river, but that doesn't suit his character at all. The taxi pulled up at the traffic lights indicating a right turn at the same spot where he had turned off before, and when they turned the corner and followed the road, curving behind the high street, a row of new apartment blocks came into view. They overlooked the river, explaining the name. They turned into a side road sign posted *The Moorings* and Dean directed the driver to the far end.

"See the windows on the top floor, at the end, where the building juts out." He pointed. "That's the back of my apartment, number 30."

"You must have an awesome view from up there, but how do you know I won't become a weird stalker?" She pursed her lips.

"I know where you live, so it's only fair you know where I live. Besides, having a stalker would make life much more interesting!" He raised his eyebrows with a sparkle in his eye.

As much as she longed to see his view, she hoped he wouldn't invite her in. After having had a few drinks, she risked making a fool of herself. Luckily he didn't. He had a brief chat with the driver, organised a morning pickup, paid and waved her on her way.

—  —

Taking a taxi to work next morning felt strange. She

had always been self reliant, but despite her concerns, the taxi arrived on time. Collecting Dean was a new first too. Those fancy new apartments had really surprised her. She knew nothing about the riverside development at all despite it being so close to where she used to live.

Houseboat, really! She smiled.

Dean joined her in the taxi and they continued the journey to work together. His freshly applied aftershave smelled divine, fresh and woody with spicy overtones. She longed to get closer and breathe him in, but didn't. It reminded her of the night they spent cuddled up – when he sheltered her from the thunderstorm – but much much stronger.

He looked so fresh, cleanly shaved, and his neatly combed blonde hair was still damp. The attraction felt too strong. She had to put some distance between them because she couldn't live with the consequences of her doing or suggesting anything he wasn't up for. He had been very clear about his intentions, but she had stupidly allowed herself to continue to fall for him, and that was wrong.

During the day, she had no difficulty keeping her distance, and felt relieved when he couldn't walk with her at lunchtime due to a meeting. Relieved in as much as not having to make an effort to avoid him, but disappointed at the conflict in her heart.

She struggled to find an excuse on Thursday, but tried to keep their lunchtime walk talk purely about work. His passion for his job made that easy, because he enjoyed talking about digital innovations.

Friday was literally a walk in the park because she had been given feedback via George from their meeting with Dixon & Newton Leisure about her presentation. They reported back how impressed they were with her knowledgeable and professional approach, and wanted to extend their contract to include a large ad campaign. They specifically requested for her to be involved in the project, giving her plenty of scope to avoid getting personal in her conversation with Dean.

As the afternoon drew to a close, feeling like she had survived the rest of the week without sinking any further into her crazy dream world, she received a message from him.

"Would you like there to be a thunderstorm again this weekend?"

She looked over, meeting his gaze, melting at his grin. It wasn't the sort a friend would offer. It felt like much more.

She typed a reply. "Can it be a pretend storm?"

He got up to walk down the office, hesitating beside her desk. He crouched down and spoke quietly. "Pretend suits me fine. Can I bring wine?"

She couldn't stop herself. "Yes!" Throwing out all her efforts to put professional distance between them.

"Saturday 7pm?"

"That's good for me." She couldn't hold back the beaming smile that had been building up.

Watching him return to his desk, Lisa caught her eye, scowling, clearly wondering what was going on there. Obviously she knew nothing about the storm night sleepover, but it was none of her business.

Keeping distance hadn't worked out well and it had been wrong to try. She enjoyed his friendship, and it would be silly to deny herself that. She just had to make sure she didn't get carried away.

— 🐦 —

She paced the floor, glancing at her watch over an over. She gazed at her reflection in the mirror, wondering if her sexy and sophisticated look might be too much. She looked like she had spent all day getting ready for their evening in, but it was too late to change. He arrived just on time, greeting her with a friendly hug and the promised bottle of wine. Living in student accommodation meant they were confined to her bedroom, but he hadn't minded last week. She had tidied up and prepared two glasses, welcoming him in and pouring the wine. She reached out to pick up her glass, but he reached out to her.

He took hold of her hand. "Do you trust me?"

"I believe so." She furrowed her brow, not sure what to think.

"Before we drink, I want to try something." He lowered his head, raising his eyes to meet hers. "It'd lose meaning if I waited until later."

A tingle ran up her spine, unsure but hoping. He took her hands into his, pulling her closer. Her heart pounded. Her hopes were coming true. He really was going to kiss her. Everything suddenly felt like slow motion, her mind racing ahead, doubting it, telling her to stop dreaming, but when his soft lips made contact with hers, the earth moved. She wasn't dreaming and responded with all the passion she had been holding back for weeks. She was, at last, breathing him in, and his aftershave, fresh and strong, just as intoxicating as it had been in the taxi. He moved away from their full mouth kiss and nibbled her lips, each in turn, running his fingers through her hair. He eased away slowly, eyes closed, lips still parted, leaving her breathlessly yearning for more.

"Was that okay?" He gazed longingly into her eyes.

She licked her bottom lip, savouring his taste. "I think so."

"Think so?" He pouted.

"Well. Unless there's a silent storm outside, my world just moved." She broke into a smile. "I would struggle to call it *okay* because it was... Wow."

They smiled timidly, kissed again then drank wine. She felt overjoyed and totally contented, unable to remember the last time she felt so relaxed and uninhibited. There was no question of Dean going home, they were inseparable and slept the whole night in a warm embrace. They kissed and caressed each other, but as relaxed as they were, neither made any attempt to seduce the other. There seemed to be a mutually shared understanding that it was too soon.

— 🍎 —

They lay, gazing into each other's eyes in the glow of the morning sun. He stroked her hair and she ran her fingers along his jaw line and across his lips.

"Any regrets?" His words only just audible.

She shook her head. "No regrets. Just a question."

"Fire away!"

"Remember the day in the park, after that night when you brought me home slightly—"

"Slightly? You mean inebriated?"

She giggled. "Yes. You said you didn't want me to get the wrong impression. I thought you were trying to tell me you were only acting as a friend and wanted nothing more. But—"

"No. That's not what I meant." He shook his head. "I didn't want you to think I was only after one thing. I brought you home to make sure you were safe. I really liked you but wanted to get to know you. I wanted you to get to know me too." He brushed his hand down her cheek. "God knows I wanted to, but impulse decisions are normally bad decisions, and I didn't want you to become a bad decision."

"And now, any regrets?" She parted her lips, heart in her mouth.

"None at all, not even for waiting." He smiled. "I love your company and your warmth. I love how you expect nothing and always act with caution."

"Really?"

"Yes, I've noticed you don't dive into anything head first. You always appear to weigh things up carefully." He ran a finger over her lips. "You're such an inspiration."

Jessie blushed. Her lips slightly parted, feeling his finger, missing it as he pulled it away. "I could say exactly the same of you."

"I guess you could, but I figure that every action has a consequence, and consequences must be lived with for a lifetime."

She pulled back, cocking her head. "Am I a consequence then?"

"I guess you are now. Yes."

"Nice. Though I'm not sure you'd want to live with me for a lifetime." She began to giggle.

"Never say never, but one step at a time!" He smiled, slipping a hand over her hip, pulling her closer.

Her pulse raced. "Good plan, next step breakfast?" Diverting him, worried things might be moving too quickly too soon.

"No. Not just yet." He kissed her very softly. "Mmm it is now, Sweet Lips."

8 SOMETHING FOR THE WEEKEND

A new chapter of Jessie's life was dawning and she couldn't believe what was happening. She had built herself up to expect nothing more than friendship from the man whose spine-tingling smile left her weak at the knees. She wanted to shout her news from the rooftops, especially desperate to tell Lisa, but couldn't. She had given up on their friendship.

Driving to work on Monday, a new emotion took over. Worry. Would they feel awkward at work? She tried not to let it overshadow her joy. Arriving in the office, meeting the warmth of his gaze, she needn't have worried. Walking on air after their weekend felt so much better than lusting after a man who, she perceived, wasn't interested in her.

She had a spring in her step. So did he. They were both extremely professional and functioned completely normally in the office, apart from sharing occasional cheeky smiles. They somehow managed to keep their lips off each other all day, even in the park at lunchtime, where they just held hands and gazed into each other's eyes.

It had been over twenty-four hours since their lips had connected, and she longed for him. As the afternoon went on, she began to daydream about how she could get him alone, the printer room, the stationary cupboard, even the lift, but they were all monitored by CCTV and she didn't want them to become the latest covert movie phenomenon.

She rested her elbow on the desk, supporting her head with a hand, drifting into a trance. She suddenly felt a presence beside her. It was him, crouching down, filling her space with his fragrance again. His eyes pulling her in, begging for contact. Keeping her feet on the ground, she recalled the last time he crouched like that, arranging their Saturday evening together, the night of their first kiss.

"Have you parked in our usual car park?" He kept his voice low.

She smiled, gazing at his lips longingly. "Yes, my car is directly behind yours."

"Good, wait for me. We can walk down together." He looked around and broke into a whisper. "I can't wait to hold you again."

The hairs on her neck stood on end. Just the thought of him holding her felt as electrifying as his kiss. She couldn't wait, and kept an eye on the time.

As she logged out of her computer, she glanced over, studying his face as he concentrated on his screen. His eyes turned to meet hers and he suddenly relaxed into a gentle smile. She felt a magical tingle in her fingers, spreading through her body.

"Are you ready to go?" He mouthed towards her.

She nodded, got up and walked over to him. Lisa was sat beside him. She shuffled some papers into a drawer, and scurried off at speed. He logged out of his computer and they walked out together, maintaining their professional distance. When they reached the car park, he pressed the button on his key-fob to unlock his car.

"Hop in!"

"Where are we going?"

His eyes twinkled and he licked his lips. "Paradise."

She slipped into the car, lowering herself into the bucket seat, closing the door behind her. A pleasant mixture of smells filled her lungs, new car and the freshness of his aftershave. It filled her with desire.

Dean climbed in the other side, turning towards her.

He reached over and took hold of her hand. "Are you okay?"

She smiled and nodded.

"Still no regrets?" He looked nervously inquisitive.

"Are you kidding?" She smiled with wide excited eyes.

She felt braver than ever, leaned over, heart pounding, lips parted, physically inviting him to kiss her. The limited space prevented full body contact, but Dean took her lead and leaned in, joining her midway with the kiss she longed for. The secretive feel to their car kiss made it even more exciting.

He lowered his gaze. "What do you have planned for this evening?"

She suddenly worried he might be about to propose something more. Something she wasn't ready for. She didn't want to ruin the magic of their relationship by going too far too soon. Her cautious side stepped in and rescued her.

"I'm having my hair done." She wasn't. She felt bad about lying, but it seemed better than rejecting any further advances. It wasn't that she didn't want more, it was more a case that she did, but not yet.

"I love your hair as it is, you're not having anything radical done are you?"

"Oh, no just a conditioning treatment." She realised she could easily grab herself a hot oil kit or something.

"Okay well give me another dose of your sweet lips before I let you go." He sounded slightly disappointed.

Knowing she would have to make it last, she devoured his taste, breathing in his fragrance, enjoying their passionate embrace. She climbed out, full of regret, and waved as he drove away.

Just a few steps away, she climbed into her own car and sat for a few minutes, feeling extremely guilty. She thought of Lisa and her history of jumping in and out of bed with men she hardly knew. Jessie wasn't like that, and any man worth being with would respect her moral values. She could have just been honest with him and explained her wish to take it one step at a time. She took a deep breath and set off.

— ❦ —

On her way home, she called in at the town centre to pick up some sort of treatment for her hair. It was the least she could do to make herself feel better about her feeble cover story. She walked into Boots and browsed the aisles in search of the hair care shelf. She hesitated next to the family planning shelf and wondered if she might be wise to ensure she was prepared, just in case she suddenly decided to take the next step.

No, being prepared could force me to make an impulse decision, and as Dean said, impulse decisions are usually bad decisions. She moved on and continued her search.

She picked up a couple of different intensive hair conditioning treatments, then opted for a conditioning treatment mask. As she wandered through the store, towards the checkout, she paused and turned back. She stood in the family planning aisle cluelessly studying the rows and rows of condom boxes, feeling completely overwhelmed. She had never actually bought condoms before and found the vast selection quite daunting.

"Flavoured, ribbed, pleasure, latex free, real feel, extra long, extra wide, extra safe, extra thin, how much more extra could you need." She spoke under her breath, looking around to make sure nobody could hear.

Lisa would know what to buy.

She continued to look from one box to the next, becoming more and more confused.

How should I know what size I should be buying? Maybe he's got some. What if he hasn't?

She picked up a box labelled *real feel*, because he's a real man, and before she could change her mind, she hurried to the checkout to pay. The young lady, barely 16, serving, greeted her warmly, picked up the box of condoms and scanned them, then glanced at Jessie – who had turned a dark shade of pink – and began to blush. Jessie could only imagine what was going through her young mind, but tried not to dwell on it.

After washing her hair and applying the conditioning treatment, she wrapped a towel around her head to let the mask work its magic while she wrote in her diary. She filled in her entry for 9th September, placed the diary back into her drawer and picked up the condoms. She examined the box, wondering if she had made the right choice. Maybe she could have bought a box each of the extra wide, extra long and extra thin as well, just in case. Then she remembered the young lady on the till.

What would she have thought of that? She stifled a giggle.

She slipped them into a drawer to keep them well out of sight. Not wanting him to get the wrong impression if he happens to see them. She had no immediate plans to use them. They were purely there for emergency use.

— ❧ —

On Tuesday morning she sat in the morning traffic, tapping her fingers on the steering wheel in time with her music. She ran her fingers through her hair, taking in the *fresh from the salon* fragrance. She glanced in the mirror. Her hair looked glossy and smooth, so the treatment had worked well.

After greeting Jane, she stepped into the lift with a lady from the third floor and psyched herself up for seeing him. After leaving the lift, she paused outside the double doors, took a deep breath, then pushed and entered. She felt fresh and gorgeous, more so when Dean eyed her with parted lips.

He hesitated every time he walked past her desk, throwing her smiles that melted her heart. Lunchtime couldn't come soon enough. They had another meeting scheduled with Dixon & Newton Leisure after lunch to discuss their new contract, so she looked forward to a relaxing walk in the park followed by an afternoon out of Lisa's piercing gaze.

As soon as it turned noon, he jumped up from his seat and approached her.

"Walking?" Something had changed. He had never been big on lunchtimes, normally just having a sandwich at his desk or going for a quick walk to stretch his legs. The last week had seen a gradual change, making it obvious that he wanted to share the time with her.

She picked up her bag. "Silly question."

They left the building together and even before they reached the park, he leaned closer, smelling her hair.

"Your hair smells amazing, I've been desperate to get a closer smell all morning." He took another breath, eyes full of awe.

She smiled. "Now you know how I feel!"

He cocked his head. "What do you mean?"

"I've been absorbed by your aftershave for such a long time. Last Saturday was my first chance to get close enough to enjoy it fully without looking like a crazy woman."

He smiled approvingly as they walked into the park hand in hand. It was a lovely sunny day and they stopped at a different bench to normal, further around the pond, quiet and more private.

He sat, pulling her close to his side, turning. "What have you done to me? I just can't resist you." He kissed her even more passionately than he had before.

Luckily they were in a public place because his spellbinding embrace completely absorbed her, arousing uncontrollable feelings of desire. Risking a very big impulse decision. They held each other closely, eating their sandwiches, smiling, giggling and touching. A closeness she had longed for.

He looked at his wrist and sighed. "Keep an eye on the time, I'm lost at the moment because I lost my watch."

"We probably need to set off in the next couple of minutes." She pouted.

He stood, took her hand, and pulled her to his side, wrapping his arm around her. They walked slowly, relaxing their embrace at the rusty archway before walking slowly back to the office to get ready for their meeting.

—  —

After a very successful meeting, they walked back to the office together slowly, enjoying every moment together.

He revisited his question from yesterday. "Do you

have anything planned for this evening?"

She swallowed hard, hesitating, but decided she couldn't just avoid being alone with him. He made her feel so incredible that she wanted to be with him. "I don't have anything planned, what about you?"

"Good. I didn't before, but I do now. Hopefully" He blushed. "There's something we need to do. Tonight should be the night."

A lump formed in her throat. She tried to find the right words because her rehearsed ones didn't quite fit.

"We need to go on a date. Do you like pasta?"

Stopped mid thought process, she nodded. "Pasta? Erm, yes. I love pasta."

"Good, then we're going to my favourite Italian restaurant for dinner."

What a relief. They hadn't yet been on an official date, just the two of them, candle-lit and all. That must be what he meant.

He paused outside the double doors to their office. "I'll pick you up at 6:30pm. I'll drive."

— 🍒 —

She focussed on getting ready as soon as she arrived home, pulling out a long purple dress and matching shoes. She tidied up her windswept hair, and looked at the box of condoms wondering if she should take them with her just in case.

Emergency use only.

She opted to leave them behind, checked the time and looked through the window. Dean was never late for anything, and as it was almost 6:30pm, she collected her bag, phone and keys, and made her way downstairs to meet him. She arrived at the door just as his car pulled up. He looked ultra sexy in his dark shades with his hair neatly styled with gel. She opened the door and got in. He looked gorgeous, wearing dark trousers and a pastel lilac shirt. She had only ever seen him wearing a white shirt when formally dressed, but this new colourful look was seriously hot.

She leaned over and kissed his soft moist lips, taking in a breath of his freshly applied aftershave. "Hello gorgeous, you smell amazing."

"Don't I always smell like this?"

She smiled. "Yes. You always smell amazing."

"Just like you always look amazing!" He stroked her cheek. "You really suit purple."

"It's my favourite colour."

He nodded. "I thought so."

He drove to the restaurant, just around the corner from their office. He parked in the secure carpark and they walked towards the restaurant.

"I'm going to leave the car here overnight so we can relax and have a drink. We can get a taxi home."

"That's a good plan." She gripped his hand, grinning. "Then I can pick you up in the morning to get to work."

He lowered his gaze, breaking eye contact. "I was considering asking you to stay over at mine."

She began to panic inside, but kept calm on the outside. Wondering how best to respond. She wanted to, really, but not yet. She took a very deep breath. "On a work night?"

"Good point, see how much more sensible you are than me!" He squeezed her hand softly and held the restaurant door open for her.

It was quiet inside, with only a few other couples dining. They sat at an intimate table, tucked away in the corner, providing them with privacy and an opportunity to talk without being disturbed. After ordering their meals they were sat holding hands and talking about their week, then he changed the subject.

"Okay. Sticking with your sensible plan, how would you like to stay at my place on Friday?"

It caught her slightly off guard, but as nervous as she felt, she really wanted to go. Waiting until the end of the week would give her time to consider how to play it. His invitation also meant she had bought herself some time with her *work night* comment, so she could relax.

She followed her instincts, took a deep breath and smiled "I'd love to. Do you like Martini?"

"I'm not sure I've ever tried it."

She squeezed his hand and kissed him gently. "You'll love it, I'll bring a bottle with me on Friday."

So the plan was made and she felt unexpectedly happy with her decision, whatever the outcome. She couldn't wait to see his amazing view. They gazed into each others eyes for a moment longer, then the waiter served their food; carbonara for Dean, tomato and basil fusilli for Jessie, and a bowl of garlic bread to share.

Jessie picked up a slice. "That'll keep the vampires away!"

"Unless the vampire has some too!" He raised his eyebrows, smiling, and picked up a slice.

They laughed flirtatiously and she felt more and more at ease with him. It might have been the wine, but the atmosphere and her decision to go with the flow helped. When the time came to order dessert, they both went for tiramisu, agreeing it was their favourite.

He flashed his eyes at her. "That's the number one sign of compatibility. Seriously!"

"Why?"

"Because I've seen marriages crumble in the dessert aisle of the supermarket. If we can agree on dessert, we'll have a long and happy future together." He kept a very straight face, then smiled.

Jessie laughed. He was so funny, not just incredibly sexy, but also fun to be around.

They left the restaurant more than slightly tipsy and shared a taxi home. She confirmed she would pick him up in the morning to save him the cost of a taxi. He accepted, thanking her sweetly.

Just before the taxi arrived at The Moorings, he put his arm around her. "I love you because you're gorgeous and gentle, sensible and caring, relaxed and not pushy. I love your smile, and your hair, and your hands and all of your body, and I think your lips are the nicest lips in the whole world."

She found it flattering, but knew he wouldn't have said it if he had been completely sober, even though he probably really meant it.

"Good. Now see if you can still say that in the morning." She smiled cheekily as he got out of the taxi.

When she arrived home she felt bad for not giving him a better response because what he said was actually very sweet. She picked up her phone and called him.

He answered in a flash. "Hello my very beautiful girlfriend."

"Hi! Does that make you my boyfriend, my very sexy boyfriend?"

"Yes, as long as that's what you want."

She smiled, imagining his shy smile on the other end of the phone. "I do, but I wanted to respond to what you said in the taxi, everything you love about me."

"I love everything about you, I just love you." He still sounded quite drunk.

"I'm blushing! I just want you to know you're the best thing to ever happen to me. I've never known anybody so caring and gentle, funny or sensitive, and the fact you're so damn gorgeous to go with it is a massive bonus, so I'm honoured to call you my boyfriend."

"I wish you were here right now so I could kiss you and fall asleep with you in my arms. But I want you to know, if ever you think I'm taking things too quickly, please please tell me because I love you, Sweet Lips."

Jessie punched the air triumphantly. "I will do, thank you."

There was a moment of silence.

"Dean. Sexy Boy?"

"Yes?"

"I love you!"

"I love you too!"

"Sleep well."

"And you."

She was content and reassured. Their short conversation had cleared up so many niggles in her mind. He had declared himself officially her boyfriend, and he demonstrated absolute responsiveness to her feelings.

She lay back on her bed with a great big smile. *He loves me, and all of this happened because of a flash of lightning.*

—  —

The rest of the week sailed by, and she felt confident. Friday would be just fine desp_te her longterm superstition about Friday 13th. He extended his Friday night proposal to the whole weekend, and wanting to treasure their time together, she didn't hesitate for even a second before accepting.

They spoke on the phone every night before going to sleep, and she felt closer to him than she ever thought she could with anybody after Mike.

She spent Thursday evening packing her overnight bag and decided she should take the condoms with her, just in case. It was so much easier now that she knew she could talk to him about it if she needed to. Her only remaining concern was whether or not she should have bought one of the extra varieties, be it long, wide, or thin, and even that felt like a very minor concern.

9 CONTRIVED SCENES

It was a very warm Friday afternoon when Jessie and Dean made their way to the car park together, blowing sweet kisses before getting into their separate cars to drive home. Excitement building because this was a new side to their relationship. She felt confident having him to her place, but entering his space would be different.

In all the time she was with Mike, she never went to his place, though he had never actually invited her to. Now, almost four months after meeting Dean, she was going to spend the whole weekend with him at his apartment, the man who told her he loves her, the only man to ever tell her he loves her.

After having a shower to freshen up, she gathered her bags together, tucked the bottle of martini and two bottles of lemonade into a sports bag, took a deep breath and set off. As she pulled into The Moorings, her knees felt weak and all her nerves were replaced with excitement. She parked her car, picked up her bags and headed towards the L shaped building in the corner. She approached the main door and pressed the buzzer for number 30.

"Hi, Sweet Lips. Come on up." His voice came via the intercom.

The door clicked and she walked inside. Not wanting to arrive out of breath, she pressed the call button for the lift and stepped in, selecting the top floor. As she felt the lift moving upwards, she took some deep breaths to relax herself because her nerves began to return. She felt like she was meeting a stranger for the first time.

The lift door slid open and she stepped out. Dean

stood waiting for her, freshly showered and looking as irresistible as he smelled.

"I love your intercom system, I wish I had one at my place, but how did you know it was me?"

He chuckled. "There's a camera, I could see you!"

"Amazing!"

They stepped inside the door to his apartment and he took her bags, put them to one side and kissed her whilst running his hands smoothly down her body. He held her at waist level with one hand whilst bringing the other hand back up to hold her head while he devoured her sweet welcoming lips. She was in awe of his presence and pulled his body closer to hers until he released his grip.

"I'm so pleased to have you here, I bought some things to make you feel at home, come and see."

They walked through a door to their right, and there were three fluffy purple cushions on the sofa, and a vase full of purple and white flowers on a table next to the corner window. She hugged and kissed him, taking a sneaky feel of his silky soft jaw line.

"Lasagne is in the oven and should be ready in fifteen minutes, so how would you like a tour?"

She beamed. "Yes please, I've really been looking forward to seeing your view."

He had a delightful apartment, and an incredible view over the river as it stretched into the distance.

"So this is where I have the best view, my living room, dining room and kitchen, all in one."

It was an L shaped room with the kitchen jutting off to one side. He had a small table with two chairs, set neatly ready for their meal. The living room had a white leather corner sofa – now decorated with three fluffy cushions – facing the big corner window.

"This is lovely, big and bright. So clean and new. How long have you lived here?"

"I bought it three years ago as a new build. I knew it would have an exceptional view over the river, so I didn't hesitate and bought it from plan. Knowing the developer was a big plus though."

They moved to the opposite end of the hallway, to the spare bedroom which was bigger, almost twice the size of her student room, then through the next door to the right, the luxury bathroom complete with a large jacuzzi style bathtub.

"I brought the martini and you have a jacuzzi, I feel a movie moment coming on."

"Next you're going to tell me you want me to pretend I'm Roger Moore or Daniel Craig!" He laughed. "Movie scenes are so contrived, real people would never do half of the things movies portray."

"I like a challenge!" She gave him a big smile. "But I much prefer you to be you."

"We'll see! Come on, only two more rooms to see, the main bedroom and ensuite." He rolled his eyes. "If I'd known you were into contrived scenes, I might have thought differently of you!"

They entered the door directly opposite the bathroom. The bedroom was vast and had a king sized bed with pure white linen. There was a walk-in wardrobe to the left of the door, a large window opposite the end of the bed, with a panoramic view down the length of the river, and the wall to the right of the bed was covered with mirrored panels. A door beside the walk-in wardrobe led to a fully tiled wet room with bright spotlights, sandy coloured tiles on three sides and one fully mirrored wall. She had expected the apartment to be nice, but she couldn't have imagined it to be so amazing.

The lasagne was almost ready, so they retired to the kitchen where she prepared martini and lemonade while he served their lasagne. She noted another first, Dean cooking for her, and he was good at it too.

After dinner, he put on some quiet music and they cuddled up on the sofa. She was desperate to try out his jacuzzi, but allowed time for their food to go down and a little more for the Martini to numb her body consciousness.

"I think it's time to relax, contrived scene style. I've never been in a jacuzzi, and you don't believe in contrived scenes, so, shall we?" She raised to her feet and offered him her hand.

"You really want to, with me, together?" He looked shocked. "Naked?"

"Yes. Come on! Well, as long as you want to?" She felt braver than ever. "We have to make the most of our weekend."

He smiled and pressed a button on his remote control. They took their martinis to the bathroom, where the piped music continued to play. Will.i.am filled the room singing *This is love.* Dean turned on the taps and poured in some bubble bath.

"I bought it for you just in case you fancied a soak. I know you only have a shower." He sniffed the bottle. "It's lavender, I hope that's okay. I didn't expect to be getting in with you though. If I had thought about it, I could've bought candles too!"

She shushed him with a finger to his lips, then replaced her finger with her own lips, kissing him sweetly. "You've done enough, you have well exceeded my expectations. Besides, candles are far more contrived than even *I* could have imagined."

The jacuzzi looked just about ready.

He tested the water. "Perfect. I won't look. You can get in first."

She felt grateful because she still worried about him seeing her fat bits, but he stood politely facing the other way whilst she stripped and climbed in. The water felt lovely and warm, and the bubbles collected around her bust, protecting her modesty.

She pulled her shoulders under the water. "Ready! I'll hold the drinks and look away for you."

He passed her the drinks, and began to strip off. "You can look now."

He was naked, climbing in, covering himself with a hand. She blinked twice before passing him his drink.

"I wanted you to see me because I've always been self conscious of my body." He raised a pile of bubbled on his hand and blew them towards her. "Getting it over and done with means I can be more relaxed with you."

She blew bubbles back at him playfully. "I understand that feeling, though I'm not sure my hands could cover all the bits I'd like. The important question is, did it work? Are you more relaxed now?"

"Oh, the hand was for your benefit, not mine. It wouldn't be very polite to invite you into my home and flash my, erm, myself at you." He replied as his cheeks turned pink. "But yes, I feel much more relaxed now, so I won't need to worry about you accidentally catching me in the nude!"

They relaxed and drank their martini and lemonade.

After a few more tracks played, She made a confession. "I had no idea you had a jacuzzi before I arrived, so this wasn't planned, but laying like this in a jacuzzi with a sexy man, sipping martini has always been one of my fantasies." She smiled. "And now I can tick it off my list!"

"You have a list?"

She giggled. "Only in my head!"

"Does it live up to your expectations?"

"It exceeds them. I could never have imagined how truly sexy the man would be."

After a relaxing half hour, Dean climbed out, took the glasses and placed them outside the door. His body was amazing, nothing to be self conscious about at all. He was certainly no body builder, but he had lovely smooth, silky skin. He wiped himself down with a towel, and she couldn't help but notice he appeared to be excited by the event.

Breathe Jessie, breathe. Good things come to those who wait.

He slipped into a bright white bathrobe, and she suddenly felt guilty about hiding her body from him. If she is ever to be relaxed with him, she had to follow his lead, reveal herself and relax, after all that was the biggest thing holding her back. She took a deep breath and climbed out, making no effort to cover herself. He turned away quickly.

"It's okay, I want you to see me so I can relax too."

He turned to face her and passed her a towel. She felt quite exposed as she dried herself, but he didn't stare, he glanced at her then emptied away the water before passing her a matching white bathrobe.

"I bought it for you so you'll always have one here."

"Thank you." She picked up the clothes from the floor. "You really have made an effort for me."

"Only what you deserve. I don't want you to need for anything."

He was right. She felt better about her body once he had seen it, especially when they snuggled up on the sofa to share passionate kisses. He hadn't been put off by her, and they felt closer than ever.

"So what other fantasies do you have on your list?"

She smiled. "That'd be telling! What about you? Surely you have some too?"

"Nothing too adventurous, not like your jacuzzi one. How about we both write down three fantasies, then compare them?"

She nodded. "That sounds like fun!"

He fetched a notebook and two pens from a drawer in his desk, which stood behind the sofa. He ripped a page out for each of them, and they both started writing furiously, pausing occasionally to think of what else to write.

"Done!" She pulled the sheet of paper to her chest.

"Hold on... okay done."

They held their lists side by side, reading.

He gasped. "I've got the same one there, look, being fed strawberries mouth to mouth!"

"Do you have any?"

"What, strawberries? Sadly not, but we could get some tomorrow, then we can both tick it off."

She nodded.

"Oh, just to clarify." His voice sounded panicked. "We don't have to tick them all off. That wasn't the aim. I don't want you to get the wrong idea or think I'm taking advantage."

"I know. It's just for fun. I think we can tick them all off at some stage though, just not this weekend."

She had written *being massaged by a naked man*, and he had written *naked massage (not sexually)*. They agreed they were practically the same thing, then blushed.

"Winning a game of strip poker?" He almost choked. "Do you know how good I am at poker?"

"Well I could have fun trying to win!" She giggled.

They had got through a few martinis by this stage, so they were falling all over each other giggling.

He pulled his paper from her view. "Don't read my last one, I changed my mind."

"No you didn't." She grabbed it and leaned away.

She smiled, her eyes firmly fixed on his words. "Making love in the shower?" She peered over the paper at him. "Talk about contrived scenes!"

"Okay, I'm a sucker for contrived scenes too, though I'm definitely no Daniel Craig!"

"I'm glad because as cute as he is, I prefer Dean Whittle, my very own super sexy boyfriend." She felt her cheeks heating up. "I'm not sure we're ready to go *that* far yet, but at some stage, I can probably try to help you tick that off."

His mouth dropped open, his face a picture. She could feel herself falling under a magical spell, but for the first time, she felt completely at ease with the thought of making love with him. No more body concerns, and definitely no more lingering worries about him trying to force himself on her. He's not like Mike. She composed herself and relaxed into his arms again, content with just being close, just cuddling and kissing. More would follow at the right time.

"I meant what I said. I want you to feel completely relaxed here. I don't want you to feel like you have to do anything you don't want to." He kissed her forehead. "Especially not just to please me."

"I know."

"You're not here because I want to have my wicked way with you." He pulled her close to his chest. "You're here so we can be close and get to know each other."

The music, Vance Joy's *Riptide*, continued to play in the background, it was a truly relaxing moment and she felt safe. He wanted her. It showed in his eyes, but there really was no hurry.

He stroked her hair. "Ready for bed?"

She nodded.

"We have something to do in the morning."

She cocked her head. "We do?"

"Yes, shopping for strawberries and ticking off one of our fantasies."

She smiled, kissed him, then followed him into the bedroom. He went to the bathroom first, and when she finally came out of the bathroom, he lay on the bed wearing only black silk shorts, a sight she could never have imagined. She joined him on the bed, his arms pulling her close. He kissed her and pulled a white sheet over them to keep the night chill off.

Jessie woke to an air of absolute silence, something she had never had in her student accommodation. She glanced around. The only trace of Dean was his black shorts on the bed beside her. She gasped and tried to fight herself, but couldn't help but pick them up and pull them to her face, inhaling the smell of his body. A sound outside the door warned her of his return, so she quickly put them back.

Dean walked through the door. "Good morning, Sweet Lips, sleep well?" He looked fresh and sexy.

"Very well, thank you."

He sat beside her on the edge of the bed and kissed her tenderly, his aftershave fresh and strong. "I'm preparing breakfast. Do you like poached egg on toast?"

"Yes. That's my favourite. I'll have a quick shower and join you in the kitchen."

"Okay. If you need anything, just give me a shout." He gave her a sweet smile.

The wet-room felt lovely and warm, the mirrored wall still covered in mist. She stripped off and turned on the shower, lowering the shower head to avoid the wide spray getting her hair wet. Water rippled over her body while she imagined making love to Dean in the steady stream of water. She took a handful of shower gel, spread it over her body. A woodland fragrance filling the air, reminding her of him. She closed her eyes and ran her fingers down her body slowly, feeling her nipples harden.

"I think I'd like that." She smiled, a little tingle washing over.

She rinsed the bubbles away and dried herself with the towel he had left neatly folded over the heated towel rail, then pulled on her clothes and joined him in the kitchen.

"Just in time, how do you like your egg yolk?"

"Soft but not runny." She sat at the small table, turning to face him.

"Same as me." He grinned. "Are you sure you're not just me imagining my perfect woman?"

She giggled. "No, I'm definitely me, a real woman."

He buttered the toast and placed the poached eggs on top, joining her at the table to eat. "So what would you like to do today?"

"We're going to buy strawberries remember!"

He squeezed her hand and smiled. She blushed. The atmosphere felt electrifying as they sat gazing at each other while eating.

"Then later." She placed her knife and fork on the

plate, dabbing the sides of her mouth with kitchen paper. "I believe you should be giving me the opportunity to try and beat you at strip poker."

"You really want to do that?" He looked surprised.

"Yes, as long as you're okay with it?"

"I'm fine with it." He raised his eyebrows, breaking into a grin. "But I won't be the one stripping off."

She cleared away the dishes while he searched through one of the drawers in his desk. He pulled out a pack of playing cards and placed them on the table ready for later.

— ❦ —

They walked hand in hand to the high street and picked up some strawberries, then he paused.

"Wait here, I just need to get something."

He walked ahead whilst Jessie sat down on a bench, wondering what he was doing, but she trusted him implicitly. He got further and further away, then he turned and walked into Boots. She widened her eyes, her heart beating faster.

Well if he's doing what I think, it will save me worrying about all those extra options.

How would she feel if he made a move to seduce her? The daunting feelings had lifted. Despite her earlier apprehension, she felt ready, especially after their naked jacuzzi. If nothing else, she had seen what she was dealing with.

He returned a few minutes later, but whatever he had in the bag looked too big to be what she expected. She looked at him inquisitively.

"Don't look at me like that, it's a surprise." He tapped the end of her nose. "For later."

"Meanie!"

"You'll like it, I promise, just trust me."

Her trust in him was greater than any trust she had ever felt. Whatever it was. She would love it.

Jessie washed the strawberries, removing the leaves and stalks. She placed them into a bowl, then joined Dean on the sofa. He picked up a strawberry, placed it in his mouth, closing his lips around it, then beckoned her to take it from him. She clambered over him trying to get close enough, giggling, but he kept moving away. She lay down on the floor to catch her breath and he crawled over, lowering the strawberry into her mouth, kissing her softly as he did so.

She retaliated to his teasing by placing a strawberry between her teeth, straddling him and holding his hands down. She lowering it enough to allow him to touch it with his lips, but not quite low enough for him to take it. He wriggled and managed to free a hand, rolled her over, pinning her, then calmly taking the strawberry from her, mouth to mouth.

"You're not playing fair!" She giggled as he kept her pinned down.

"You never said it had to be fair. Fair would be boring." He released her hands from where he held them and kissed her passionately, rolling around on the soft cream carpet.

"You taste like strawberry!" She reached out to pick up another strawberry from the bowl.

"Strange that." He smiled. "I wouldn't notice because you always taste this sweet."

She held the next strawberry between her lips and gently placed it into his mouth, stroking his soft ash blonde hair as he chewed it. He responded by doing the same thing for her. Much calmer, less teasing, more passion.

He brushed his fingers over the soft cream carpet. "I'm glad I didn't go for laminate now. Come here." He rolled her over, pulling her on top of him, hands on her bottom, tongues entwined.

An air of sexual tension began to build. She bravely picked up the next strawberry, placing it between her cleavage, his eyes glowing. He kissed his way down her neck and chest, slowly moving towards the strawberry.

He peered up from where he rested his chin on her bust. "Now who's not playing fair?" He smiled and gently removed the strawberry with his teeth.

They reverted to rolling around on the floor, then paused near the window to watch two small boats racing along the river.

He ran a finger over her lips. "How were your strawberries?"

"Very tasty. I should eat strawberries like that more often."

"We could have whipped cream with them next time." He began to blush.

"Mmm you're so adventurous. I just thought we would pass them backwards and forwards one by one. Anyway, as we're getting to know each other, tell me three things I don't know about you."

He looked thoughtful. "Any three things?"

"Yes, anything you like."

"Okay. Erm, my feet are a size 9. I have one brother, older, more handsome and very muscular. Erm, thinking." He raised a hand to his chin, looking thoughtful. "Okay, I should confess this before you find out by accident. My favourite TV programme is Neighbours."

"Really?"

He lowered his head. "Yes."

"Good because I like Neighbours too."

They both smiled. He met her gaze, cocking his head. She realised it was her turn.

"My parents live in Australia. I have no siblings, and I can play the piano."

He nodded approvingly. "I'll tell you one more because mine were rubbish compared to yours. I probably owe you this. I'm actually not very good at playing poker, and I've never played strip poker."

"Good, can we play later?"

"Yes. That's what I got the cards out for." He pointed to the table.

Her mind raced, anticipating another glimpse of his naked body. She tried to read his expression, sensing him having the same thoughts about her. As her mind wandered, becoming lustful, she realised she was racing too far ahead. She needed to slow down, take one step at a time, else she could end up hurt again. Mike ruined her faith in men.

After a relaxing afternoon listening to music, then a Chinese takeaway, Dean picked up the set of cards and passed them to Jessie.

She smiled. "Are you ready to lose then?"

"We'll see." His poker face already in play.

She shuffled the cards and dealt five each. Dean looked at his cards and looked at her, his face perfectly straight. He was good. He discarded three cards and she gave him three more. He grinned at her. She couldn't decide if he was bluffing or if he actually had a good hand. She looked at her own cards, a pair of kings. She discarded the other three, hoping for another king, but ended up with a jack, a two and a nine. She revealed her hand and he smiled.

She raised her eyebrows. "Can you beat it?"

He shook his head and placed his cards face down. She looked suspiciously at him, then picked up his cards. He only had two jacks.

"Come on then." He stood. "Take something off me."

She looked him up and down. He wore a pair of dark blue shorts and a white polo shirt, and presumably some sort of underwear, but nothing else. She unfastened the button on his polo shirt and lifted it over his head, revealing his silky soft chest. It made her mouth water.

She eyed his remaining clothing. "I assume you're now two hands from losing?"

"Yes, but you must be only one ahead, so don't look too smug!" He winked.

He shuffled the pack and dealt. She looked at her cards and smiled before putting two on the discard pile. He gave her two more and she smiled again, before watching carefully as he discarded one card. She swallowed hard as he picked up a new one, then placed them down on the table. A four, five, six, seven, and a nine, all different suits. Jessie revealed her three of a kind; three eights.

He sighed. "No wonder I couldn't get my eight, you had them all!"

She giggled. "Well, you dealt, so it's down to you!"

She stared at his chest, then the buttons on his shorts, wondering what she would reveal by taking them off him.

"Feeling shy?" He stood up to allow her to remove his shorts.

Her hand trembled, but she managed to unfasten three buttons, then let go. The shorts fell to his feet. She tried to avert her gaze but curiosity got the better of her. Her mouth dropped open and she gasped. He wore skimpy black tanga briefs. They left very little to the imagination, but she tried hard not to imagine, then looked up and met his gaze.

"Don't look so scared, you're not the one who is almost completely naked!"

She glanced back at his briefs, bit her bottom lip, then shuffled the cards again, dealing another hand. He discarded two cards, and collected two new. She didn't want to win again, spoiling his fun, so she discarded her good cards including half of a pair, collected three new ones and ended up with a pair of threes. She placed her cards down and Dean smiled as he revealed three jacks.

"I guess I can't win them all." She stood up, nervous but glad.

She raised her arms and waited for him to lift her lilac dress over her head. He looked incredibly nervous about it considering he was the one standing there wearing nothing but his briefs. He visibly took a deep breath, then removed the dress, sitting down quickly, cheeks all pink. She blushed as she stood in front of him wearing just a white lace bra and matching thong.

He picked up the cards, shuffled and dealt. She couldn't decide whether she wanted to win or lose, so she played it seriously and left her fate to the luck of the cards. They sat staring each other in the eye before revealing their hands together. She had two queens, but he had two jacks and two fours. His previously pink cheeks turned a distinct shade of red and she stood up, turned around and allowed him access to unfasten her bra, then turned back to face him. Suddenly they were equals. She put her arms around his waist to pull him closer, partly to hide her naked breasts, but also because she wanted to kiss him. The feeling of his bare skin on hers was arousing, adding to their obvious sexual tension.

"One hand left." He passed her the pack, "And as an added incentive, the loser gets their naked massage today, but the winner has to wait until tomorrow."

"We can stop if you want. If you're uncomfortable."

"Are you uncomfortable?"

She shook her head. "No, I'm feeling quite liberated. Nobody can see through that window can they?

"No, this side of the building is not overlooked at all." He tapped the cards. "Let's play."

It was her turn to deal. He looked at his cards thoughtfully, then discarded two. He looked at her, his eyebrows raised. She looked at her cards and discarded three, then placed all five on the table to reveal three queens. His eyes widened, then he took a deep breath and presented two fours and three kings.

"Full House I believe." He turned pink.

She gave him a brave smile, stood up and presented herself to him, arms open wide, a definite feeling of butterflies in her tummy. Despite the nerves, she wanted to live out her fantasy, and there was no better person to do it with.

He peered at her panties, then into her eyes. "Are you sure?"

"Yes. You won fair and square." Her eyes fixed on his. "You've seen it all before, so just take them off me."

"Okay, but I should admit, I was being polite, I didn't really look yesterday." He stood and slowly slipped his fingers under the waistband of her thong, lowering it gently.

She put her arms around him and kissed him. "Thank you for shattering my fantasy. I'm heartbroken." She held a straight face for a moment before laughing.

"You've got a beautiful body and as a reward for winning, I get to touch it." He bit his lower lip. "Come to the bedroom. I've got something to show you."

She followed him nervously, then spotted the Boots bag from earlier.

He revealed a massage gift pack, opened it up and held up a candle. "This is what I wanted. A massage candle. My brother told me about these because his wife loves them. You relax while I light it." He disappeared through the open door.

She lay on the bed face down, and he walked back in with the lit candle. He placed it on the bedside cabinet and joined her on the bed, gently running his fingers over her back.

"You've got beautiful soft skin. You don't mind me touching do you?"

She kept her eyes fixed on his. "No. I feel perfectly safe in your hands."

He poured some of the melted candle into his hand and began to massage it into her back and shoulders, moving slowly down her arms, then back up to her shoulders, her neck and back. She glanced over her shoulder, catching a glimpse of his expression. He was completely focused on what he was doing. His eyes full of desire, and his lips parted slightly as he licked his lips. Her attention was distracted when she noticed his briefs, clearly stretching across his building excitement. She smiled warmly and closed her eyes.

He whispered close to her ear. "Is this okay for you?"

"It's lovely, I'll be asleep soon if you're not careful."

He continued to massage down her back, around her hips and across her bottom before moving onto her thighs, one by one. She felt completely relaxed.

He blew out the candle and lay beside her. He whispered softly in her ear. "I love you, Sweet Lips."

"I love you too, Sexy Boy." Her voice almost a whisper.

Jessie woke feeling invigorated on Sunday morning. Dean continued to sleep beside her. He had clearly got up at some point because he had swapped out of his tanga briefs, and wore his black silk shorts instead. Fresh visions of his bulging briefs flashed though her mind, making her smile, wishing she had been the one to take them off him. He rolled over, showing off his gorgeous long legs and the shape of his pert bottom beneath his shorts. She brushed her fingers over the silk and he stirred, turning and opening his eyes, meeting hers with a content smile.

She smiled back. "Can I give you your massage and let you rest some more?"

"What time is it?"

She leaned over to check. "6:45am."

"Don't you want to sleep?"

"No." Daring herself to tell the truth. "I really want to touch you, and I owe you a massage."

"Mmm I like your thinking."

She went to the kitchen to light the candle, returning to find him laying face down – naked – ready to allow her to caress his bare body. The silk shorts lay on the bed beside him. She grinned, recalling how she examined them cheekily yesterday, but now she had all six foot of him, waiting for her, naked.

She felt nervous, and as her fingertips brushed past his silky soft skin, she felt an electrifying connection to him and all her nerves vanished. The candle had melted enough to collect the oil, so she poured it into her hand just as he had done. She rubbed it between her fingers and placed her hands firmly on his back, devouring his skin, along his shoulders and down his back, hesitating to take a deep breath before moving lower, squeezing his bottom and working the warm massage oil down his long slender legs before gently working her way back up to his shoulders and down his arms.

"Thank you." He reached for her hand.

She blew out the candle, took his hand and cuddled into him.

Packing her bag and preparing to go home was a sad moment for Jessie because she felt closer to him than ever. She had loved every minute of their weekend and felt like they were on the verge of taking the next obvious step. Dean had been such a gentleman, and was maybe waiting for a sign, some indication that she was ready. Daydreaming as she made the bed, she hoped she was right, then picked up the Boots bag to put the massage candle back into the gift set, and there in the bag was the sign she needed; a box of condoms.

10 NEWS

Jessie lay on her bed reflecting on the events of the weekend, wondering why she had ever been nervous of becoming too close to Dean. Ever since the first time she saw him walking in the park, when he smiled, he has been nothing but gentle and caring towards her. She smiled and ran her fingers over her skin where he massaged her, it felt so soft, then she remembered the box of condoms in the bag.

She got up and sat at her desk to fill in her diary, but her phone began to ring, disturbing her.

She picked it up, saw Dean's name and answered. "Hi Sexy Boy."

"I wanted to check you got home safely. I also thought I should talk to you about something."

She felt extremely nervous about what he was about to say. Had he decided not to take things further because he had changed his mind?

"What's that?" Her nerves were on edge.

"Am I right that we're serious about each other?"

"Yes, that's how I see it, why?"

"I want to make our relationship public at work. I think it'll take pressure off us because we won't have to be discreet. It'll also nip the gossiping in the bud."

She was aware that at least one such episode had already occurred, so he was right. "I'm happy with that, but won't it be seen as a conflict of interest?"

"No. I'm not your boss, so as long as we're open, it couldn't be seen like that."

"Okay, that sounds reasonable enough." The prospect excited her. "How do you intend to break the news?"

"Meet me in the car park. We can arrive together

hand in hand, then we'll announce it."

"I like that idea. Also, thank you for a lovely weekend. You're a true gentleman."

"I was going to say that to you, well, all except the gentleman part! Thank you, it was amazing, especially ticking off those fantasies."

She twirled her hair around her finger, licking her lips. "Yes, we still have one of yours to look forward to at some time though."

"No hurry. It can wait until you're ready."

She almost gasped down the phone, but cleared her throat and tried to be natural.

"Okay, Sexy Boy. I'm going to sleep now."

"Okay, night night, Sweet Lips, I love you."

"I love you too."

Dean had just pulled into a parking space when she drove into the car park on Monday morning. She parked beside him and got out to join him where he stood waiting nearby. He put his arms around her, raised her chin and kissed her softly.

"Are you ready for this?" He stroked her hair.

"Yes." She smiled. "I feel proud to be able to walk in there and claim you as *my* boyfriend." Her words sending a warm tingle through her body.

He offered his hand and led her down the road towards the main entrance. They walked into the building and straight into the waiting lift. That alone was a good sign.

"Are you okay?" His eyes drifting to their hands.

"Yes, you?"

He nodded and kissed her just before the lift doors opened, delivering them to the fifth floor. They both took a deep breath as they walked through the double doors, still holding hands tightly. Beaming as they raised their adjoined hands to chest hight for people to see. The office went quiet after some initial chatter and psst sounds. Almost a hundred eyes pointing in their direction, including Lisa's.

"I thought you might all like to share our news. Jessie and I are now officially a couple." He looked at her. "I know there have been a couple of whispers over the last week, so to save any further speculation, yes it's true." He kissed her hand and released her when they reached the side of her desk.

During the morning, various people congratulated them, saying how great they look together.

George approached Jessie with a beaming smile. "I'm so pleased to hear your news, I couldn't think of a more perfect couple."

She was even more focused on her work because she felt so content with their decision to go public. She caught Lisa's eye a couple of times, and Lisa smiled warmly. It felt slightly disturbing, but she smiled back politely. Later in the morning, she went to collect coffee from the canteen when Lisa approached.

"I know I'm the last person you want to talk to, but I want to say I'm happy for you." Lisa stared at her feet. "I also want to apologise because it has made me realise something that should have been obvious."

Unsure how she felt, Jessie remained calm. "What's that?"

"Everything you said was true. I've been really stupid, but it's more than that. I accused you of being jealous when you walked out and left me with Rob and Dan." She looked into her eyes. "But it's clear now that you didn't want to jeopardise your chances with Dean." She looked serious.

Jessie felt sympathetic. "Thank you for saying so, it means a lot."

"I suddenly understand the difficult positions I put you in when we were out together, and I understand your reasons for walking away. I truly respect your moral feelings."

They returned to the office. an air of peace between them. Jessie missed her best friend, and this was the longest they had been upset with each other for.

She paused just outside the double doors. "Lisa."

"Yes?"

"I miss you. If ever you want to meet up after work to catch up. You know where I am."

Lisa smiled. "I might just take you up on that because I miss you too."

— 🦋 —

Jessie sat down next to Dean on their bench in the park. She was still feeling positive about her chat with Lisa. She told him about it as they walked.

"It's worth reconciling your differences because long term friendship is something to treasure." He opened his lunchbox and offered her a chicken and mustard sandwich.

"I know. I can't wait to tell her about the storm, and how you looked after me. She'll appreciate that." She poked her own floppy cheese sandwich. "I wonder if we would be sat here now if it wasn't for that storm."

"We would have ended up together eventually." He grinned. "The storm just accelerated the process."

She cocked her head. "Do you think so?"

"Yes, I was so close to kissing you the first time we went to The Old English." He began to blush. "I worried you might reject me, so fear held me back."

"So what about the night you came over to look after me? When you stayed and held me all night." The thought flooded her with warmth.

"What about it?"

"Were you tempted to kiss me then?"

"Yes and no. I wanted to. I really really wanted to, but I wasn't going to because you were vulnerable."

"You're quite the gentleman." She leaned in and kissed him.

Her phone buzzed, a message from Lisa, asking if they could meet up after work at The Red Lion.

"Do you think I should accept?"

He nodded. "Yes, I think you should."

She replied to accept, not expecting a complete, immediate reunion, not after all that had happened.

"You're a good friend." He rubbed her arm. "But don't let her walk all over you."

— 🐦 —

At the end of the day, Jessie walked down to the end of the road with Dean, giving him a kiss before letting him go to his car. She continued further down the road to join Lisa at The Red Lion.

They ordered two lemonades and sat in the corner near the window.

Jessie started their conversation. "How are you?"

"Mmm life is interesting, what about you?"

"I could call it interesting, but probably a different sort of interesting to yours. You don't seem like your normal self. What's going on? Life at home troubling you?"

Lisa sighed. "If only it was that easy. You're my oldest friend in the world, the only person I could ever trust as we grew up. Apt that you are now the only person I can trust with this."

"What happened?" She frowned.

Lisa looked tearful. Jessie put her arm around her.

"At lunchtime, today, I did a test." She hesitated to wipe her eyes. "I'm pregnant."

Jessie gasped. "Are you sure?"

Lisa nodded.

"Who?"

"Rob or Dan. I don't know because they were both the same night, 27th July, so about seven weeks ago, and that probably fits."

Jessie could probably have guessed, but she didn't suggest it. Considering how Lisa had been behaving, it wasn't a surprise, but it was shocking. "Why didn't you use condoms? STDs and all that." She swallowed hard, wishing she hadn't been so blunt.

"I know." She lowered her head. "It was stupid but I was very drunk. They flattered me and I've long fantasised about being with two hot men, and there they were." She frowned. "Surely you've slipped up at least once. It's easily done."

"Me?"

Lisa nodded. "How often do you forget to use a condom?"

Jessie froze, unsure how to respond. Lisa just stared at her.

She shook her head, looking down. "I've never used one."

Lisa looked confused.

"I don't get it." She furrowed her brow. "You're lecturing me about not using one, just this once, but you've never bothered." She almost looked angry.

"Lisa, it's not about bothering or not bothering." She took a deep breath and looked her in the eye, dropping to a whisper. "I'm still a virgin."

Lisa's face froze for a moment, then she looked confused. "But you and Dean?"

"No, we haven't." She blushed.

Lisa's eyes widened. "I don't know how he can keep his hands off you."

"He's very sweet, polite, never pushes. Everything happens naturally with us."

"So he knows?"

Jessie smiled, relaxing. "No, of course not."

She felt extremely embarrassed, but Lisa had forgotten about her own problem. This was headline news to her, something she should have known.

Lisa's face suddenly became suspicious. "Hold on, what about Mike?"

"Nope, that'll be why he went off with someone else, probably why he tried it on with you too."

"I'm so sorry. I just thought you did."

"There was no chance." She shook her head. "He put me under too much pressure, even tried to force me. I wanted to do it for me, not because someone wanted me to do it for them. He pressured me from day one and I knew if he couldn't wait, he wasn't worth it."

"So Dean is different?"

Jessie smiled. "He's the complete opposite, extremely respectful and gentle."

"Are you sure he's not gay?"

"Going by when we were in the jacuzzi together at the weekend." She raised her eyebrows. "I'm thinking not. He was excited to be there, trust me."

Lisa's face was a picture, clearly shocked by this information. "You were in a jacuzzi together. Naked?"

Jessie nodded, pursing her lips.

"He's clearly waiting for you to make the first move then." Lisa would know with her wealth of experience.

"Good, that's how I want it to be." She smiled.

Lisa broke into a big smile. "Well, good on you. I'm quite proud of you for respecting yourself enough to hold out, especially when you have a hot guy on a plate in front of you."

"So what about you? What are you going to do now?"

"I made an appointment at the doctors, but it's not until the end of next week. I'll have to see what they say." Lisa looked distraught once more.

They finished their drinks and walked to the car park together.

Lisa looked around, as if checking who was nearby. "You won't tell anybody will you?"

"No, I'll keep your secret if you keep mine."

Lisa hugged her, then got into her car and drove away.

— ❦ —

True to her word, Jessie said nothing about Lisa's problem to anybody, not even Dean, but on Wednesday lunchtime he inadvertently backed her into a corner. They were sat on their bench in the park eating their lunch.

"Have you spoken with Lisa today?"

She shook her head. "Only briefly to say good morning, why?"

"Don't you think she looks a bit unwell? She was backwards and forwards to the bathroom all day yesterday."

Her cheeks flushed with warmth. "I think she might be lactose intolerant or something."

Wondering if he would buy that feeble stab in the dark.

"She was the same last week too, but never before." He looked inquisitively at her.

She tried to think of what to say, remembering her promise to keep the secret in exchange for Lisa keeping hers. She didn't want to keep any of it from him, but her inexperience worried her.

"Do you think she might be pregnant?"

Unable to control it, her face was enough to tell him he was right, she didn't even have to open her mouth.

"You were sworn to secrecy weren't you?"

"Yes." She pursed her lips, nodding. "Please don't let her know I told you, and don't tell anybody else, especially Rob or Dan." Then she realised what she had said, closing her eyes.

He put his hand on her lap, jolting her to open her eyes. He gazed straight at her. Shocked. "You mean she's been with them both... hold on. Was it her?" He stared at her. "They were bragging about a girl who was all over them a while back and suggested they share her for the night. I thought they were making it up." His mouth hung open.

"Sadly not, just please, please, please don't let on you know anything."

"I'm staying well out of it." He shook his head. What a mess."

11 EVERYONE HAS A STORY TO TELL

The alarm hadn't yet gone off when Jessie woke on Friday morning. She lay thinking about how much had changed over the last week. The time felt right. Like Lisa said, he was waiting for her to make the first move, and that move was imminent.

I'll talk to Lisa and get some tips from her.

The alarm went off and she got up, ready to face the world and conquer her fears. Just as she got out of the shower, her phone buzzed with a new text message. She wrapped herself up in a towel and checked the message. It was from Lisa.

"I won't be at work today, the morning sickness is really bad and I feel quite rough. Have a good weekend with that sexy boyfriend of yours. See you next week x"

She replied to tell her to take it easy, but decided not to elaborate on her plans, after all, she had got this far on her own. Rather than wait, she decided to send Dean a message to organise an evening at his place. The student accommodation wasn't exactly a romantic spot, certainly not somewhere to create lasting memories.

"Morning Sexy Boy, do you have any plans for this evening? I'd love to have a dip in your Jacuzzi if you're free?"

Less than thirty seconds later, he responded.

"Hey Sweet Lips, I was planning to invite you over to watch a DVD, how would you feel about staying for the weekend again? After all, if you won't stay over on a work night, then I must make the most of our weekends. I can cook for us again."

A plan was coming together, so she replied straight away.

"I'd like that very much, consider it a date. See you at work."

She packed her weekend bag and ensured the condoms were still safely in the side pocket, then dug out her sexiest underwear: a low cut black lace bra and matching black thong. She placed it on the end of her bed then rifled through her wardrobe and picked out a sexy red dress she had only ever worn once before. Having laid them out on her bed, ready to get changed when she arrived home from work, she stood back to look at them and smiled.

Project seduction is now in operation.

During the morning at work, she gave Dean a flirtatious look every time she caught his eye. She knew something he didn't, and she couldn't wait to present her new seductive self to him. When lunchtime arrived, she started to get nervous and worried about him rejecting her. The way he held her in the park reassured her though. He was definitely fired up and responding to her flirting in way she could only interpret as a man who wanted to be seduced. She recalled how passionate he was when he fed her strawberries, and how excited he looked when he got out of the jacuzzi.

They walked through the park and found somebody else sitting on their bench, so they walked slightly further to the privately positioned bench on the other side of the pond. She decided to test him and see how keen he was.

"Are you sure I'm not intruding by coming over tonight?"

He smiled. "No, I really want you there."

"You know I only want you for your jacuzzi, don't you?" She fired him a cheeky grin.

"Of course you do, just like I only want you for your gorgeous lips." He winked and kissed her. "The rest of you is just an irresistible bonus."

"Irresistible? Powerful word." She giggled.

"Do you want to come over for 6pm and I'll make sure dinner is ready?"

"That's good for me."

They began to eat their sandwiches.

"I wish we had strawberries for lunch." She waggled her eyebrows.

"I'm glad we don't have strawberries today, you've already got me feeling rather frisky, if you don't mind me saying so."

"No, I don't mind. It's a nice thought." She grinned.

Having played it calm outside, she was doing cartwheels inside. She was doing the right thing.

—  —

She had just finished drying her hair when her phone dinged with a message from Lisa. She saw enough on the preview screen to know she was asking to come over. She couldn't say no, but if she hadn't opened the message, she wouldn't be saying anything. She ignored it. This was her night, and after the way they had been for the last few weeks, she wasn't about to give it up for Lisa. She finished getting ready, inspected herself in the mirror and took a few deep breaths. It was time to go and she felt more ready than she ever had. She picked up her bag, slipped her phone into the side pocket and set off.

Arriving, she stepped out of the lift, his eyes firmly fixed on her, his mouth open and eyes full of desire. Her sexy red dress certainly enhanced her voluptuous bust line, as she planned.

He wrapped an arm around her waist and kissed her softly. "I'm cooking a hoi sin chicken stir fry, but you look good enough to eat, so I'll skip the main, and have your sweet lips for dessert instead."

She smiled and squeezed his bottom. "Good things come to those who wait."

He pouted, then took her bag and led her inside, placing the bag in the bedroom. She felt completely relaxed, but suddenly remembered Lisa's message. She was about to open it and reply to say she was out, but changed her mind. The best thing to do was to turn the phone off and prevent a string of messages from disturbing her evening.

The stir fry tasted delicious. She helped clear away the dishes, running through her plan in her mind. Gentle music played in the background, and as they walked out of the kitchen area, he put his arms around her and started to dance slowly with her, kissing her neck and running his hands down her back to hold her bottom seductively. It felt amazing.

"Is it okay if I do this?" He squeezed her bottom.

"Yes. I like that." She held him closer.

They danced for a short time before she released her grip, breaking up their embrace.

She took his hand and led him towards the bedroom. "I want to show you something."

Once there, she unfastened her dress and pulled it over her head, exposing her skimpy black underwear.

"That's gorgeous." He gave her a timid smile. "Is it jacuzzi time?"

She lowered her chin, her eyes still fixed on his. Breathing through her parted lips, she shook her head. "No, in the words of a very wise man. I want to try something first."

She reached into the side pocket of her bag, pulled out the box of condoms and held them up for a moment before placing them on the bed. His eyes lit up and he distinctly gasped. He didn't say a word. Instead, he reached into the bedside drawer and pulled out an identical box and threw them onto the bed with hers. They grinned at each other, then began to kiss. She lowered her hands and fumbled to undress him. She felt terrified, but this was the point of no return. Everything was right. She felt ready, and she could feel it, he was ready too. He kissed her and caressed her, then eased away gently to speak.

He gave her a fearful gaze. "I need to warn you about something."

She had no idea what he was about to say, but she worried it would end in rejection. He looked concerned, nervous, then he took a deep breath, still holding her firmly in his arms.

"I'm twenty-five years old and I can't believe I'm admitting this, but I love you and I trust you entirely." He paused again. "I really, I mean really really want to, but you'll be my first." He swallowed hard. "I've never done this before."

She rested her head on his chest, feeling his heart pounding. No wonder he hadn't made the first move, even after buying the condoms. She looked up at him, his eyes so gentle, and so wanting. His flushed cheeks showing off his embarrassment. She took a deep breath and looked him in the eye with absolute desire.

"I'm twenty-one years old and this is my first time too, so if you're gentle with me, I'll be gentle with you."

There was an air of intense relief. His shoulders relaxed in time with hers, and they grinned as their lips met again. Nobody was being judged or compared, it was just the two of them in their own magical passionate world.

They took it very slowly, guiding each other, whispering and giggling as they made love for the very first time. The passion in their eyes was enough to say they felt comfortable with each other. Jessie felt glad she hadn't given in to Mike's demands because Dean was the one, he always treated her like she was the most important person in the world, unlike Mike who treated her like she was just there to serve him.

They lay face to face, gazing into each other's eyes, still full of passion, but fulfilled and relaxed. Waiting had made it mean so much more than a drunken fumble. They chatted openly, and Jessie admitted to being surprised, not because of his age, which he had just given away for the first time, but because she finds him completely irresistible and cannot understand why he hasn't had the opportunity before.

He chuckled. "I had two bad experiences at

university. They were enough to put anybody off."

"Really, that bad?"

He nodded. "The first time, I invited a girl back to my place and instead of politely declining, she made a show, shouting about how I thought so much of myself that I thought she would want to have sex with me. She was drunk and slightly presumptuous, but I was young and naive."

"Well she wouldn't have been worth it."

"That's what I thought too, but it left me with the nickname *Desperate Dean*, which made girls avoid me." He blushed.

"Their loss, my gain." She ran her hand over his body, resting it on his smooth, naked bottom. "What about the second one? It can't be as bad as that."

"Worse unfortunately." He frowned. "I'm not even sure you'll want to hear it, but, there was a girl on my course who had been flirting with me for couple of weeks. I was in the bar with Rob, and she was sat on her own while her friend visited the ladies. She sat smiling at me, so I went over just to talk to her. I remember it so clearly. She stunk of alcohol but it seemed like my only chance to talk to her alone. I only planned to ask her out on a date, but when I sat next to her, she leaned over to kiss me, burped, and threw up all over me." He pulled a repulsed face.

She screwed up her face to match his. "That's awful."

"Yes, nightmare inducing. After that, I decided my perfect woman would find me when the time was right. I've never felt confident enough to initiate more than one kiss with one woman. You."

How sweet.

She kissed him tenderly. "I'm glad you did, but put the rest down to fate. You were waiting for me, but just didn't know it."

"I can live with that, now tell me about you." He pushed a strand of hair off her face.

She felt nervous, but he had been open with her. "Mostly all study, no play. Boring compared to your reason. I was seeing someone for a few months earlier this year but it didn't feel right. He tried to pressure me and I didn't want it to happen like that." She shook her head. "Anyway, he went off with someone else and proved he was the wrong one for me."

"Well he definitely didn't deserve you."

"No he didn't, I even found out he had been trying it on with Lisa, but she rejected him out of loyalty to me."

"What a loser!"

"Agreed." She leaned over to get off the bed. "Now, how about that jacuzzi?"

12 THE LOVE OF DEAN'S LIFE

Waking up in Dean's bed on Saturday morning, remembering their passionate evening, filled Jessie with warmth. She picked up her phone and turned it on to check for messages, but the only one was the one Lisa had sent before she set off from home. She placed it back on the bedside cabinet and rolled over to watch Dean sleeping just as he opened his eyes. He gazed at her for a moment, then broke into a beaming smile.

"Good morning Sexy Boy."

"Hey, Sweet Lips. Kiss me quick so I know I'm not dreaming."

She leaned in ready to kiss him, then stopped. He looked confused.

"If you were dreaming, I would have kissed you, so now you know you're not."

He rolled over and pinned her down, kissing her tenderly. She felt like she was the one dreaming. She wanted more, then his outstanding fantasy popped into her head.

She squeezed his bottom. "How would you like to join me in the shower?"

He smiled. "I'd love to." Rolling over to stand.

She picked up a condom from the side pocket of her bag, and his eyes twinkled. He led her into the luxurious ensuite where she caught sight of their naked bodies in the mirrored wall opposite the shower. At first she felt self conscious, but when Dean put his arms around her, she knew he didn't mind her lumps and bumps.

Trying to live out his fantasy was an interesting experience, but definitely unlike the movies. After slipping and sliding, trying to make love in the steamy shower for fifteen minutes, she admitted defeat. "That's clearly a contrived scenario."

He smiled, nodding in agreement. It had been fun trying. "I thought you didn't believe in my *contrived for television* theory?"

"Maybe just this once." She giggled.

They wrapped themselves in towels and returned to the bedroom, throwing themselves on the bed giggling. She gazed into his eyes and ran her hand down his chest, over his navel, moving lower. Suddenly, her phone began to ring. She looked at the screen, saw Mike's name, and immediately swiped the screen to reject his call. Dean looked intrigued.

"Mike. My pestering ex." She wanted to be as open as possible.

"Pressure boy?"

"Yes. He's a pain, probably drunk again. He's on placement somewhere up north."

Just as she finished speaking, the phone rang again.

"Can I answer it?" He smiled.

She passed it to him.

"Hello... Who?... What do you want from the love of my life?... Sorry, she's busy looking extremely sexy on my bed right now... No, she can't talk with her mouth full, besides, she doesn't want to talk to you so don't bother calling back." He held the phone out in front of him and shrugged.

Her mouth was half open, speechless.

He passed it back to her. "Aww, he put the phone

down on me."

A smile spread over her face. "I can't believe you said my mouth was full, that'll wind him up no end."

"Shame he actually hung up when I said you were the love of my life." He began to laugh. "I was just practicing what I would like to say to him."

She looked relieved but saw the funny side.

He wrapped his arms around her. "I'll protect you from him. Of course, he might give up now he knows you're with me."

She frowned. "You clearly don't know him." She flipped the phone to silent, not wanting him to distract them again, and lost herself in his embrace once more.

—  —

Walking along the river side, Jessie was surprised by how much the old industrial area had changed. Back when she was a child, there was no parkland or housing, no wildlife, just smelly old factories. They approached a long bridge just before a bend in the river and she remembered playing there during her summer holidays when she was about ten.

"We used to come down here on our bikes. There was one time when Lisa got caught writing on one of the concrete pillars by a passerby, and as we ran with our bikes to try and get away, Lisa slipped and almost fell in the river."

"Hooligans." He shook his head.

"Look, there. *Lisa 4* Tomn." She pointed, laughing. "It was meant to say *Lisa 4 Tommo*, but she didn't get to finish it, and we never did come back."

He chuckled. "That passerby must have really

scared you."

"No, it wasn't that. Lisa cut her leg on some wire when she fell. She had to have stitches, so when her Mum found out where it happened, we were barred from coming back."

He shook his head in disapproval. "So you've known Lisa for longer than I thought?"

"Yes, as long as I can remember. She's always been the adventurous one, living dangerously. Little changes there, but look at this place."

They emerged from the other side of the bridge, and approached a row of large houses, all brand new. The front lawns stretched down to the path at the riverbank. Ducks quacked in nearby reeds.

"This is beautiful, I could never have imagined this." She shook her head. It really had been just wasteland last time she saw it.

"You couldn't live here though because Lisa wouldn't be allowed to visit."

"Why?" She furrowed her brow.

"Because her Mum barred her from coming back down here." He broke into a chuckle.

She gave him a playful slap on the arm. They continued to walk until the next bridge, then turned back to return to his apartment, just in time because the late September sky was becoming dark and it looked like rain was coming.

— 🍎 —

Their relaxation continued as they spent the afternoon listening to music, comparing their favourite tracks. They were sprawled out on the floor beside the full length corner window, watching the rain make patterns in the river. James Morrison sang *If the Rain Must Fall* in the background.

"Apt." She pointed into the air.

"What's that?"

"The music."

He laughed. "I picked this one specially."

She smiled. Happier than she had ever been, rolling around on the floor with her dream man. This was one moment when she couldn't agree more with the words of a song, because dreams really *can* come true. So many words in that song applied to them, right back to the darkening sky on the day of the storm.

"I find your view relaxing, so much unspoilt sky."

"You should come over for the bonfire night fireworks on 2nd November. I've never had a better view than this. One of many advantages I've found for being on the fifth floor."

"That'd be great, I've never found a perfect spot to watch them from."

He pulled her head onto his chest. "What would you like to do later?"

"I would love to stay like this forever." She stroked his cheek. "But maybe we could play pool at The Old English."

"Good idea. I often walk over there on a Saturday evening because it's nice and quiet there when most people head off into town for the wild night life." He shuddered.

"You don't like wild night life?"

"No!" He looked outraged. "It's definitely not my thing."

"I couldn't agree more."

131

— ❧ —

It had stopped raining when they set off for The Old English. It wasn't far, just a pleasant stroll. She suddenly remembered the night when he dropped her at home in his taxi, clearly going well out of his way.

"Remember the first time you took me home, when you didn't want me to get the wrong impression?"

"Yes, why?"

"If I hadn't been there, would you have walked home?"

He blushed and raised his eyebrows. "I was looking after you. I took you over there, to unfamiliar territory, so I wanted to make sure you got home safely."

"But, would you have walked if I wasn't there?"

"Yes, I would have walked." He pulled her into an embrace and kissed her. "In all honesty, if I hadn't been too nervous, I would have invited you to come home with me, but you know why I didn't." His blushing cheeks gave away his shyness. "I thought you were adorable but I didn't know how to tell you."

— ❧ —

Arriving at The Old English, the open fire was lit, most welcome on a damp evening. Jessie spotted Rob and Dan on the far side of the bar, and suddenly remembered leaving Lisa with them. She tried to put it out of her head while Dean ordered their drinks. They made their way over to the pool table where the lads sat, Dean holding her hand firmly.

"Woooo are you two...?" Dan raised his eyebrows to finish the sentence.

Dean glanced at Jessie. "Dating. Is that what you

mean?" He proudly put his arm around her.

Rob smiled. "Congratulations both of you, ignore jealous pants." He sounded entirely genuine.

They sat down, staying close.

Dan took a swig of beer and slammed his glass down. "Where's your gorgeous friend tonight?"

She hadn't expected that. Admittedly, she didn't know where Lisa was or what she was doing because she had forgotten to check the message she had sent. Hopefully her face hadn't let on that she knew what they did.

"She's on leave at the moment." She looked at Dean from the side of her eye.

Dan nodded in response then made his way to the bar for another drink. Rob took it as his opportunity to go to the gents, leaving Dean and Jessie alone.

"I'm struggling with the image of them with Lisa." Dean kept his voice to a whisper. "How could they be so confident that they could do that, well, together?"

"I don't understand it, drunken lust maybe?"

"I've known them for most of my life, that's why I'm so shocked!"

Jessie cleared her throat and nudged him as Dan walked towards them. Dean got up and prepared the pool table, inviting her to play. She didn't have much hope of winning based on last time, but it was the taking part, and being with her sexy boy that counted.

"Hey, Jess." Dan disturbed her shot. "Can I have that girl's number?"

She knew who he meant, but she wasn't in the habit of giving people's numbers out. Besides, you would expect him to know her name after getting so close to her.

She played dumb. "What girl?"

"Your gorgeous friend. I don't remember her name, cute ass, little tattoo on her hip."

Dean almost choked as he sipped his drink. "Sorry, it went down the wrong way."

Jessie glared at him, trying to keep a straight face. "Her name is Lisa, but I can't give you her number without her agreement. How about you give me yours and I'll pass it on."

"Wow Deanie-lad, your lady is requesting his number." Rob jeered. "Aren't you worried?"

Dean wrapped his arms around her and gazed into her eyes dramatically. "No, not in the slightest bit worried because this beautiful lady is the love of my life." He stroked her cheek passionately just before kissing her tenderly so they could see their electrifying lightning attraction.

Rob chuckled. He seemed to be much more relaxed than Dan.

He didn't push the subject and he didn't give her his number. He probably couldn't hack the heckling of his drunken friend, but neither could Dean. So after a few more games of pool, they set off for their walk home. It felt much colder than it had been on the way there, so when they arrived back they snuggled up with a warm drink before retiring to bed to warm each other up with their naked bodies.

Jessie woke feeling much warmer on Sunday, except for the chill she felt when she remembered about going home. Dean lay awake beside her, having woken early and lay quietly to watch her sleeping.

"You look like an angel when you sleep." He stroked her hair. "I can't believe you're going home later, running away and taking my virginity with you."

She smiled, she hadn't had much chance to think too much about it since Friday. The thought of them losing their virginity together sent warm tingles through her body. She kissed him softly, pulling him closer. "Make love to me then, it'd be a shame to waste our time together today."

Dean rolled over and knelt between her knees, leaning over her, kissing her tummy, then her breasts, working his way up until he could reach her lips. She pulled him closer and wrapped her legs around him so they became one.

"Is this what you wanted?" He spoke softly, breathing in her ear.

She rubbed her hands along his back, kissing his shoulder. "Yes. I wish we had done this last week too."

He rolled over, pulling her on top of him, reaching up to feel her breasts. "We'll just have to make up for it now and every time we see each other."

"Even in the lift at work?" She giggled and moaned.

He rolled her back over, taking control once more. "That might be one fantasy too far. Maybe every other time."

She gasped, breathing heavily. His warm breath making her want more. Friday had been magical, but this felt different, more natural. It wasn't overshadowed by nervous tension, and she could concentrate on how it felt to be loved so deeply.

He looked more relaxed as he groaned, moving slowly, circling his hips, pulling her body to match his movements. She gazed into his eyes, his desire obvious, and the power of his presence washing over her in shattering waves. She arched her back below him, crying out, squeezing his bottom as she pulled him deeper.

"I just..." He panted. "Can't stop."

She felt all his passion flooding out as he groaned, his legs twitching, filling her with the warmth she had been longing for. She clung to him, perspiration between them, hearts pounding, together.

They lay holding each other, fulfilled, like lovers do. Nothing else in the world mattered. In a few hours time they would be torn apart by a cruel life dictated by work and warped moral boundaries.

"You don't have to go home today, stay for one more night." He cupped her face with one hand. "We can go to the cinema, eat out, then collect some bits from your place. I can drive you to work in the morning, then bring you back."

She hesitated, then wondered why not. Going to work shouldn't be a barrier to life, and where she sleeps should have no effect on work. She wasn't sleep deprived, and Dean wasn't the sort of man to keep her up late.

"Okay, one more night."

— ❧ —

As they sat eating their meal in the restaurant, chatting about the film they had just watched, Jessie changed the subject.

"Did you mean what you said yesterday to Mike,

and then to Rob?"

He cocked his head. "Which part?"

"About me being the love of your life."

"Yes." He smiled, nodding. "My life is so much brighter with you in it. I feel like I have true purpose when I'm with you."

"I couldn't agree more, you're like the final piece of a jigsaw that makes me complete." She looked down, biting her lip. "I remember so clearly the first time I saw you in the park. You strolled past and smiled at me. I didn't know who you were or where you worked, but I felt something inside me, pulling me towards you like a magnet."

"I remember. You looked so beautiful with the sunlight shining in your hair, and your eyes glowed as you smiled back at me." He rubbed her cheek. "If I hadn't been so afraid of rejection back then, I would have stopped and spoken to you, but I had convinced myself that my perfect woman would come to me when the time was right."

"Which in some ways, I did."

He smiled. "Yes and I'm pleased you did."

On their way home to his apartment, they called in at Jessie's to collect her work clothes. Even before they had parked the car, she spotted Mike sitting outside the main door to her building. She directed Dean to park his car at the side of the building out of Mike's view.

"Did you see the guy sitting next to the door?" She waited for his acknowledgement. It's Mike."

"Is it now?" He sounded like a man on a mission.

"Please don't wind him up, he gets violent." Fear in her voice.

They walked around the back to the other side of the building, making it look like they had walked from the main campus. Jessie felt terrified, not just for herself, but for Dean too.

"Where were you last night?" Mike's voice loud enough to attract attention from nearby windows.

"What I do and where I go is nothing to do with you." She acted calm, hiding her true fear inside.

"I thought we were getting back together."

The atmosphere felt tense. Mike had completely ignored Dean's presence, but Dean held her hand firmly and reassuringly. Mike's eyes were full of rage as he changed his focus to glare at the two of them.

"Last time you landed up here and suggested that, I had to call security to drag you away." She clenched her teeth. "Didn't you get a clue from that?" Her hands were shaking.

Dean squeezed her hand and stepped forward. "I think you should just leave her alone."

Mike looked at him with venom in his eyes. She felt afraid. He could hurt Dean, and she didn't want that. She was poised, ready to throw herself between them to protect the love of her life.

"Oh the mysterious man on the phone! Love of your life indeed." Mike sneered. "Don't waste your time with her. She'll never let you screw her, she's so uptight I doubt she's even capable."

Dean laughed. Mike just stood looking confused. She wasn't sure anybody had laughed at him before through fear of repercussion.

"You obviously don't know her very well at all because she looks like an angel every time I make love to her." He puffed his chest out. "And she's definitely given me more pleasure than any woman ever has."

Mike turned to her and looked at her like dirt on the ground. "You filthy tart. I'll get you when he's not here. You owe me for all those months I wasted on you."

"I suggest you leave and don't come back or you *will* regret it." Dean pulled his phone from his pocket.

Mike backed away with a look of concern. Jessie held her breath. The tension between their glares made her feel bad. Dean didn't deserve any of that. Suddenly, Mike turned around and began to walk away.

"I get the message, just you watch yourself, you worthless whore." He snarled over his shoulder at them.

Once inside, Dean comforted her. She trembled, terrified by the confrontation and threat. He sat her down and cuddled her, stroking her cheek, kissing her softly. She fought back her tears, not wanting him to see her with red eyes and a blotchy face.

He stood near the window, peering out. "Collect as much of your stuff as you can. I want you to come and stay with me for a while."

"I can't do that." She dropped her head into her hands. "It's your space and you don't need me invading it. Mixed feelings ripped through her body. She liked to be with him, and she felt flattered by his offer, but it was too much of a burden for him to take on.

He placed his hands on her shoulders. "I don't want Mike to hurt you. I would never be able to live with myself if…" He lowered his head. "Well, you know. If you were hurt."

Her mouth dropped open. She hadn't thought along those lines, but he was right.

He kissed her forehead. "My space feels better with you in it, please let me protect you."

She nodded softly and proceeded to collect some clothes. Dean pulled a suitcase from under the bed.

"Fill this, bring as much as you like, you can even use my spare room, make the whole room yours if you like, I just need you to be safe."

She opened the suitcase and pulled out a smaller case, then proceeded to fill them both up. She remembered her diary, she needed that, so she slipped it into one of the cases with her underwear.

Dean helped her to zip up the cases, then held her firmly in his arms. "I'll protect you, I promise. My brother is in the police force, so I can get some advice from him about getting an injunction, make it a criminal offence to approach you again. But only if you want to go through that process."

"Thank you, you're my hero."

She placed her cases in Dean's spare bedroom and sat on the edge of the bed to check her phone. Mike must have been trying to call when her phone was set to silent. She had no missed calls, only a string of messages from Lisa. First the one from Friday which she had ignored. She wanted to hang out because she needed a friend to talk to. Then a whole string of messages sent during the day. The phone had been on silent since Mike's call on Saturday morning. She hadn't realised.

Dean walked in. "Are you alright?"

"Yes, I just realised I have a load of missed texts from Lisa." She scrolled down to the next message. Her face dropped.

"Lisa's in hospital. She fell down the stairs on Friday" She gasped. "Oh man."

"What's up?"

She read out the messages that followed.

```
"Just so you know, Mike has been
looking for you. He was drunk when he
called me last night, then again today.
I wasn't well enough to deal with it
last night because I was sleepy after
my anesthetic, but he said he came back
because he missed you and wanted to get
back together. Please be careful."
```

Dean opened his mouth, about to speak when she moved on and read out the next message, sent a couple of hours later.

```
"I just called Jordan because he's on
placement at the same place as him. It
turns out he got sacked for touching
himself and telling a female colleague
he was getting ready for her. Police
got involved and everything."
```

She sank her head into her hands.

Dean sighed. "What a slime ball, no wonder it didn't work out with the two of you."

"I need to call Lisa and find out what's going on with her."

He stood and approached the doorway. "Okay, and

I'm going to talk to Matt, see what he can find out."

"Matt?"

"My brother, the police officer."

She sat feeling extremely guilty. If she had been a better friend and supported Lisa on Friday, she wouldn't have been wherever she was when she fell down the stairs. She took a few deep breaths before calling, then faced the music.

— ❦ —

What was supposed to have been another pleasant evening, had turned into a nightmare. Dean had been verbally abused by her ex, she had been threatened to the point of having to take refuge, and Lisa had been struggling so much emotionally that she got extremely drunk and fell down stairs. Dean comforted her.

"It's not your fault. She's not your responsibility. What about the baby?"

"She lost it." She felt extremely guilty.

Lisa's outcome was probably Lisa's version of fate, not wanting the baby and the tragedy of how the whole thing came about. Everything happens for a reason. But it didn't prevent her feeling of guilt. She had to keep reminding herself the Lisa hadn't wanted a baby, that's why she felt so emotionally torn, but the circumstances of how it happened were devastating. Regardless, Jessie would always carry the guilt of not answering her friend's call for help.

13 TAKING REFUGE

A difficult week followed. Lisa had been signed off work to recover from her miscarriage, but she was going through emotional turmoil about the whole situation, and how she actually ended up there. Jessie had her own emotional battle, not only about abandoning her friend, but about her need to take refuge at The Moorings.

She loved being at his apartment, and she felt honoured that he wanted to have her there, but she would have preferred it to have been a natural and spontaneous move, not forced by the actions of her evil ex. Dean reassured her constantly that he liked having her there, in the best place to protect her. He had spoken with Matt, and he also thought they had made a wise move to keep Jessie in a safe place, somewhere where Mike wouldn't find her easily. Matt explained that taking out an injunction would be an emotionally draining process for Jessie, and given that Mike was already on the run from the police, would serve little purpose. He was a loose canon, and once caught, would no doubt be taken into police custardy and charged for his outstanding offences, apparently there was an ongoing investigation. Matt promised to keep them posted if he heard anything further.

By the next weekend, Jessie became more relaxed about Dean looking after her, and she started to enjoy the closeness they shared as they explored each other's desires, making up for all the time they had wasted. They sailed through October like they were on a honeymoon, enjoying nights out, erotic massages, and lots of passion. Jessie kept her diary up to date, as she always had, but it was starting to read more like erotica than her life experiences.

Moving into November, Dean made an effort to make Saturday night special by organising a bonfire supper in preparation for the firework display. After their meal, they sat on cushions in the window with all the lights turned off and watched the sparkling explosions in the sky.

"Thank you." She rested her head on his shoulder. "This is definitely the best view I've ever had of any firework display, and the bonfire supper was the perfect meal."

He put his arms around her. "This is my best bonfire night ever because I have you to share it with."

They felt completely relaxed and at ease with each other, living together suited them well. Jessie still had flashbacks to their confrontation with Mike, and thinking about how that day had gone from pleasure to torment, she remembered that when they made love on that morning, they had got so carried away in the moment that they forgot to use a condom. Lisa had been right, sometimes it can be easy to forget. She didn't want to worry Dean by pointing it out, but she did plan to make an appointment at the medical centre to talk about future birth control options.

As another long week came to a close, Jessie and Dean curled up on the sofa to relax and listen to music. She felt incredibly happy, but suggested to Dean that as they had heard nothing more from Mike, maybe it would be safe for her to return home soon.

"That crazy man is still out there somewhere, and we don't know where. Please stay until he has been caught."

"I just don't want to outstay my welcome or get in your way. I've been here for over two months now, but this is your apartment, your private space."

"Jess, honey, my very own Sweet Lips. I love having you here. I love sharing precious moments with you and getting to know you, and most of all, I love your companionship. You're good for me, and you make me whole." His eyes were relaxed and longing. "I know a day will come when it'll be safe for you to go home, and I'll be happy for you to do that, return to your own space, but right now, you would be in danger there and I couldn't live with myself if I let anything happen to you."

She felt extremely lucky to have him in her life. She understood what he was saying, and he was right. They continued sipping their wine and cuddling, and she decided it was a good time to discuss the birth control situation with him.

"I've got an appointment at the medical centre on Tuesday." She stared into his eyes. "I'm going to talk about birth control options so we don't need to use condoms."

He rubbed her arm. "As long as you're sure, they *are* a nuisance but I can cope with them if you don't want to go down the hormone route."

"Do you remember the weekend at the end of September, Sunday morning, the day when we went to the cinema and met Mike?" She bit her lip.

He looked curiously at her. "Yes?"

She shook her head.

"Yes.... oh no, we didn't..." He clasped his hand to his mouth.

"It's ok, I'm not pregnant, but that's what made me consider going the hormone route. I'm going to ask about injections or implants because it saves me having to remember pills."

"You'd go through that for me?" His eyes wide, shocked at the mention of invasive options.

"Yes, I'd do anything for you, plus your shower fantasy might be worth another try when we're less restricted." She blushed.

"I look forward to that. Would you like me to come with you on Tuesday?"

"I should be okay, unless they do something there and then." She began to giggle. "I've been known to pass out at the sight of a needle."

"Okay, I'll take you just in case. I feel like they should give me a needle too, after all, you're going through it to protect yourself against me."

"It's too late to protect myself against you. I'm a lost cause."

He smiled, pulled her close and kissed her.

— 🦌 —

On Tuesday morning at work, Jessie was gearing herself up for her medical appointment when Dean suddenly got up and rushed over to her.

"I've got a message from Matt, I need to give him a call about Mike." He squeezed her hand. "I'll be back soon."

Curiosity took over. What news might Matt have to share with them? He had been extremely supportive considering they had never met. She was on the edge of her seat waiting. It wasn't long before Dean returned and smiled, giving her thumbs up.

"What happened?" She mouthed at him.

"I'll tell you when we set off." He mouthed back, holding up his open hands, indicating ten. "Ten minutes."

It was the slowest ten minutes in history, but his smile and thumbs up would most likely mean Mike had been arrested, and that would be great news. She watched the minutes melt away, then gathered her things ready for their early lunch break. They set off, and once outside the building and out of the earshot of their work colleagues, he filled her in on the news.

"Mike has been arrested and charged with the rape of two colleagues." He looked triumphant. "Matt said there are other charges pending, but the investigation is ongoing so he can't give any other details at this stage. The positive part is that bail has been refused at this stage, but he's likely to get a lengthy sentence when the case goes to court."

It was delightful news. Knowing he was safely locked away, Jessie could relax. Dean put his arm around her and they continued to walk to the car with a huge weight off their shoulders. When they reached the car, she sent a message to update Lisa and to ask if she could find out anything more from Jordan.

At the medical centre, she asked him to stay with her, not just for reassurance, but also so he knew what was happening and to remember any important details like when they would be protected from.

She was given a full check over, height, weight, blood pressure, and although she was advised to lose some excess weight, her blood pressure was good and she was deemed to be just within the safe limits for a three monthly injection.

They walked back to the car. Jessie felt pleased to have got it over with, but embarrassed about discussing her weight in front of Dean. She recalled him mentioning an intention to get fit and wondered if they could get fit together.

"So we're safe as soon as we're ready." His words sounding like an invitation.

"Yes, that's positive." She smiled, her thoughts still on her embarrassing chat with the nurse. "And how about I join you on the fitness regime you've been putting off? Get you those muscles you want and save me from getting told off next time I have to go in there."

He looked surprised, but happy. "One of the reasons I put it off is because I find keep-fit lonely, so if you want to join me you'll be doing me a massive favour."

"Can we shake on it?" She held out a hand.

He shook her hand and started the car.

She checked her messages on their way back to work and Lisa had responded to say she had spoken with Jordan and would talk to her about it later. "I'm just going to give Lisa a quick call." She called on hands-free so Dean could hear what was going on.

"Hi Lisa, how are you doing?"

"So-so, what about you?"

"Better with the latest news that The Snake is behind bars. What's the latest news from Jordan."

"Okay, Jord said that after the touching incident, two women came forward to say he raped them, another was groped, and one more is behaving out of character and won't talk about him. All the incidents have some CCTV evidence, one of the rapes was entirely caught on film as well as the touching himself incident, and the others ."

"So pretty damning then." She looked at Dean.

He nodded.

Lisa giggled. "I would think so."

"Thanks for doing that." They neared the carpark at Webber OMC. "I'm just about to go back into work so I'll catch up with you soon."

"How's the sexy boy?"

She looked him up and down, grinning. "He's very sexy and he's here, you're on hands free."

"Hi Lisa." His cheeks glowed.

"Oh, Hi Dean. Thanks for looking after her. I'll talk to you both soon."

Jessie laughed at Lisa's sexy boy comment. "Do you know why she said that?"

Dean looked blank, shaking his head.

They climbed out of the car and walked together.

She gripped his hand. "The very first time we saw you in the park, the day when we smiled at each other, I said you were a sexy boy and it stuck."

He smiled. "I like that." Nodding and firing her a sideways glance.

—  —

Later that evening – back at the apartment – rain lashed against the window. Gabrielle Aplin sang *Home* on the stereo system. Jessie watched the rain pour down the window pane, listening to the words of the song. It wasn't her home, and although her heart was firmly settled on being with Dean, she couldn't help but think about her position and living arrangements. She didn't want to outstay her welcome.

Dean had been taking a shower. He walked in and joined her on the floor next to the window. "You look deep in thought, is everything okay?"

She wanted to be honest. "I was just thinking that although I'm really happy here, it'll probably be safe for me to go home now Mike has been caught."

"Please give it more time just in case something happens and he ends up on the loose again. I'll be more confident when he's been formally sentenced." He stroked her leg. "If it's space you need, use the spare room. You can go in there and pretend you're not here. I would rather that than put you in danger by sending you home."

"I don't want to go. It's not about space. I just worry you'll get fed up of having me here."

He shook his head. "That's not going to happen, I've told you before. I love having you here. Please stay until sentencing, then if you want to go home, you can, but if you don't, I would be more than happy for you to stay."

He had a valid point about needing Mike to be sentenced. Her deepest fear was about what Mike would do if he got to her.

"Okay, but promise to tell me if *you* need space."

He pulled her into a tight hold. "Deal!"

— 🐛 —

A deal was done, and as the weeks went by, she started to feel like she had always been with him, living in his apartment. They were happier than ever, living mostly in their own little bubble. She had shared her news about Dean with her parents –

omitting the whole Mike situation – and they were excited by the news. Catching up was always difficult with the time difference, but they managed to arrange for a Skype call one Saturday evening.

They had huddled together on the]sofa and made the call. Her Mum was more than happy because he was – in her words – quite charming. After their call, they sat chatting while the laptop powered down.

"Your parents are quite cool, I would've expected them to be uneasy about you living with a strange man."

She slapped his arm. "Strange, as if! They only want the best for me, and agree that sleepless nights in the noisy student accommodation wouldn't be good for my career."

He nodded. "That was a good way to avoid telling them about the drama with you-know-who."

"It's better than letting them worry, trust me. They felt extremely guilty about leaving me here when they went to Australia, but I had just secured my place at university, so I really didn't want to give that up." She pulled her legs up onto the sofa, turning towards him. "What about your parents anyway, do they know about me?"

"Yes, I was going to tell you." He lowered his gaze. "I wanted to find the right moment."

"That sounds scary."

"I told Mum my beautiful girlfriend had moved in and she wanted the whole lowdown about who you are, how we met, when, where, whatever, you know, all that—"

"This is bad isn't it?" She widened her eyes.

He averted her gaze. "Not really. Depends how

you look at it."

"With that sort of information." She frowned. "I'd expect her to come over here and chase me out armed with a feather duster."

"No, she wouldn't do that. She has a dust allergy." He chuckled.

She grabbed his hand, pulling it like a petulant child.

"Come on then. What did she say?"

"She has invited us to Christmas Dinner, with the whole family, Matt and his wife Angela will be there with their son Patrick."

She gazed at him, frozen, her mouth gaping open.

"Are you going to say something?" He waved a hand in front of her face. "They're all very nice. Honestly." He looked slightly tense.

She broke into a laugh. "I was joking, I'm sure they'll be lovely."

"You had me there." He threw a cushion at her. "Does that mean we accept?"

"Yes. It'll be nice to have a family Christmas again after the last couple of years." She recalled the last two Christmases, spent alone in her student room. "Plus it'll be nice to be able to say thank you to Matt in person."

He pulled her into a big hug. "I'll let Mum know in the morning."

Meeting his family was going to be an honour, but she couldn't help but feel apprehensive. She felt a lot more body confident as a result of their new fitness drive, and having lost just over 8kilos, looked forward to going to buy a new dress for the occasion.

The one huge worry she did have, was what they

would think about a young student just turning up and worming her way into his apartment, taking over his space and restricting him. From their own point of view, it had all happened quite slowly and naturally, to a point. From the outside, their relationship may look like she had just walked into his life and bewitched him. This was something she would have to work through on her own. He probably wouldn't understand.

—  —

The next morning, after their morning jog along the river, Jessie filled the jacuzzi and relaxed with a good romantic fiction. She had always loved reading, but studying had made it feel like more of a chore. She finally felt relaxed enough to lose herself in a book. While she lay back, he spoke with his mum about Christmas. He popped into the bathroom to tell her his mum was ecstatic that they had accepted her invitation.

He noticed her apprehension, and reminded her he had never had a girlfriend before, so it was going to be a real treat for his family to meet her. She had forgotten all about that, and started to feel less anxious.

With only two weeks left until Christmas, she busied herself trying to organise gifts for his family. Not knowing them made it difficult, and Dean didn't have any ideas. They sat down with a bottle of wine and a notepad to make a list.

"So, should we start with your Dad?"

He shook his head. "No. Dad's always been difficult to buy for. We can't even buy him chocolate because he's diabetic."

"Okay, we'll come back to him." She moved her finger down the list. "So what about your mum?"

"Mum is quite difficult too, she normally ends up with chocolate of some sort, but then I feel guilty because she complains about her weight."

"So what does she do in her spare time? Any hobbies?"

"Not really." He frowned. "She's a self confessed homemaker."

She already felt slightly exasperated, letting out a huge sigh. "She must do something when she puts her feet up in the evening."

"She loves doing puzzles, especially Sudoku, but we can't exactly buy her a puzzle book for Christmas because that's way too small." He shrugged.

"Maybe not just a puzzle book, but how about a 12 month subscription to a monthly Sudoku magazine?"

"You know, that's actually a really good idea." His eyes twinkled. "You're excellent at this gift buying thing."

She waved a hand at him, embarrassed. "That's only one gift, besides, wait until you find I've bought you a pair of Paisley socks."

He laughed. They ploughed on and decided that luxury toiletries and relaxation candles would be good for Angela, Matt's heavily pregnant wife, and after some probing, he said Matt had an interesting hobby of collecting novelty socks.

"So if you don't want the Paisley socks, we can just give them to Matt."

"Oh, you actually have bought them for me?"

She rolled her eyes. "No. Of course not."

He looked relieved. It left just the two most difficult people to buy for, his dad and two-year-old nephew, Patrick. They had made a lot of progress, so they decided to think about them for a little longer. Besides, she had a more pressing issue, what should she buy for Dean, apart from those socks.

The list lay on the table for a few days, staring them in the face as a constant reminder that they had to finish it off and brave the high street. Jessie stared at it every day when they got home from work, but as another week neared the end, she picked it up and waved it at him.

"I hope you're aware I know absolutely nothing at all about babies and children beyond where they come from."

He looked at her confused. "What makes you say that?"

"I need to think of what to buy for a two-year-old, then I have to spend a day in his company."

"Well maybe we can go to a toy shop and have a look around for inspiration?" He shrugged. "But don't worry about Christmas Day. You won't need to have much to do with him, I promise."

"Cross your heart?"

"Definitely."

"What about your dad?"

"You don't need to have anything to do with him either if you really don't want to." He kept his face completely straight.

Jessie smiled, rolling her eyes. "Not that part. His present."

He sat up suddenly. "Slippers, let's get him some slippers."

She looked at him like he was mad.

"No, seriously, mum is always going on about dad needing new slippers, it's a diabetic thing."

"Okay, that completes the list then." She smiled and ticked the list.

He gave her a high five. "Then tomorrow is our day of action."

She suddenly remembered she still needed to think of something for him, and as if like magic, it came to her. A while back, he lost his watch, and she hadn't seen him wear one since. He is a great believer in good time keeping, she decided to buy him a new one.

— 🐭 —

Shopping on the high street on the last Saturday before Christmas was hell, absolute pure hell. The toy shop was packed full of demented parents, sparsely stacked shelves and stressed out staff. Jessie gripped Dean's hand tightly as they weaved through zombie-like shoppers who had also left it to the last minute. Browsing the shelves was incredibly difficult as they searched for the perfect gift for Patrick.

She tugged his hand, forcing him to stop. "Come on, if you were two-years-old, what would you want?"

"How am I supposed to know that, I'm twenty-five!" He looked bemused. "I don't even remember being two."

"Hypothetically?" She pressed him for some idea of where to start.

"Trains, anything to do with trains. I loved trains

when I was a child."

She looked up, scouring the signage hanging above them. Suddenly, she tugged his hand again and set off, weaving through the great masses once more.

"Here we go, trains." She pulled him closer, at least twenty other people within touching space.

They worked their way down the aisle looking for one suitable for a two-year-old.

"Okay, not wanting you to get the wrong idea, but if I had a son, this is what I would buy him." He looked like he had just discovered the magic of Christmas all over again, eye's twinkling, smile wide. He reached out and picked up the last one from the shelf.

It was a chunky blue train, ten inches long, and came complete with a large oval track. Jessie pulled out her notepad and crossed out Patrick's name with a smile of accomplishment.

When they left the toy store, she went off to collect the socks, toiletries, relaxation candles, and slippers. Dean went in the opposite direction, on a *message*, but it most likely meant he was going to get her present. She took the opportunity to sneak into the jewellers for his watch her way.

There was a massive selection of watches to choose from, but one stood out from all the others, a smart black one with silver edging. It reminded her of his car, so it was perfect. She tucked it away in the massive bag from the toy store before rushing off to collect the last few bits.

Dean met up with her in Boots just as she picked up the final item, but she couldn't help but notice he wasn't carrying anything. Maybe he hadn't been to buy her present after all. Maybe he was just trying to avoid spending too long in another crowded shop. She didn't dwell on it too much though because he wouldn't forget her.

— 🦌 —

With just two days to go until Christmas, Jessie had been to see Lisa when she returned to discover her early present. She was right. He didn't forget her. She opened the door and took less than two steps into the hallway.

"Don't come in yet." He rushed out from the living room, closing the door firmly behind him.

She didn't know what to think. It was a strange reaction.

He held her at arms length. "Right, I had to have your present delivered early, and as it's rather big, I have no way to hide it."

She pulled a puzzled expression. "So I'm not allowed in there until Christmas Day?"

"Yes, of course you are. I just wanted to tell you in advance. Your present is in there, and I want you to have it early."

She felt apprehensive. "Okay, I can't imagine what could be so big you couldn't just hide it for two days."

He turned her around, placing his hands over her eyes before leading her to the door. She fumbled around to find the handle, then walked inside.

"Happy early Christmas Sweet Lips." He removed his hands.

She gasped, unable to say a word. She stood with her hand clasped to her open mouth. Just in front of her stood a shiny new, electric piano. His cheeks turned pink as a smile stretched over his face, clearly as excited about giving her it as he hoped she would be about receiving it.

"That's, wow, no, that's..." She struggled to find her words. "Dean! That's too much!"

He shook his head. "No, it's not. That's nothing compared to what you've given me over the last few months."

"How did you know I would like it?"

"Remember when we were getting to know each other and we shared facts about ourselves? You said you can play the piano."

She nodded, her mouth still gaping.

"Now I've been to your place and never seen anything resembling a piano, so I kind of thought it might be a nice, meaningful gift."

She wrapped her arms around him, hugging and kissing him.

"Thank you." She tapped at the keys and threw her arms around him again. "Of course, you realise I haven't played for a few years?"

"Well you can now. I'll get us some drinks."

They spent the rest of the evening sitting at the piano, taking turns to play short tunes, putting off their gift wrapping for another day.

14 A FAMILY FOR CHRISTMAS

Christmas Day was finally upon them. Dean placed their overnight bags in the back of his car. Jessie was still checking herself over in the mirror, straightening her new purple glittery dress, fluffing up the golden waves in her hair. He returned for the bag of gifts.

"You look fabulous, come on, let's go."

She took one more glance at herself in the mirror and they set off on their way to his parents' house. They arrived in little over half an hour because there was virtually no traffic just after breakfast.

They pulled up outside the house, a large double fronted detached, got out and walked across the driveway holding hands. As they approached the front door, her hands trembled.

He squeezed her hand reassuringly. "They're going to love you, I promise."

Before they even reached the door to knock, it opened wide, and there stood Sue, Dean's mum. She was a large framed lady with silvery blonde hair and the same greenish blue eyes.

She greeted them with a great big welcoming smile just before putting her arms around them both, hugging them warmly, together. "It's so lovely to finally meet you, but what have you done to my little boy?"

Jessie looked at Dean, worried. Sue didn't notice, she had moved on to make a fuss of him, pinching his cheek and sniffing at his aftershave embalmed jaw line.

"Just look at you, my little boy has suddenly become a man."

"Leave it out mum. I haven't changed that much since I saw you a few months ago." He batted her hand away with a look of extreme embarrassment.

"Trust me, you've changed, there's a warm glow around you, and I know who I can thank for that." She turned to Jessie. "Thank you, my love. You're clearly very good for him."

"It's a pleasure to meet you, Mrs Whittle." Jessie gave her a shy smile.

"Please call me Sue, or mum. Consider yourself family."

Jessie felt slightly shocked, not sure she could go as far as calling her mum, but it was nice to be so well accepted. Sue led them into a large, warm looking, living room with an open fire and two comfortable, cream sofas adorned with frilly edged claret cushions. In the bay window stood a big pretty Christmas tree surrounded with brightly coloured gifts, framed by ornate claret curtains.

"This is my husband, Marvin, Dean's dad."

Marvin stood to greet her. He was a tall man with medium build, grey haired, but mostly balding. He wasn't as openly affectionate as Sue, offering a gentle handshake rather than a hug. "I'm pleased to meet you. Welcome to the family. Make yourself at home. Matt and Angela are just putting Patrick down for a nap."

"Thank you, I'm delighted to meet you at last." She stopped herself before calling him Mr Whittle.

Marvin left the room with Sue, leaving Jessie and Dean to unload their bag of gifts, placing them under the tree with the others. They were about to sit down when they heard footsteps coming down the stairs.

Dean popped his head around the door to acknowledge the owner of the footsteps.

"Hey Deano, I thought I heard your voice, kid. Where's your…" An older version of Dean walked in. "Jess, I've been desperate to meet you. I can finally put a face to a name. How are you feeling?"

Wow. He's so like Dean.

"Much better now. Thank you for helping with my situation. Especially for keeping us in the picture and reassuring us. I'm not sure I can ever thank you enough." Her emotions stirred.

"No need. Family means a lot to us Whittles." He rubbed her arm.

He grasped Dean's hand, pulling him into a man-hug, then squeezed his upper arm, shaking his head. Matt was as gorgeous as his brother, just a few years older. He had the same ash blonde hair and greenish blue eyes, but his tall structure was broad and much more muscular. That's obviously why Dean wanted to start going to the gym. Sibling rivalry, but there was certainly no malice between them.

Sue and Marvin had brought in some drinks, then Angela, Matt's heavily pregnant wife, walked in. Angela was a similar height to Jessie with light brown, highlighted hair. Jessie was shocked at just how heavily pregnant she actually was. Looking at how she struggled to walk, it is unlikely that any relaxation candle in the world would be enough to help her.

"Hi Jessie. Sorry I wasn't here to meet you before, Patrick was really playing up." Angela looked like she was in extreme discomfort.

"No problem. It's very nice to meet you."

Angela didn't give off the same enthusiastic warmth

as everybody else had, but there was little wonder when she looked so uncomfortable. Matt helped her get down onto the floor to sit, where she crossed her legs and looked like she was doing some sort of yoga with rhythmic breathing exercises. Jessie felt equal measures of fascination and relief, pleased not to be at risk of falling pregnant after her injection.

Sue and Marvin proceeded to chat, directing Matt to distribute presents, but Jessie could feel Dean breathing near her ear.

"I'll be surprised if she gets through the day without going into labour."

She nodded, unsure what to say. She didn't know enough about the subject to know if Angela was close to labour or not.

She felt brave enough to speak out. "So when is your baby due?"

Angela waved her hand towards Matt, keeping her eyes closed, maintaining her breathing rhythm.

He smiled enthusiastically. "It was due on 21st December, so realistically, it could come at any time. Patrick was three days late, so now that we're four days over, it feels imminent."

"Just so long as it doesn't happen on my carpet." Marvin fired a piercing gaze at Matt.

Angela didn't seem impressed by his comment, opening her eyes for the first time since sitting down, only to narrow them in Marvin's direction. There was no way to know if they were being serious, so nobody made an effort to get involved.

After exchanging presents, Matt went to collect Patrick from upstairs, and everybody else moved into the dining room for Christmas dinner. The Whittles obviously had regular gatherings and dinner parties because the large oak dining table, complete with ornate candlesticks and matching napkin holders, could have seated at least a dozen people.

Marvin directed them to their seats while Sue served bowls of steaming food into the centre of the table. Jessie offered to help, but Sue was having none of it.

"Not today, I want you to relax and enjoy the day without having to do anything."

Matt arrived with Patrick and strapped him into a high chair. Patrick just sat staring at Jessie whilst banging his hands on the tray in front of him. She had absolutely no idea how to relate to a toddler. The idea was completely alien to her. She smiled, recalling what Dean said about not needing to have anything to do with him.

Dean chatted to Matt about his sock collection enthusiastically, and Angela continued her shut-eye deep breathing ritual. Jessie couldn't help but think she was being slightly antisocial or at worst competing for attention, but without much experience of pregnant women, wasn't sure. It certainly looked strange, but not as uncomfortable as the piercing stare of the nearby toddler. It was a relief when Sue and Marvin arrived and directed everybody to tuck in.

Angela continued to look uncomfortable throughout the meal, but Jessie seemed to be the only person to notice. Most of the focus was on Patrick who wore more of his dinner than he had eaten. Luckily the novelty of staring at the strange lady opposite had worn off once there was something more exciting to do.

As they were all just about finished eating, Angela

finally made eye contact with Jessie, probably for the first time all day. She used the best body language she could to ask if she was okay. Angela's reaction was a definite no. Soon after, she let out a very definite ouch, attracting the focus away from Patrick, with mixed reactions around the table.

"It's started." Angela held a hand to her bump. "That was definitely a contraction!"

"Try to relax love, it normally takes a couple of days." Sue tried to reassure her.

Even with her limited experience, Jessie had heard it was a long drawn-out process, so she was reassured, even if Angela wasn't.

"Well, she's been sat there all day willing it to happen, so what do you expect." Marvin had clearly forgotten to bite his tongue.

Matt raised his voice, adding urgency to the situation. "Last time it was three hours from the first contraction to arrival. The Midwife insisted that as soon as she feels the first one, we must go in."

Marvin waved a hand, sighing. "Fuss about nothing, in our day—"

"It's not your day Dad, this is our day, and unless you fancy delivering the baby here, on your precious carpet, we best go." Matt sounded anxious. "Mum, you're the only one, apart from Ange, who hasn't been drinking. Can you drive us please?"

Marvin looked at Jessie and Dean, rolling his eyes as the others started shuffling around. Jessie couldn't help but like his carefree, but flippant attitude.

"Looks like young Jessie here has been left holding the baby, or whatever it is you call him now." Marvin waved a hand towards Patrick.

She looked at the child in horror, then at Dean, then at Marvin, unsure what she would call him either. This wasn't just a toddler she was being expected to look after, it was a messy, pile of mushed-up food with scary green eyes.

Jessie and Dean cleared the table while Matt rushed up and down the stairs. Angela bellowed at him, far less calm than she had been in her yoga pose. She could probably do with lighting up the relaxation candles. Marvin just sat watching Patrick, smirking.

"You'll have to give this one a bath when you've finished." Marvin's eyes fixed on Jessie. "Did I already say, welcome to the family."

"We'll do it together." Dean turned to her. "I'm so sorry."

She just gave him a reserved smile and approached the child apprehensively.

Patrick did the sweetest thing, held out his plastic fork and babbled. "Ooo now."

She was slightly taken aback, realising he was human after all.

Angela appeared in the doorway, clutching herself awkwardly. "Thanks for looking after him, I'm sure he's in great hands."

She probably had no idea that this was the closest Jessie had been to a child since she was one herself, but she still felt honoured that Angela would trust her to look after him. The whole idea of not having to have anything to do with the child had just flown out of the window. There really is nothing quite like being thrown in at the deep end.

Working together, Jessie and Dean managed to bath Patrick, and after some confusion over which way his nappy should go, got him dressed. She expected to have to finish cleaning up after the food monster in the dining room, but Marvin had done it, clearly not a belligerent old man after all.

In an attempt to keep Patrick amused, Dean gave him the present they had bought him, and allowed him to rip the paper off.

Patrick squealed with delight. "Tain et." He beamed from ear to ear.

The two boys, Patrick and Dean's child-side, proceeded to unbox the train and lay out the large pieces of track. Still unable to relate to the scary blonde haired child, Jessie sat chatting with Marvin about her studies and work placement. She was surprised to discover Marvin was the executive director of a large property development company, a company he had started himself forty years earlier. It certainly answered a few questions in her mind; what they did to have such a magnificent house, what inspired Dean to work so hard, how he could have afforded to buy a luxury apartment when he was only twenty-two, and how he knew *the developer.*

It wasn't quite the family Christmas Jessie had expected, but it was entertaining nonetheless. Patrick was her gremlin, but she managed to overcome her green-eyed monster perception by the time she put him to bed. They were exhausted when they finally sat down at the end of the day.

Jessie lulled her head to one side, then the other. "I'm not in a hurry to do that on a full-time basis."

Dean looked at her sympathetically. "Shame, you were just getting the hang of it."

She glared at him, only realising he was joking when

he laughed. Marvin walked in, bringing them each a warm mug of his traditional family recipe mulled wine twist. They all sat quietly watching television, and soon after 9pm a crunching sound alerted them to a car pulling up on the gravel driveway. Sue and Matt returned to share the news that Angela had given birth to a 9lb baby girl called Sapphire Holly Whittle.

Matt sprawled on the sofa opposite. "I just wanted to call her Holly, but Ange had a sense-of-humour bypass."

Jessie chuckled. "Well it is a bit of a cliché."

"Women!" Matt rolled his eyes.

Marvin served two more mugs of his delicious mulled wine, and they all toasted to the arrival of yet another Whittle.

Sue raised her glass. "It'll be your turn next Jessie."

Jessie and Dean looked at each other with a combination of horror and bemusement, but nobody said another word.

— ❦ —

It had been an interesting Christmas, but Dean suggested leaving early next morning to avoid the drama of Angela returning with the new baby.

"You know they'll plonk it in your arms and say how much it suits you." He pursed his lips.

Jessie frowned. "Based on your mum's toast last night. Yes I can see that being inevitable."

They made sure their bags were packed before going down to breakfast.

"Are you sure you can't stay for the rest of the day?" She fussed around in the kitchen. "You'll miss seeing the new baby."

Jessie felt awful because Sue had been desperately wanting to meet her and the visit had been totally overshadowed by Angela and baby Sapphire. She hadn't really got to spend much time with her at all, but Dean was right, it would only get worse once they arrive.

"Angela won't want to come back to a house full of people. It's an intimate time and we don't want to intrude." Dean poured a glass of orange juice. "You focus on them, and we'll visit again soon."

Their departure was as warm as their arrival had been, and even Marvin gave Jessie a hug when she said goodbye.

Arriving home, Dean flopped on the sofa looking exhausted while Jessie prepared some warm drinks.

He propped his head up on one of the fluffy purple cushions and watched with eyes full of desire. "I'm so pleased to be home, but you know, I'm even more pleased to have you all to myself for the rest of the holidays."

She joined him on the sofa, laying her head on his chest with her lips just a few inches from his. "I have no idea how we could possibly make the most of a whole week off work." A cheeky smile spread across her face.

He gazed longingly into her eyes and kissed her gently. "I can think of a few things." His voice just a whisper. He ran his hand across her breast.

A warm tingle followed his touch, stiffening her nipples. "I suppose we could use the time to prepare for our next presentation." She kept a straight face.

He shuffled her head off his chest and made his way over to the desk. "I hadn't thought of that, what a good idea."

Her face fell into absolute disappointment. He proceeded to fire up his laptop, turning to face her innocently. Meeting her gaping expression, he broke into a laugh. She realised he was joking and threw the fluffy cushion at him.

"Right, you're in trouble now." He climbed over the back of the sofa, pinned her down, tickling her.

She wriggled and squirmed, begging for mercy until he stopped. There was a moment of calm followed by intense passion as she pulled him closer, running her fingers through his blonde hair, kissing him with vigour.

The atmosphere was electrifying as Dean broke off their kiss, leaving her wanting. He stood, reached for her hand and led her to the bedroom.

"Bedtime already?" She squeezed his hand. "We've not long got up."

He shook his head. "If I can't tickle you, I'm going to have to kiss you all over."

They peeled layers of clothing off each other before he lowered her gently onto the bed, beginning to kiss her softly. He started at her feet, moving up her legs, across her hips, along her naval and torso, and around her breasts.

She giggled. "That still tickles."

He paused. "Do you want me to stop?"

She didn't reply. Instead, she pulled him onto the bed beside her, rolled over and pinned him down. She straddled him, switching roles, kissing him along his neck and jaw, inhaling his arousing fresh woody scent.

He squirmed and giggled. "You spoil all my fun."

She whispered breathlessly in his ear. "You're just a tease, and I could be too if I didn't find it so hard to resist you."

He smiled as she eased back, running her fingers down his chest as she relaxed her knees, pushing down, overpowering him and absorbing his obvious desire as he slipped inside her slowly. He ran his hands along her hips then took hold of her hands and pulled her body closer so she was face to face with him. As she leaned forward to kiss his longing lips, she raised her hips, freeing him from her firm hold.

"I've got you now." He rolled her onto her back, taking control once more.

She was satisfied that he couldn't tease her any longer because she had him longing, just like she wanted him. Their love became so intense that he couldn't hold back. Neither wanted to because they had become completely lost in their passion. He cried out, breathing warmly into her neck, sending her over the edge.

Spending a whole week together with no distractions or diversions was going to be a whole new experience. Work usually allowed them space to focus on something other than each other for the greater part of the week, so their Christmas holiday was an opportunity to see how their relationship would stand the test of time.

Jessie worried that they might run out of things to talk about, but she needn't have worried at all. Their taste in music and movies was virtually identical, so they had plenty of scope to enjoy shared experiences. A couple of days into their holiday, they returned from a jog along the river and relaxed in the jacuzzi together, Bon Jovi sang *Always* in the background.

She had been putting off going to her place to collect some more of her things, but she couldn't put it off any longer because she needed some more clothes and wanted to collect her music books.

A lingering fear of Mike turning up had haunted her thoughts whenever she considered going there, and it was becoming more intense. They sat in the jacuzzi, completely relaxed, but she gave in to her pride and asked Dean if he would go to her place with her.

He looked surprised. "Why didn't you tell me, I would've gone with you any time."

"I didn't like to put on you."

"That's not putting on me, it's allowing me to protect you." He rolled his eyes. "Besides, I didn't realise you still worried about him."

She looked ashamed. "I guess I just let it build up more and more each time I put it off."

"You should have just told me. Promise me you'll ask me in future. Please don't go without."

— ❦ —

The student accommodation was extremely quiet because most – if not all – of the students had gone home for the holidays. Being there made Jessie feel extremely uncomfortable, even more than she had expected. As she looked around, the hairs on the back of her neck stood up. She would probably never be able to go back to living there.

They collected what she needed and left promptly.

As they drove away, her mind was swimming, she was more than aware she couldn't stay at Dean's indefinitely. A day would come when she would have to move back, probably when Mike was sentenced. All she could do for her own piece of mind was to ask the university for a transfer. As there was nothing she could do before the start of term, she put the thought to the back of her mind and returned her focus to enjoying the Christmas holiday.

The rest of the week felt like a winter honeymoon, packed with relaxation and romance. She had put all her worries aside and returned to her new carefree lifestyle. They continued going for morning jogs, and although it didn't make Dean more muscular, she felt fitter and discovered the clothes she had collected were too big. She was full of contentment, loved by a man who had accepted her as she was, feeling fitter, healthier and happier.

Sinking into a warm jacuzzi after being out in the cold winter air was the perfect start to every day, and she enjoyed the luxury of returning to her piano playing. She even began to write a song for Dean. She didn't tell him. She just composed it, making notes in her notebook quietly.

Dean walked into the room. "That sounds heavenly."

She stopped suddenly. "I'm just doodling, playing with harmonies."

"Well I like it." He kissed her and went to the kitchen.

She smiled, not ready to tell him the truth yet.

New Years Eve brought snow, delicate, perfect flakes of pretty virgin snow. They planned a romantic evening-in to watch the fireworks with champagne, and a playlist of their favourite music. The lights were dim and Jessie was laying on the floor near the window, watching snowflakes sparkle as they drifted past. Dean joined her, placing a bowl of strawberries and another of whipped cream beside them.

Her face lit up. "You remembered!"

"Yes. I wanted to help you send the year out on a high. I think you deserve that after the last few months."

"The last few months have been lovely, just slightly overshadowed." She stroked his cheek.

He placed a strawberry between his lips, lowered it into the cream, then passed it to her, mouth to mouth, kissing her gently as he did so. Fireworks started to erupt outside the window, reflecting on the snow and the water below.

"That'll be it then." She flung her arms around him. "Happy New Year."

He rested his head on hers, nose to nose. "Happy New Year, Sweet Lips, I have a feeling this will be a very special year."

15 A FRESH START FOR LISA

The lift had stopped but the doors wouldn't open. Jessie began to panic. Mike's voice echoed through the steel doors from outside. His shouting made her tremble. She wanted to escape but her limbs felt too heavy. A heavy hand on her shoulder startled her. She looked up, alarmed with fresh tears in her eyes. Dean stood over her.

"Hey, you were dreaming." He stroked her cheek. "It's okay now."

She sat up and looked around his bedroom, wiping the tears that had collected around her eyes.

He put his arm around her. "Give me a cuddle before we have to get up."

She relaxed back and he held her securely in his arms, kissing her forehead tenderly. She felt safe, he always made her feel safe. A nasty vision flashed through her mind. Mike shouting. Like in her dream, but the memory of Dean confronting him reassured her that he wouldn't let Mike hurt her, ever.

She sniffled. "I love you."

He squeezed her in his arms. "I love you, and whatever that dream was about, I'll protect you from it."

She managed a feint smile. "I was stuck in the lift at work."

"Oh, I'm not sure I can protect you from that." He sighed. "Unless you want me to carry you up and down the stairs."

She laughed. She couldn't tell him about Mike shouting because that would allow the snake to slither into their personal space again. Her eyes started filling with tears, but luckily he didn't notice because the alarm went off.

Returning to work felt strange after a long and relaxing break, but she looked forward to seeing Lisa. No doubt Lisa would be apprehensive after her extended sickness leave, so she sent her a quick text message just before they set off.

"Looking forward to seeing you back at work today."

Lisa replied almost instantly.

"Thank you, it'll feel odd to be back, but I know I need to make a fresh start."

Jessie pushed the phone into her pocket and picked up her bag.

Dean walked in. "Ready to go?"

"Yes, let's go."

They set off in his car, arriving at work in plenty of time, so they took a detour into the canteen for coffee. Dean spotted Lisa walking in and waved. Jessie turned to see who was there.

"Lisa!" A big smile stretching over her face.

Lisa looked extremely well. She waved, then indicated – with a tipping hand to her mouth – that she was just getting coffee. A moment later, she drifted over, looking Jessie up and down.

"Blimey Dean, what did you do to her? She looks amazing."

He nodded. "She sure does."

Jessie cleared her throat. "I am here you know!"

They both laughed and apologised together.

He stood up. "I'm going to leave you two ladies to catch up. I'll see you in a while." He kissed Jessie, picked up his coffee and left.

Lisa had a massive grin on her face, and when Jessie made eye contact with her, she raised her eyebrows.

Jessie shrugged. "What are you grinning at?"

"You two look amazing together. How's it working out with you living at his place."

She quickly corrected her. "Staying, temporarily at his place."

"Minor detail."

"He's very easy to live with, a perfect gentleman, and he looks after me very well."

"I can see that, but you deserve it after Mike."

"Thanks." She blushed. "Now less about me, we only have ten minutes, how are you doing?"

"I'm good, the whole thing has been a massive wake up call. My parents have been extremely supportive and helped me get a good counsellor."

Jessie looked at her sympathetically. "I suppose emotional upset is to be expected, but you're strong."

"Between you and me, and probably Dean because I can't expect you to keep things from him, can I be honest?"

Jessie nodded. "You can always be honest with me, you know I always want the best for you."

She looked around, lowering her voice. "I'm having therapy to deal with a sex addiction. That's how I ended up in that situation."

"How's that going?"

Lisa raised a hand to her chin, eyeing her up inquisitively. "You don't look surprised."

"No, I'm not because I knew."

"You probably tried to tell me, but I was such a

mess. I was in complete denial."

Jessie shrugged. "Normal for any addiction."

"When I kissed you, that was probably part of the same thing." Lisa looked embarrassed. "I'm really sorry about that."

"Water under the bridge. As long as you're on the mend now."

Lisa looked at her phone display. "I am, but it's time we went up to the office. We can talk another time, but thanks, it really helps to know I can talk to you about it."

"No problem." Jessie gave her a hug and led the way to the lift.

— 🐦 —

Settling back into routine wasn't too difficult, and the professional distance between Jessie and Dean returned quite naturally. She continued to have nightmares about Mike shouting at her, but didn't share the details with Dean in case it caused a rift. He was always comforting when she woke flustered, but didn't push her to discuss it. He may have suspected, but didn't let on.

Lunchtime walks in the park were shorter than normal because the snow had turned to ice, leaving a bitter chill in the air. The main paths had been cleared, but the pond was frozen and the trees were adorned with sparkling icicles.

There was another flurry of snow overnight on Thursday, but the temperature dropped again, making the snow crunchy under foot. Jessie still wanted to walk in the park on Friday because the fresh air gave them chance to relax away from the office. They stood next to a small stone wall near their bench, watching birds scurrying along the snow encrusted icy pond. Jessie admired the pretty footprint patterns the birds had left. Suddenly Dean's phone rang.

He looked at the screen. "It's Matt." He answered. "Hi Bro, how's it going...?"

Jessie suspected it was about Mike. Daytime calls usually where, and he was due in court soon.

Dean looked serious, not making eye contact with her. "Oh okay. When was that?"

Fear overcame her, wondering if he had been released.

"Thanks, that's a huge weight of our minds. I'll catch up with you soon." He put his arms around Jessie. "Mike was sentenced this morning. He got ten years."

She looked extremely relieved. "Is that it? Is it over?"

He nodded. "Yes. The evidence against him was solid and stacked a mile high."

They stood, clinging to each other for a few minutes. Jessie had tears of joy in her eyes. She felt free. Safe. But when she dared to imagine being able to return home, she was awash with the same dread; the *what if* she felt before. Her nightmares were fresh in her mind. She could never go back there.

Dean tugged her hand. "Come on, let's go and have our sandwiches in the warm."

She followed his lead. "We should share the news with Lisa too."

Lisa was equally pleased and reminded her that his

sentence meant he wouldn't be returning to Uni with them for their final year. It was a mighty relief.

Jessie had some time over the weekend to think about her living arrangements, and eventually plucked up the courage to talk to Dean about her fears. They were snuggled up on the sofa listening to music.

She struggled to make eye contact with him. "The nightmares I've been having. They're about—"

"Mike?" He took the words out of her mouth.

She kept her head low, but nodded slowly. "Yes, and although he's locked away and unlikely to get out for quite some time, if I go back to live in my old room, I'll always be in fear of him turning up." She avoided his gaze.

Dean shrugged. "So don't go back there."

"That's what I was thinking. I'll probably need a week or two to organise it, but if I talk to Student Services, I should be able to get a transfer to one of the older blocks on the edge of town."

He stroked her cheek. "Why don't you just stay here?"

She looked up, meeting his eyes for the first time since she started the conversation. "Because this is your space, and I don't want you to get fed up of me."

He took hold of her hand. "I like having you in my space, the closer the better."

"I know, and I can still stay over regularly, but you don't need me here all the time."

"Would it help if I rephrase it. I was considering doing this over the holiday, but my nerves got the better of me. Now I fear I wasted the opportunity."

She looked confused. "What do you mean?"

He got down on one knee. Her subconscious screamed. She wasn't against *ever* marrying him, but this was just too soon.

He held her hand, kissing it. "Jessie, would you please consider officially moving in with me, here, sharing my space, my life, my love and my everything."

She was shocked but relieved. "I don't want you to feel obliged."

"I don't. I have a two bedroomed apartment and I want to share it with you. Make the other room your own, pretend that's your room, your space, but please stay."

"So I can rent your spare room?"

"You can *have* my spare room."

"I need to pay for it though, if I plan to live here as my only home."

"If that makes you feel better, yes, but I'll just save up the money, for us, for our future."

She just gazed into his eyes indecisively.

He was still on one knee but beginning to shuffle slightly. "Please say yes so I can get up. My knee is numb."

She smiled. "Okay, yes."

He jumped up from the floor and pounced, hugging and kissing her.

"Now you're looking desperate." She giggled. "Desperate Dean!"

"Hey cheeky! I could change my mind."

She called the university to give notice on her room, and Student Services understood her situation. Instead of the usual month notice, they allowed two weeks because they had a long waiting list for the North Campus accommodation block. She felt happy enough with that because it gave her plenty of time to clear out her belongings the following weekend.

Lisa offered to help with the move so Dean offered to cook them all a meal as a sort of housewarming celebration. They invited Lisa to stay over, as she often had done at the old place.

The week flew by, and Saturday was soon upon them. Jessie picked Lisa up and they made their way over to the North Campus. Just as they arrived and climbed out of the car, Lisa paused.

"You know I'm really happy for you. Dean is perfect."

"Thank you, but he's too perfect sometimes. I feel like I don't deserve him."

Lisa frowned. "No way, there's no such thing as too perfect, but you totally deserve him."

Jessie began to blush. "Come on, let's go and close this chapter of my life so I can get on with the new one."

They went inside. It was still eerily quiet, but term didn't start until Monday, so many students were still away.

Jessie shuffled through her desk drawers. "We can just put everything in bags, there's not much, mostly books and things."

Lisa started putting folders and notepads into a bag while Jessie collected her post and flicked through it. It was mostly junk, but there was one official looking letter. She realised it was from a prison and opened it quickly to see what it was.

Lisa looked over. "What's that?"

"A letter from Mike asking me to visit."

Lisa was aghast. "You've got to be kidding."

"Forget it, he's an idiot." She tucked the letter into the side pocket of her study bag.

Lisa smiled, appreciating her sentiment. "That's the spirit. You should burn it and forget he ever existed."

It didn't take long to pull everything together. Jessie used the vacuum from the cleaner's cupboard to freshen up the grubby carpet while Lisa wiped around the ensuite, ensuring there would be no quibbling about the return of the deposit.

As they made their way to the security office to hand over the keys, Jessie looked back at her window. She had taken down her pretty lilac curtains and replaced them with the boring beige ones that most of the windows had.

"Well, this is it, the end of a very unpleasant chapter of my life."

16 BACK IN THE SADDLE AGAIN

Even though she had technically been living with Dean for a few months, Jessie found it strange to call Dean's apartment home, but she tried to say it as often as she could. She stood in front of the full length mirror in the bathroom practicing.

"Let's go home."

"I'm glad to be home."

"We live in an apartment overlooking the river."

"Our apartment."

"Our home."

She heard a sound from the other side of the door, then it opened slowly.

Dean peeped inside. "Who are you talking to?"

She laughed. "Just myself. I'm trying to get used to this being home, reminding myself."

"You've lost the plot." He chuckled and walked out, closing the door behind him.

He was probably right, but she wasn't fazed by it. She carried on repeating different phrases, then paused, laughing. "If he thinks I'm crazy, he might throw me out, then it won't be home after all."

She followed him into the living room where he was stood with his back to her in a star shape holding up two bottles of water. She watched quietly for a moment as he squatted, counting, then straightening up.

"We're slightly short of plots here this afternoon, you seem to have lost yours too."

He turned suddenly and placed the bottles of water on the table. "That makes us equal then."

She smiled. "No, it's just a sign that we're relaxed enough to be ourselves."

"Seriously? You mean you always talk to yourself in the mirror?" His face was solid and serious.

She just laughed as she put her arms around him, pulling him close enough to smell his delicious aftershave. He kissed her with passionate nibbling movements, sucking her lips each in turn. She reciprocated then licked her lips to savour his taste.

He held her at hip level. "Do you want to walk up to The Old English tonight?"

"Yes, we can practice my pool moves, then walk home to *our* apartment."

He gave her a high-five. "You've got it, Sweet Lips."

She grinned. "See, talking to myself in the mirror works."

— 🐛 —

They walked slowly up to The Old English, hand in hand, throwing smiles at each other.

"Hey, Sweet Lips. When's your birthday?"

She was surprised. They had never discussed anything like that before. "9th of May. When's yours?"

"Wow. 11th of May, so close, and both Taurus."

"We best not visit any china shops together then." She gave him a sideways smile.

Dean looked confused for a moment, then laughed. "We should do something to celebrate. Can I plan something, as a surprise?"

She looked alarmed. "Not a party?"

He laughed. "No, definitely not a party, something

for us, just the two of us."

"Okay, as long as I can trust you."

He lowered his head and towards her, raising his eyebrows to look from the top of his eyes. He had a big beaming smile. She responded by pinching his bottom.

They arrived at The Old English and inside, the fire crackled. Rob and Dan sat in the corner near the pool table, just like part of the furniture. Jessie ordered drinks while Dean greeted the boys. She joined them at the table.

Rob stood to kiss her cheek. "So you've moved in."

"Yes, just to keep him company, obviously." She smiled.

"Obviously." He returned her smile, raising his eyebrows.

Dan cleared his throat. "How's Lisa?"

He had asked the same thing every time she had seen him.

"She's fine."

"Fine?"

She shrugged her shoulders. "Busy? What did you want me to say?"

Dan blushed. "No, fine is good. When are you going to get her to come over here?"

"I'll have to talk with her, see when she's free." She turned to look sharply at Dean.

Dean jumped up and grabbed a pool cue. "Ready to play?"

"Of course." She was relieved.

Dean was setting up the pool table while she reflected on Dan asking about Lisa. Rob never did, he always appeared to distance himself from the conversation. It was very strange.

After a few drinks and three rounds of pool, Jessie and Dean strolled home together admiring the moonlit sky. It was much darker than when they arrived, but the sky was the darkest shade of blue, almost black. There wasn't a cloud to be seen, just bright sparkling stars and a beautiful crescent moon. All the snow and ice had melted, but it was still bitterly cold, so when they reached their apartment, they had a warm, relaxing shower together, and slipped into the onesies Lisa bought them as a *moving in gift*.

"Birth control indeed! I can't believe she said that." Jessie pulled her cow-head hood up. "Only Lisa could go for such a silly mooooving in present."

Dean pulled his hood up and laughed. "It's good she can joke about birth control though, given what happened, and they *are* nice and warm."

They galloped around, laughing, before collapsing on the sofa together. Jessie took a selfie of them and sent it to Lisa.

He widened his eyes. "We might live to regret that picture."

Jessie quickly sent a text.

"For your eyes only, remember the secrets."

Dean looked intrigued. "Secrets?"

"She said I could share it with you, but only you. We've been so busy that I totally forgot to tell you."

"What has she done now?" He put his head into his hands.

"Nothing, it was about her therapy, she has finally

opened up and admitted to having a sex addiction, but she's having counselling for it."

He smiled. "I've got a sex addiction too. I always want to have sex with you, everywhere, every day, because I'm addicted to you."

She tried to kiss him, but the cow-head kept getting in the way. "I feel udderly ridiculous in this." She giggled.

He hesitated, looking up thoughtfully. "You'd be Friesian cold without it."

"Not if we take them off and snuggle up together in bed."

"Feeding my addiction again." He raised to his feet with a glint in his eye.

— 🐛 —

The next morning at work, she decided to tell Lisa about Dan asking incessantly about her. It was only fair. They walked down to the canteen for coffee at break time, so she took that as her opportunity. Lisa's response shocked her slightly.

"Can I come over there with you one night?"

"Erm, I, well, are you sure?" She felt awkward. She hadn't expected that, and hesitated. Lisa's therapy was going well, and an encounter with a man like Dan could potentially knock her off course.

"I can't avoid going out forever, but I know I'll be in good hands with you."

"Okay, I'll have to talk with Dean to see when we're going again."

She spoke with him about it at lunchtime and asked for his opinion.

"The best thing we can do is let Lisa make her mind

up, especially given your previous arguments over your protectiveness. How did she react?"

"She was flattered by him asking about her, and said that maybe she could try to get to know him better."

They sat down on the bench.

Dean widened his eyes. "You'd think she knew him fairly well already, intimately even."

"I'll talk to her again, she's probably in the canteen."

After a few minutes, they made their way back to the office. Lisa had just walked out of the Ladies.

She bounced over to them. "Hey! Did you talk about me?"

"Yes. We support your decision, and will be there if you need us."

Dean stepped in, hoping he wasn't overstepping the mark. "What if you look like you might be going too far?"

She shrugged. "Then just try to sidetrack me to keep me in line."

"Okay. I'll organise it. Are you free this weekend? Probably best on Friday when Rob is out with his football club buddies."

She smiled. "Yes, this Friday's fine."

"I'll text him to see if he'll be around." He tapped away at his phone. "I'll let you know when he replies."

Later that evening, Dan's replay came through. He was delighted to hear Lisa wanted to meet up. Dean suggested they pick her up in a taxi, and deliver her home at the end of the evening, promising to look after her and make sure the evening didn't turn disastrous.

— ❦ —

Friday night was soon upon them, and Jessie worried about how Lisa would cope. The taxi pulled up outside her house, and the curtain twitched.

Jessie shook her head. "I hope we're doing the right thing."

"Relax, it'll be fine."

Jessie gave half a smile. "I know, I just worry."

It was only a moment before Lisa came through the front door, down the path and joined them in the taxi. She looked beautiful, but then Lisa *always* looked beautiful. When they arrived at The Old English, Jessie and Dean walked in first. Lisa trailed behind nervously. She hadn't been out in a social situation since the night when she fell down the stairs and lost her baby.

Dan was waiting in their normal spot near the pool table. He had made a real effort, wearing smart trousers and a shirt rather than his normal torn jeans. Even Dean commented on how well he scrubbed up.

Dean pulled out his wallet. "Can I get everybody a drink?"

Dan held up his pint glass. "Another lager for me please, mate."

Lisa nodded. "Lemonade please."

Dean look firmly at Jessie.

She nodded. "I'll help you carry the drinks."

At the bar they could see Dan and Lisa chatting and smiling.

"She's probably avoiding alcohol because that always played a part in her episodes, you know, when she got carried away."

Dean joined Dan with a pint of lager, whilst Jessie had a glass of white wine. They delivered the drinks to the table, but not wanting to cramp Lisa's space, Jessie challenged Dean to a game of pool.

She played much better after all the evenings he had spent teaching her to line up her shots. The other two laughed as they watched the competitive drama.

Lisa turned to Dan. "Do you want to play the winner?"

He nodded. "Sure, then you can play me."

"What happened to the *winner stays on* rule?"

He raised his chin and scowled. "I can beat both of them, so don't you worry yourself about that."

Jessie widened her eyes and Dean smiled. How arrogant is it possible to be?

Wanting to squash Dan's arrogance was enough to make Jessie even more determined than ever to win her round of pool, and she did. She beat Dean fair and square. She stood proud and waited for her next opponent.

"Watch and learn." Dan looked smug.

They flipped a coin and he won the break. Lisa and Dean were on the edge of their seats watching every single move. He potted six balls in a row, but missed his last colour. Jessie was in the spotlight. She took a deep breath and potted three balls easily. Having a virtually clear table was a massive bonus. She lined up her next shot.

Dan sniggered. "You've got no chance."

It went in, followed by two more. He looked less smug. They were now head to head, but she had the advantage. Her next shot was a clear line, but she had to ensure the cue ball landed in a good position for a shot on the black. She looked at Dean, hoping for inspiration. Dean indicated bottom right, so she lined up her shot, hitting the cue ball on the bottom right, hard enough to get a good curve. Dan looked worried, there was no way she could miss the black unless her hand slipped. Just a gentle tap and the black went in. She had beaten Mr Arrogance extremely easily. Lisa was impressed, but Dan was less so.

Dean gave her a high-five. "Awesome play young apprentice."

It was a great achievement given how bad she was the first time they played together. As the evening went on, Dan became more drunk, and Dean decided it was time to go. Lisa gave Dan her number, and although Jessie didn't think it was a good idea, it wasn't her place to say. They delivered her home safely, then returned home themselves.

Reflecting on their evening the next morning, Jessie didn't like Dan because his attitude and showing off reminded her of Mike. It was unnerving. Lisa probably saw it as him being manly because she had always liked the rough boys at school, moving onto guys with a bad boy persona as she grew up. Her thought process was disturbed by Dean suggesting a walk along the river, so she got herself wrapped up to cope with the February breeze, and they set off.

"I was thinking about last night. You know, Lisa and Dan." She sighed. "I don't think he's right for her."

He frowned. "Rob would've been perfect, but he

wouldn't go there after their last encounter with her."

"How do you mean?"

"Rob's much more of a gentleman, but he wouldn't get involved with a woman who has been with one of his friends."

She was confused. "What they did wasn't exactly very gentleman like."

"No, but that would've been Dan's idea. Rob is easily influenced."

"So that's why he doesn't seem interested in her, and has never bothered to ask?"

"I expect so, but we can't get involved. If Lisa wants to hang out with Dan, there's nothing we can do.." He shrugged. "We can support her and be there for her, but she has to make her own mind up."

"You're right, if I tried to say anything, she would see it as me interfering, and we know how that normally ends up."

He put his arm around her and pulled her close as they walked. It was a lovely day, cold, but bright, no clouds in the sky at all. They stopped and sat down on a bench.

He shook his head. "I'm glad we're not complicated."

Jessie gave him a sly smile. "You *hope* we're not complicated."

"I *know* we're not."

She gave him a gentle peck on the lips. "No, others would say we're boring, but I think we're perfect."

"We *are* perfect." He kissed her softly.

"So confident. Should we jog home?"

"Why?"

"Ulterior motive!" She winked.

"You want to have a jacuzzi so you can get back into that cow onesie!"

"Close." She jumped up from the bench. "Catch me if you can."

They jogged all the way home, and collapsed on the sofa. She had far more energy than she had ever had, and she was feeling slimmer and more confident all the time.

— 🐭 —

Over the next couple of weeks they spent more time with Lisa and Dan at The Old English. Rob turned up on one occasion but turned pink and left as soon as he saw Lisa. It was evident Dean had been right about him. Being in her presence obviously made him uncomfortable.

Two days before Valentine's Day, Dean said he had to go out on a message, which he described as *top secret*, so Jessie had lunch with Lisa in the canteen.

"Where's he gone?"

Jessie smiled. "He said it was top secret."

"Valentine's Day!" Lisa grinned, flashing her eyes at her.

She nodded. "That's what I was thinking, the day after tomorrow."

They both sat smiling for a while as they ate their lunch.

"How are you getting on with Dan?" She worried that the conversation might turn sour.

Her expression changed to a semi frown as she rocked her head from side to side.

"Try not to look too enthusiastic, what's going on?"

She looked apprehensive. "We've arranged to go bowling next Saturday, followed by something to eat at Prezzo."

"Nice, but?"

"I'm not sure if I'm doing the right thing." She looked down.

Jessie cocked her head. "Being alone with him?"

"Partly that, but getting to know him better has been an eye-opener."

She felt brave enough to be honest. "I actually find him quite arrogant."

Lisa nodded then looked beyond Jessie towards the door. Jessie had her back to the door, but suddenly she inhaled deeply, closing her eyes.

"I can smell a handsome man. If he's got blonde hair and sexy eyes, I'm taking him home tonight."

Dean sat down beside her wearing a beaming smile, not saying a word. She smiled at him.

"Look at you two. Far too cute." Lisa rolled her eyes.

She took a big mouthful of coffee, realising it was almost time to go back to work.

"Have you been talking about me the whole time?" Dean winked.

Jessie gave him a sideways glance. "Sorry, who are you again?"

They all laughed, and Lisa dribbled coffee down her top as she spluttered.

Jessie shook her head. "We can't take you anywhere."

"Luckily you don't have to, but I've decided to go bowling with Dan, see how it goes." She caught

Jessie's expression. "Rest assured, if he's not more gentleman-like when it's just the two of us, that'll be it."

"Okay, but let us know how it goes, how about you come over for lunch on Sunday to tell us how it went?"

"Okay, thank you. As long as I'm not intruding." She looked at Dean.

Dean shook his head. "No, we want to know what happens."

Lisa Nodded apprehensively, then got up to clear the table.

17 LESSONS IN ROMANCE

Jessie had been nervous about Valentine's Day because she had never been in a relationship for it before, but this was it, everything was ready for the morning. She slipped into bed beside Dean, kissed him and turned over, allowing him to cuddle her, spooning from behind. They slept peacefully together, all night.

The alarm went off and she rolled over.

"Good morning, Sweet Lips."

She smiled. "Good morning, Sexy Boy." Her face turning to stone when she glanced at the clock. "It's 8:30, we're late."

He shook his head. "No, we're not going to work today. We have an appointment at 11am."

"We do?"

"Yes we do." He wrapped himself around her.

She kissed him softly before easing herself out from his grasp.

He pouted. "Tease."

She scurried over to the wardrobe and returned with a big red envelope. "There's something else, but you'll have to wait until later."

He opened the envelope and pulled out a card with a big red heart on the front. Opening it revealed a gold envelope. He read the card, kissed her and proceeded to open the gold envelope. "Seriously? A hot air balloon trip for two, that's amazing."

"I thought we could do that when it gets warmer, is that okay?"

A beaming smile had spread over his face. "More

than okay, I've always wanted to go in a hot air balloon."

"I know. I spoke with your mum about it because I had to make sure you weren't afraid of heights."

He pulled her into his arms firmly and kissed her tenderly. "Right, I think we should have breakfast before showering." He waggled a finger, beckoning her. "Come with me."

She followed to the living room, and the first thing she spotted was a big purple envelope on the coffee table. He stood grinning as she opened the card. Purple fabric rose petals fell out and she read what was written inside.

Sweet Lips, my Sweet Lips,
you've captured my heart,
you know that I've loved you,
right from the start.

My beautiful girlfriend,
so precious to me,
I love you so dearly,
I hope you can see.

Six gifts await you,
throughout the day,
just look for the clues,
start now with my shoes.

"Dean!" Her eyes widened, her mouth dropping open.

He smiled. "Never mind Dean. Find your first clue."

She went into the bedroom and looked in the bottom of his wardrobe. There was a little purple envelope sticking out of a shoe. She opened it and read the clue out loud.

Gift number one,
is hidden away,
not very far from,
a place where you lay.

She looked around the bed but found nothing. "Lay, not sleep, ah, it must be near the window." She went back into the living room where Dean was sat with a big smug grin. She moved the edge of the curtain, and there it was, a box of luxury chocolates. She picked them up and stuck on the bottom was another purple envelope. She looked over at him with a cheeky smile. He was grinning like the Cheshire Cat.

Gift number two,
will arrive at your door,
you had better get dressed,
to be ready for more.

He looked at his watch. "You've got under an hour."

She immediately rushed to the bedroom, prepared her clothes and took a shower. Six gifts. He had organised six excitingly presented gifts. The second was obviously flowers.

What could the other four be?

She dried herself off and quickly put the hairdryer

over her hair, still thinking what else he could have planned. No wonder he had to go off on a top secret mission. He must even have got up in the night to set this up.

She couldn't help but smile as she removed the packaging from her new silky Lovehoney underwear.

Dean walked into the bedroom. "Are you almost ready?"

She quickly tucked the underwear under her pile of clothes. "Almost."

"Okay, I'm going to have a quick shower. Answer the door if the bell rings before I come out."

She kissed him sweetly before he disappeared into the steamy shower. As quickly as she could, she slipped on her new sexy underwear, and looked at herself in the mirrored wall.

She ran her fingers over the red silky fabric. *I can see why they called it 'Adore Me'. He's going to love this.*

She had just finished getting dressed when the doorbell rang. It had just turned 10am. Never having used the intercom system before, she nervously looked at the display. A young man with dark hair and designer stubble stood waiting.

She held the button to speak. "Hello."

"Good morning. I have a delivery for Miss Jessica Williamson."

"Thank you, I'll come down." She sprinted down the stairs and the young man handed her a bunch of purple roses. After she thanked him, he went off on his way. She took the lift back to the fifth floor and as she stood looking at the delicate rose petals, she noticed another little envelope attached.

Dean was waiting for her when she arrived on the top floor. "They thought I was mad when I said they had to be purple, but I would have been mad to make you settle for red."

She kissed him, then detached the envelope, reading it out while he put the roses into a vase.

Gift number three,
just wait and see,
it's not here now,
but soon it will be.

"Another mystery delivery! You're very sweet."

He was blushing as he put on some music. "Come and dance with me." He held out his arms.

She loved his *fresh from the shower* smell because his aftershave was strong and undiluted, maximising the spicy overtones. She rubbed her cheek against his, savouring his soft, smooth skin, and absorbing the passion that radiated from him. They danced slowly as they kissed and caressed each other. Richard Marx was singing *Now and Forever* in the background, and Dean mimed the words to her with his eyes full of desire. It was one of those moments when nothing else in the world mattered.

"I made this playlist just for you." He kissed her neck.

"It's perfect. You're perfect, thank you."

They danced on until shortly before 11am. Tom Odell had just finished singing *Real Love* when Dean let go of her and looked through the window.

"You might want to see this."

She joined him, looking down at a boat moored up

below their window.

He took her hand. "We can take a closer look on our way to lunch."

They walked along the path at the side of the river, and approached the boat.

Jessie read the writing on the side. "Lilac Dream. Such a beautiful name."

At that moment, a man stepped out of the cabin and smiled in their direction.

"Mr Whittle, Miss Williamson, welcome to the Lilac Dream. My name is Spencer and I'll be your captain today."

She turned to look at Dean, her mouth open, a tear in her eye.

He smiled. "We've jogged along here watching boats pass-by many times, so today we're sailing."

She was speechless, not just lost for words, totally speechless.

Spencer helped them to climb onboard and guided them to the compact cabin. "Make yourselves comfortable." He made his way up the steps, paused and looked back. "Oh and Miss Williamson, I believe there's an envelope addressed to you in the top drawer over there."

She looked across the cabin and spotted a drawer on the side of a little wooden table. She opened it up and collected her next clue.

Gift number four,
I have it with me,
it's in my hand,
would you like to see?

She turned to look at Dean. He held out his hand, presenting her with a small box covered with purple velvet. She opened it slowly to reveal a pretty heart shaped locket. "It's beautiful, thank you." She wiped a tear from her eye.

He helped her to put the locket on, and she looked down to discover another clue inside the box.

Gift number five,
will be very nice,
it's up on the deck,
chilling on ice.

She looked through the cabin door, and Spencer appeared with a bottle of champagne in an ice bucket. They sat down and Dean made a toast.

"To make up for all the Valentine's Days we've missed."

"Thank you."

Spencer popped his head into the cabin. "Are you both ready to sail?"

Dean nodded. "Yes. Thanks, Spencer."

They sailed slowly down the length of the river, mooring up outside a renovated windmill. The cabin door opened and a mature lady – with greying hair pulled back into a bun – entered the cabin with food.

"Happy Valentine's Day. My name is Catherine. Your lunch today is duck in plum sauce with crispy roast potato and seasonal vegetables."

She placed the food on a little table and left quietly.

Dean leaned in, whispering. "Spencer's wife."

Jessie nodded, then looked around smiling. "This is incredible. I would never have thought of this."

"Having an extremely romantic older brother is useful." He smirked, giving away his secret inspiration.

Jessie didn't mind. Matt is adorable. It was touching that he would admit to being soppy because he wanted to do something extra special.

When they finished their main course, Catherine returned to take away their plates, and presented them each with a miniature heart shaped strawberry cheesecake, served on a plate alongside the word *love* written in strawberry sauce. She left quietly again.

Dean flashed Jessie a smile. "They've really thought this out. How is it for you?"

"It's wonderful. The most romantic thing anybody has ever done for me."

He kissed her hand, smiling.

— 🍂 —

They wandered into the apartment, all smiles and twinkling eyes. She clung to the Champaign bottle, and Dean pointed out the envelope on the side. She smiled. She had forgotten all about her final clue.

Gift number six,
what will you get?
it's full of rose petals,
and needs to get wet.

She looked confused, glancing around the living room for inspiration. He grinned, and turned his eyes towards the door.

"Wet, full of rose petals." She narrowed her eyes and walked towards the door, then slowly towards the bathroom, wondering if maybe it was... "Bath bombs, ah, that's why we have more champagne." A huge smile stretched over her face.

He walked in and turned the water on.

She began to blush. "Well I guess it's time for you to see what else I have for you. Just a mini gift."

It was his turn to look intrigued, but as Jessie stripped off her outer clothes, he knew. "Mmm, my very own ultimately sexy lady, carefully wrapped in silk."

His eyes twinkled as he licked his lips and touched the soft fabric of her red chemise. He ran his fingers along the black lace edging, kissing her and nibbling her lips softly with his teeth.

She glanced over at the jacuzzi. "Don't let it overflow."

He released her and turned the water off. "I feel like I might overflow if I'm not careful." He curled the side of his lip, eyebrows raised.

"You had best be careful then, we can't be dealing with messy overflowing today because that's unromantic."

He smiled and placed the bath bombs in the water, then stripped off. She gazed at him longingly, his gorgeous long legs one of his finest features. She couldn't help but notice he was looking more muscular. It must have been his water bottle squats, despite making him look silly.

He turned and lifted the chemise over her head very slowly, before running his hands over her naked body. "You've got the most adorable body."

His touch made her tingle, her breath becoming shallow. He took her hand and helped her into the jacuzzi, then slipped in behind her. They lay holding each other, completely relaxed, while Dean's Valentine's playlist continued to play through the bathroom speakers.

"Oh, Dean. I love you so much. You've put so much effort into making our first Valentine's Day special. Thank you."

"It wouldn't be special without you, so thank you for being here to make it so special."

On Monday at work, Jessie had coffee in the canteen with Lisa. She wanted the full lowdown about their day. Jessie told her about all the clues and gifts, the meal on the boat, and showed her the little gold locket. Lisa had never been big on romance, but she was impressed by his imagination.

She smirked. "I got two cards."

"Two Valentine's cards, but no boyfriend?"

She tried to stifle a giggle. Jessie looked bemused.

"Don't rub it in. They were from my little brothers!"

"Cute." Jessie cooed. "Talking of your love life, are you still planning to go bowling with Dan on Saturday?"

"I don't know, I really don't think it's going to work out between us. He didn't even send me a card, and you would have expected him to, you know, if he had any intention for us to get together."

"Did you send him one?"

"Yes, anonymously though."

Jessie shook her head and sighed.

Lisa observed her expression and sipped her coffee, clearly not in disagreement with what she probably knew Jessie was thinking. "You really don't like him do you?"

"No, he's not right for you." She looked uncomfortable about telling her the truth, but it had to be said. She was surprised Lisa didn't react as she would have done in the past, but there was no rebellion at all.

Lisa nodded. "He's incredibly annoying. He shows off constantly and is the most self centred man I have ever met."

"You sound like you're talking yourself out of it."

She sighed. "Yes, I think I am. I thought he was cute, but it's amazing how much you learn about somebody by spending time with them." She shook her head. "He might be pleasant to the eye, but as the saying goes, beauty is only skin deep."

Jessie laughed. "Don't hold anything back will you."

"No, I'm going to text him and cancel. I didn't want to let him down, but can you imagine bowling with him." Lisa frowned, shaking her head decisively. "Thank you for helping me with that dilemma."

"You made the decision, I just made you think about it."

They went quiet while a group of people walked past, not wanting to be overheard.

Lisa sighed. "Relationships are so overrated. Well, except for yours."

"What happened with you and Max anyway, do you still chat with him?"

"No, nothing. Absolutely nothing." She took a deep breath, furrowing her brow. "Probably for the best though."

Jessie raised her eyebrows. "Erm, okay, I won't ask."

On their way back to the office, Lisa gasped. "I forgot. Did you know Claire and Ethan split up just before Christmas?"

"No, I don't see them very often. What happened?" Jessie pressed the button to call the lift, the doors opened and they stepped inside.

Lisa waited for the doors to close behind them, then leaned against the hand rail and shrugged. "No idea, they never said, and I didn't ask. They seem fine about it though."

"I can't understand how people can still be friends after a failed relationship."

Lisa shook her head. "No, but since I came back to work, Ethan has asked me on a date about four times."

"Why was I not made aware of this?" Jessie looked shocked.

Lisa blushed. "I, erm, kind of forgot."

"I can't believe you're actually blushing, is there something you need to tell me?"

Lisa's face was scarlet. "No, well, not really."

They stepped out of the lift and paused before entering the office.

"You said you don't like blonde men." Jessie smiled.

Lisa shrugged again. "I said I don't *fancy* blonde men, but sometimes it's worth looking beyond the packaging."

"You like him. Go on admit it. You can't hide it from me."

She was looking extremely embarrassed. "Okay, I might have a, well a kind of, erm, appreciation of him."

"Please tell me this is level headed Lisa, not the impostor I used to know."

"Definitely level headed Lisa, I've learnt from my old ways."

"So?"

She grinned. "So, I may consider accepting his next offer. Am I mad?"

Jessie smiled. "No, you're not. Mind you, this is coming from me, someone who finds blonde men hot, but I think there's probably more to Ethan than his hair colour."

"So you think I should say yes?"

"Yes, a definite yes."

Lisa smiled and they walked into the quiet office without saying another word.

— 🐚 —

When they arrived home from work, Dean quizzed Jessie about her coffee break with Lisa. "You were definitely recovering from a man-talk session."

She grinned. "It wasn't about you, obviously I told her all about Valentines Day, but her twisted love life was the hot topic."

"Dan?" He looked worried.

"No, she's cancelling their date because he's not charming enough for her."

He wasn't surprised. "I could've told you that. He's not exactly romantic. His last girlfriend left him because he introduced her to a group of us by saying, *meet my new bitch*."

Her jaw dropped. She couldn't wait to share that with Lisa, but in the meantime she told Dean about Ethan.

"Lisa and Ethan? Young, innocent looking Ethan?" He shook his head. "No, she'd eat him alive."

"She's changed. Honestly, she's much more, well, I don't know, calm I suppose, but she's better than she was."

He took her hand and kissed it. "I love that you see the best in her. She's lucky to have a friend like you."

18 GOOD THINGS COME TO THOSE WHO WAIT

"He did it."

Jessie frowned. "Who?"

"He asked me."

"Earth to Lisa, who asked what?"

Jessie felt frustrated. They were sat in the busy canteen, drinking coffee.

Lisa looked around shiftily, checking who was nearby. "Remember the conversation we had last week?"

"Last week was a long time ago." Jessie stared at a broken ceiling tile, curling the side of her lip, clearly attempting to rewind her memory.

Lisa grinned, then suddenly nudged Jessie under the table.

She moved her focus from the ceiling tile, towards Lisa, and was diverted by Lisa's darting eyes. She followed her gaze to Ethan. "Ohhhh!"

Lisa raised her finger to her lips, still smiling. Ethan disappeared out of earshot.

"He asked you to go on a date?"

Lisa's cheeks glowed. "Uh huh, we're going out on Saturday evening."

Ethan walked towards them looking shy, probably aware they were talking about him.

"Hi, Ethan. Would you like to join us?" Jessie looked at Lisa from the corner of her eye.

"Sure, thanks."

"It seems like an age since we caught up." She

ignored Lisa's glare.

"Well you've been snatched away from us by your high-flying boyfriend. Don't get me wrong though, I think it's lovely when true love hits."

She glanced at Lisa again with a sly grin, turning back to Ethan quickly to avoid Lisa's famous eye-talk. "Talking of relationships, what's happening in your love life at the moment?"

Lisa kicked her under the table, but she didn't react.

Ethan looked stunned but didn't try to avoid the question. "There's one lovely lady in my sights, little more than that at the moment, but maybe in time."

Jessie smiled, nodding slowly, then Ethan started laughing.

"Come on, I know she told you. She tells you everything."

They all smiled, and Lisa started blushing more than Jessie had ever seen before.

"Enjoy your date, but please look after her."

"I will, she made me ask her five times before accepting, so I really can't afford to mess it up."

"She's always been hard work, so it's not just you. But talking of hard work, we need to get back."

Ethan looked disappointed. "Okay, catch you later."

Lisa threw him a smile. "I'll text you tonight."

They walked out without saying another word until they reached the lift. Jessie looked pleased with herself, and just as Lisa was about to speak, a man who they had never seen before joined them to wait for the lift. She had been saved from a grilling.

— ❦ —

Later that evening, she had been speaking with Lisa on the phone, accepting the telling off she had managed to avoid earlier. Dean had overheard her half of the conversation, smiling as he listened.

"Ethan finally asked her then."

"Yes, they're going out on Saturday, to the cinema followed by something to eat." She grinned, then slapped his arm. "We should go on another date sometime, I know we live together, but dates are fun."

"I agree, but there are two things I want to organise. First, book our balloon ride, and second, I want to take you on a little holiday next year. My treat, somewhere like, erm, how about Australia to visit your mum and dad?"

"Oh my, that's huge, and way too expensive."

"That's why we have to wait until next year, but I've always wanted to go there, and what better excuse than to take you to visit your parents."

She sat with her mouth open and tears in her eyes.

Dean wiped a stray tear from her nose. "We don't have to go if it makes you cry."

"No, no, I want to go. Happy tears." Her voice cracked up.

Dean kissed her forehead, then pulled her into a hug. "I assume you have a passport that'll still be valid next year?"

"Yes, I renewed it last year, not because I planned to go anywhere, but because a renewal must be easier than a fresh application. I can't believe I'm actually going to get to use it."

He had a sparkle in his eye. He released his hold and

picked up his iPad. Inside the cover was the envelope from Valentine's Day, containing the balloon trip information.

He found the booking website. "Do you want to do a morning or an evening?"

"I don't know, maybe a morning, what would you prefer?" She shrugged. "It's your present after all."

"I think I would prefer a morning. There's just something about the morning air that makes me feel energised."

They glanced through the available dates on the balloon ride website, and opted for the morning of 2nd May.

He entered a few details and hit confirm. "That's all booked up now, so all we have to do is hope for good weather." He hugged her. "Thank you for buying the voucher, I'm really looking forward to it."

— ❦ —

The weeks that followed felt exciting. They starting looking at dates for their Australia trip and Lisa's love life was simmering nicely. Jessie met her down by the river because she wanted to show her what their old stomping ground had become. It was a beautiful spring afternoon, almost the end of March, and Lisa was amazed by how pretty it looked.

She stood gazing at the big luxury houses. "I knew they were doing some development down here, but if it wasn't for my scribble under the bridge, I wouldn't have recognised it at all."

"Dean's dad built all of this, well not him personally, but he owns the company that did."

"Wow, I didn't realise that. So when you've got lots

of little Dean and Jessie's running around, you'll live somewhere as awesome as this."

"Maybe, but it won't be here. Dean said we can't buy one because you wouldn't be able to visit."

Lisa appeared confused. "Why?"

"Because your mum banned you from coming down here after that day when you fell."

"I had completely forgotten about that. Remember that man? He was so scary."

Jessie rolled her eyes. "Well, you were vandalising the bridge."

Lisa rolled her eyes to match and continued to walk a short way before they turned back.

"How are things going with Ethan?"

Lisa's expression changed completely. "Extremely well, he's a real sweetie."

"But you're taking it steady?"

"Yes Mum."

Jessie gave her a pointed look, she hated it when she called her mum. A few minutes passed before she unintentionally returned to her mother-like role.

"I hope you're staying safe."

"Safe?

Jessie elaborated slightly. "Using protection."

"Oh, no. No we haven't, I mean, we haven't gone that far yet. I'm still having some therapy sessions, but I've discussed my new relationship with the counsellor, and we agreed that I'm at a stage where I could take the first step towards normality."

Jessie looked inquisitively at her, not quite understanding.

"It's not like alcohol or drugs, sex is not something I

could, or should, avoid forever. I've cut right back on drinking because that was my biggest issue. It made me feel out of control and in need of affection, but I haven't felt like that for a while." She frowned. "Back then, I didn't care who it was, or what they meant to me, I just felt like I needed to be wanted."

"Well just take it steady. I expect Ethan is fine with things as they are."

"Yes, he's good, a world class kisser, but hasn't tried to push me to go any further yet."

"World class whoa. Stop right there. Way too much information."

Lisa giggled while Jessie walked along with her hands over her ears. It wasn't long before they reached the path that led back to the apartment, and Lisa set off in her silver Mini to go for a burger with Ethan.

When Jessie arrived home, Dean was behaving suspiciously. She was about to confront him, but then she saw a message pop up on his phone, which was laying on the table next to her. She didn't see the whole message, but it was an airline ticket booking confirmation. He had obviously been booking their tickets to Australia as a surprise, so she bit her tongue and said nothing. They hadn't officially confirmed a date for their trip, but his track record was enough to reassure her that whatever he had organised would be absolutely fine.

"How was Lisa?"

"She was good, she didn't come up because she's going out for a burger with Ethan."

"They're still together then?"

"Going steady, as the saying goes."

He pulled his finest *aww that's cute* face. "I remember

when we where like that, exciting and magical."

She looked aggrieved. "You mean we're not exciting and magical anymore?"

He swept her up, put her over his shoulder, and walked around the room with her squealing. "Is that exciting?"

"Nooooo, put me down."

"Not even magical?"

She kicked her legs and wriggled.

He slapped her bottom then put her down on the sofa, and lay on top of her. "In that case, no, we're beyond excitement and magic. We may as well just get married and grow old."

"Speak for yourself, I still have wild sexual desires."

He gave her his best shocked look. "For whom?"

She reached up, pulling him close enough to kiss, and whilst he was being consumed by her sweet lips, she ran her hands down his body to his bottom, squeezing and pulling him tightly against her body. "I only desire you, I've only ever desired you."

He gave her a cheeky grin. "Desires are so overrated."

She pushed her hips to meet his as she pulled him even closer. Her smile widened because she could feel his desire growing. "Really." She whispered, smiling, "I can feel your desire from here."

"That's just your imagination."

She slipped her hand down the back of his shorts and tried to move it around him to check. He started laughing and wriggling. She had forgotten how ticklish he was, but eventually reached her intended destination.

She gasped. "That's not my imagination, and for someone who thinks desire is overrated, that's a lot of desire."

He got up and moved so he was sitting on the other side of the corner sofa. She pouted with disappointment, assuming she had offended him, but he dropped his head and looked at her from the top of his eyes, smiling.

He beckoned her over, then placed his hands on the sofa beside his hips. "Face me and put your knees here." He tapped his hands at his sides.

She didn't hesitate or question him before hitching her dress up slightly and shuffling up, straddling him, resting her bottom on his lap. He put his arms around her and pulled her even closer, then began to kiss around her neck softly, moving up to her lips. She could feel his desire beneath her, twitching, desperate for freedom.

She struggled to speak through his passionate kisses. "Show me."

Dean paused. "Show you what?"

"Show me your desire."

She didn't need to ask again. He immediately shuffled below her, losing his shorts.

He smiled. "I really should get onto Lovehoney and buy you some crotchless panties."

"I had wondered what the point of them was, but now I understand." She giggled.

As he pushed her panties aside, he pulled her firmly into his lap, allowing her warmth to surround him. He continued to trail sweet kisses around her neck and into her cleavage as he made love to her. It wasn't the most comfortable position to be in, and her knees ached, but her discomfort was outweighed by the magic of Dean's gentle touch and the burning passion inside her.

It was the first time they had made love with their clothes on, in the middle of the day with the curtains wide open. She was glad they were not overlooked, and being on the top floor, nobody could see in, but the danger of the window cleaner turning up added jeopardy and a new level of excitement. She felt his love ripple through her entire body, and she cried out. He gripped her tightly, pulling her firmly into his lap, filling her with all the desire he had. They slumped, side by side on the sofa, holding each other, gazing eye to eye.

She furrowed her brow. "Did I really hear you say we should *just get married?*"

He ran his fingers through her hair. "It's open for discussion, if you want to discuss it."

"That's not exactly the most romantic proposal in history, but I'm not completely against the idea, as long as you don't mean next week."

He shook his head, smiling. "No I don't, but that's not a proposal, pretend I didn't say that because I can definitely do better when the time is right."

"I'm sure you can." She rested her head on his shoulder. "I love you."

"I love you too, Sweet Lips."

As the weeks passed, Jessie wondered when Dean was going to tell her about the Australia trip. She considered asking him several times, but didn't want to ruin the surprise. He must have been planning to tell her on her birthday, and that wasn't long, so she decided to wait until then.

In the meantime, they had their balloon trip to look forward to, and that was upon them soon enough.

"Wake up sleepy head." He rubbed her arm gently.

She stared slightly, rolled over and pulled a pillow over her head.

"Come on, we have to get up."

She lifted the pillow from her head, looked at the clock and groaned.

Dean kissed her gently. "Good Morning."

"Uh, it's 5am."

He stroked her hair lovingly. "Yes, we need to leave at 6am."

She sat up looking extremely tired, her hair all ruffled and messy. Dean gathered his clothes from the wardrobe, returned and lay them out on the bed.

He leaned over and kissed her. "Do you want to shower with me?"

A smile broke through her fatigued expression. "Yes, that's worth getting up for."

She had already prepared her clothes, so she followed him straight into the shower.

Just before it turned 6am, they collected their tickets from the desk and set off. It didn't take long to get to their take off location because there was virtually no traffic on the roads. A small group of people had gathered on the edge of the field, and a man with a clipboard confirmed their booking number.

The man tapped his clipboard with the end of his pen. "We're just waiting for two more, then we can begin."

They stood observing the people around them, mostly couples, as they waited, and as soon as the last people arrived, they moved over to the centre of the field for their safety briefing.

Everybody helped to lay out the balloon, then supported it as it began to inflate. It didn't take long until they climbed into the basket and lifted off. Dean held Jessie as they floated upwards, admiring the fields like a patchwork quilt below them. The sun hadn't long come up, glowing on the horizon, and reflecting in her golden blonde hair.

Dean's face was a picture. "This is amazing, it's so peaceful up here."

"Look at the motorway." Jessie pointed down. "The cars look like ants, crawling along in neat lines."

"Oh yes."

They drifted over fields and passed quaint villages, holding each other firmly the whole time. Before they knew it, they began to descend slowly, preparing to land. It was over far too quickly, but what an experience. They helped to pack up the balloon before being served a small glass of champagne.

She raised her glass. "Happy Valentine's Day, Sexy Boy."

A few people turned and looked at her confused, it *was* the beginning of May after all.

"Thanks, Sweet Lips. This was well worth waiting for. It was awesome!"

"My feelings exactly. There's only one thing I didn't like about it."

He frowned. "What's that?"

"It's over, so I can't look forward to sharing it with

you now."

He gave her a hug, then gazed into her eyes thoughtfully. She was normally good at reading him, but not on this occasion. Still, he has the most incredible eyes, and any chance to lose herself in them was a bonus.

He nodded. "You do have something else to look forward to."

She wondered if it was time. Was he about to tell her about the flight to Australia? The decision she had to make was whether or not to let on she already knew.

"I wasn't going to tell you until the day, but I guess you'll want to pack in advance. Next week, on your birthday, we're going to Paris for the weekend."

She was stunned. She had always wanted to go to Paris. "Seriously?"

"Yes, remember the day when you went for a walk with Lisa along the river?" He cocked his head. "I booked the flights then. You almost caught me, but I managed to put the laptop away just in time."

She smiled, knowing he had been up to something, but she didn't let on. "You always know how to make me happy. Thank you."

19 LA VILLE DE L'AMOUR

The plane taxied to the runway and stopped. Jessie squeezed Dean's hand tightly, preparing for the moment of takeoff. He leaned over and kissed her, then the engine roared and the aircraft began to move faster and faster, thundering down the runway. Everything around them shook, including Jessie, but she gripped Dean's hand like her life depended on it. Suddenly there was silence. The plane tilted back and the land outside the window began to move further and further away.

He squeezed her hand. "Are you okay?"

She nodded, still clinging. The plane banked to the left, making the colour drain from her face, but it soon straightened out and levelled off. The seatbelt light went out and she released his hand. She let out the biggest breath, as though she had held it since takeoff.

He stroked her cheek. "Okay?"

She took another deep breath. "I am now. Takeoff is always the hardest part."

"You had me worried there."

"Why?"

"Paris is just a short hop across the Channel, but Australia is a very long way away." He raised his eyebrows. "If you couldn't cope with this, next year would've been more like torture than a treat."

She looked much calmer than before. "No, it's just the takeoff, all that shaking and tilting."

It wasn't long before they began their descent ready to land at Paris Charles de Gaulle Airport, landing smoothly and making their way to an awaiting coach.

After a straightforward journey – on the wrong side of the road – they arrived at the Hôtel Eiffel Trocadéro. It was a tall, thin building that didn't look big enough to be a hotel, and after checking in, they started to make their way up to their room on the sixth floor.

"Est la chambre de luxe avec vue." He sounded enthusiastic and confident.

She smiled. "It's a chamber of..."

He giggled as she struggled to work out what he said.

She shook her head. "I was never good at French."

"Neither was I. You wouldn't believe how much I had to practice saying that."

"Which means?"

He grinned. "The luxury bedroom with a view, or something to that effect."

"Nice. What is the view of?"

"Mademoiselle, est la Tour Eiffel!" He unlocked the hotel room door.

Her face lit up because they had a spectacular view. She flopped on the kingsized bed, beaming from ear to ear.

"Paris, I'm finally in Paris."

He propped himself up on his elbow beside her. "Yes you are. Happy birthday."

She pulled him closer and kissed him, the French way.

He reciprocated, then pulled away. "We shouldn't waste time here, we have a tower to climb."

"Now?"

He jumped to his feet. "Yes, right now, let's go."

— 🐛 —

The Eiffel Tower looked so much bigger from below. They stood gazing up, amazed.

"I should ask somebody to take a picture for us." He looked around. "A memory to treasure."

He continued to look, spotting a young couple who looked like they might speak English. He quickly rushed off to speak with them. He shuffled around in his pocket and took out his phone, fiddled with it, then handed it over and returned to Jessie.

The young man stood holding the phone steadily, pointing in their direction. "Ready."

They stood, posing, cuddled together with the tower behind them. The camera flashed.

"Another one for good luck."

At that, Dean slipped out of their embrace and dropped to one knee. Jessie was gobsmacked as he pulled out a little velvet box and opened it. She looked at the couple with the camera and they smiled. They knew. He had clearly told them.

"Jessica, my Sweet Lips, my lightning attraction, will you marry me?"

Her eyes filled with tears and her smile widened. She took a deep breath and wiped a tear from her cheek.

"You soppy old romantic, you brought me all the way to Paris for this."

He didn't move, neither did the camera couple. They all waited with baited breath.

"Yes, yes, yes!" Her heart pounded.

The camera was still on them as Dean stood up, put his arms around her, lifted and twirled her round.

There was another flash of the camera, and the

camera couple handed the phone back. "Congratulations."

"Thank you." Her tears continued to seep from her eyes.

Dean was beaming. "Thank you for your help."

The couple walked away and left them to enjoy their moment. They stood with their arms around each other, kissing for what seemed like an eternity, but was actually just a few minutes.

"Ready to join your fiancé at the top of the tower to take in the view?" He turned, leading her towards the tower.

"Yes, I think I am, Mr Whittle." Her smile was solid. "Hmm Jessica Whittle, Jessie Whittle, Mrs Jessica Whittle."

Dean laughed and shook his head. "Mrs Sweet Lips Whittle. I bet you'll be doing that in the mirror later."

She slapped his arm as they walked along.

The view was incredible. They could just about make out their hotel in the distance. They stood snuggled together, looking at the hotel for a few minutes.

"This is so surreal. When we get back to the hotel, we can look out and see our tower, knowing that when we arrived, I was your girlfriend, but when we left, I was your fiancée."

"That was my plan." He wrapped his arm around her waist, holding her close, running his fingers through her hair. He glanced at his watch. "Hungry?"

"Yes, but please, no snails or frogs legs."

"No, I don't fancy any of that. I've booked a table

at a nice intimate restaurant on the other side of the river."

They took some more photographs, then made their way along the River Seine, hand in hand. They were the perfect picture of happiness as they crossed the bridge, exchanging sweet smiles, soon finding themselves standing outside L'Astrance.

She stared at the sign on the wall. "We can't eat here, it's got three Michelin stars." She had a look of horror on her face.

Dean gave her his finest smile and opened the door to lead her inside. She wouldn't win that battle, Dean had made his plans, and if that's what he wanted, well, that's it.

"Bonjour, erm, bonjour, une table resev, erm réservée pour Dean et Jessica Whittle." He looked less confident than she had ever seen, but she was proud of him for trying. She had no idea what he had tried to say, but it had sounded sort of French.

"Oui, ah, she said yes?" The head waiter gave them a big smile.

Dean smiled and nodded whilst Jessie looked at him amazed.

"Congratulations. We hope you enjoy your celebration with us today." He escorted them to their table, presented them with the menu and returned to his position near the door.

Jessie leaned in, speaking quietly. "I'm glad he speaks English, I have no idea what you said to him back there."

"Hopefully I just told him we had a reservation, but I was pleased that he replied in English because I wouldn't have had a clue either."

She looked inquisitive. "How did he know?"

"I told them when I booked."

Of course he did. She relaxed and tried to forget how much it was going to cost, after all, you only get engaged once.

It was, by far, the most romantic meal they had ever had, topped up with plenty of wine. She kept going back over her name variations while Dean laughed and smiled. It could have gone so badly wrong. She could have said no, but it all worked out well. It was an evening to treasure forever.

They walked slowly back to their hotel via the river, admiring the beauty of the Eiffel Tower; all lit up and looking magnificent. It was their special place, somewhere they would remember forever. Jessie expected to have a sleepless night, with thoughts and excitement running through her head, but the expensive wine and sheer comfort of the bed allowed her to fall fast asleep in her fiancé's arms the moment her head hit the pillow. Dean gave a sigh of relief and joined her in dreamland.

As the sun began to break through the crack in the curtains, she woke and met Dean's gaze.

She rubbed her eyes. "What time is it?"

"Early. Actually, too early." He yawned.

He rolled over and climbed out of bed, shuffling through their weekend bag, eventually pulling out a box of Paracetamol.

"Good thinking, can I have some too please?" She lay with a hand to her thudding head.

"Too much wine, not enough water. We should know better." He passed her a glass of water and two tablets.

She widened her eyes. "Did I dream it, or did we get engaged last night?"

He lay on the bed, raised her hand to his lips and paused. "Yes. You're going to become Mrs Jessica Sweet Lips Whittle."

She grinned, eyes fixed on her sparkling new diamond ring. "Amazing."

"I love you. Now, should we get some breakfast and prepare for our sightseeing day?"

She kissed him and got up.

After breakfast, they walked down to the coach tour pickup point, and waited with a large group of tourists, all excited about visiting some of the iconic Parisian landmarks. They hadn't been waiting for very long when the coach arrived. They travelled along the Champs Élysées and around the Arc-de-Triomphe.

She nudged him. "I never really knew what to expect, but I hadn't imagined the Arc-de-Triomphe would be on a roundabout."

"Aww bless you. We all have our issues. Hopefully you'll get over the shock soon." He pretended to flinch.

She gave him a playful slap. They continued on, stopping a while later at The Cathedral of Notre Dame. They had three hours to explore and have lunch before they needed to be back at the coach, so after a quick look around the cathedral, they stopped and had their portrait sketched by one of the local artists in the square.

Dean didn't attempt any more French speaking, but

he didn't need to, they were in a busy tourist hotspot where it seemed like almost everybody spoke English.

He led her around the edge of the square, looking at the vast selection of cafés. "Frogs legs for lunch?"

"You're very welcome to them, but I'll settle for a plain chicken sandwich." She threw him a smile.

It was extremely busy, so they kept tight hold of each other's hands until they got inside the café. They sat admiring their sketch while they waited for their food.

He pointed at her sketched lips. "It's good, very realistic."

"It is. We'll never forget when it was done." She held up her new engagement ring. "I still can't believe you asked him to get my hand and ring into the picture."

"It was important. Now we can get it framed to hang on the wall as a constant reminder."

She smiled. "I like that."

The time flew, and they arrived back at the coach just in time. Their next destination, a familiar and precious spot, the Eiffel Tower. Despite having already been there, they were more than happy to go back.

"Less than 24 hours ago." He squeezed her hand. "It seems like so much longer."

They stood gazing up at the tower from the spot where he proposed.

Her smile was wide and proud. "Would you do it any differently if we had gone back in time?"

"No I wouldn't, it was perfect, very memorable, plus I have a video of it." He held up his phone.

They didn't go up the tower again, spending time on their spot was much more important while they waited to set off on their short cruise along the Seine. The perfect end to their day out.

The coach had left and their tour was over, so they strolled back to their hotel to freshen up before their evening meal.

— 🐞 —

After their evening meal, the perfect weekend was finished off with a relaxing jacuzzi.

Dean flicked bubbles at her. "This is just like being at home."

"Except we don't have a view of the Eiffel Tower from home." She flicked bubbles back.

"True." He giggled. "Maybe we could get a picture of it for the bathroom wall."

She was grinning like the cat that got the cream. There was a lot to be happy about.

"What are you grinning at?"

"I'm just feeling very happy and lucky. I can't wait to go home and tell everybody the news."

"Our parents already know."

She looked confused. "Mine too?"

"Yes, of course. I had to ask for permission from your Dad."

She started laughing. "What, you actually did that?"

"Of course, that was very important."

"Oh my perfect gentleman." She felt proud. "I think that's why I love you."

He pulled her closer and swished water over her body while she rested her head back onto his chest, her eyes closed, savouring the moment.

— 🍎 —

She woke him with sweet trailing kisses on Sunday morning. It took him a moment to fully wake up, but she enjoyed his surprise. She had already opened the curtains enough to expose a view of the tower.

She whispered in his ear, still nibbling his neck softly. "Happy birthday my fiancé."

He smiled, remembering it was indeed his birthday. "Thank you."

"Now, I *have* got a present for you, but I left it at home because I didn't want to risk it getting lost. Can you wait until later?"

"Yes I can. In the meantime I've got you, and what more could I need on a Sunday morning in Paris?"

She was happy enough with that response, and made sure their last morning in Paris was filled with passion and romance. It had to be memorable. After a relaxing lay in and a continental breakfast, they gathered their bags and set off for the airport.

The journey home was smooth, once they got over the plane taking off, and Jessie was excited about giving Dean his present. They had hardly got through the door when she rushed into the bedroom, returning with a small flat gift box.

He chuckled. "You don't waste any time."

"Well, I want you to open it *on* your birthday."

Once in the living room, he opened it. "Two tickets to the..." He looked at her open mouthed. "Jessie. This is amazing, tickets to the VIP party at Madonna's concert."

"Yes, it's a while off, but I knew you would like it."

She wore the smuggest grin.

He put his arms around her, lifted her and twirled, just as he had at the Eiffel Tower on Friday. She squealed until he put her down.

"I remembered you said you were distraught about missing one of her concerts when you were on holiday with your parents."

"You're good at picking out the fine details, first the balloon trip, then this."

"Well you're not exactly easy to buy for." She shrugged. "So I have to think *way* outside the box."

He kissed her. "Thank you, that's perfect."

The next morning at work, they walked into the office looking extremely pleased with themselves.

Lisa bounded over. "Obviously a good weekend then."

Jessie lifted her left hand enough to draw attention to the sparkling diamond solitaire ring.

Lisa's eyes almost popped out. "No way!

She nodded. "Yes way."

"No."

She didn't respond again, just smiled as she held out her hand. People gathered around, admiring her diamond, even people she didn't really know. Dean played it cool and just carried on walking to his desk, logging into his computer as normal. She stared in his direction. He smiled, then blew her a kiss. It took a while, but eventually all the gabbling people that had been congratulating her started to drift away, so she finally got to her desk.

She didn't normally like being the centre of

attention, but found it interesting to see how bright and chatty everybody became after all the excitement.

Lisa leaned over Dean's desk towards her, practically pushing him out of the way. "A party, you need a party."

She shook her head. She didn't like parties. Neither did Dean. His disapproving look confirmed it as he leaned out of her way, shaking his head with a smirk.

They discussed it at lunchtime in the park and Dean suggested inviting everybody to drinks at The Red Lion on Friday lunchtime. "Then it won't drag on into the dark hours, and nobody will get completely paralytic and make a show of themselves."

She giggled. "Good plan. I hate the whole dramatic drunken fiasco that normally goes hand in hand with these sorts of celebration. Plus it saves us looking like hermits."

"That's what I thought."

He announced their lunchtime celebration when they got back to the office, and it went down well. George gave them both Friday afternoon off so they could relax and celebrate without needing to worry about getting back to work.

Later in the afternoon, Jessie walked down to the canteen to collect her coffee with Lisa, and told her all about Paris, how he proposed and took her to L'Astrance.

"I've never heard of it."

Jessie shook her head. "He's crazy. It's got three Michelin stars, need I say much more?"

"That's got to have been expensive."

She nodded. "He spoils me. Sometimes he feels

too good to be true. It's like I'm waiting to wake up one day, only to find I've been dreaming the whole time."

"Why?"

She shook her head. "I don't know what I did to deserve him, and that scares me."

Lisa put her arm around her. "Relax. You're amazing together."

They sat down in the canteen for a few minutes before returning to the office. As they walked, Jessie changed the subject.

"Talking of being amazing together, how is it going with Ethan?"

Lisa's smile widened. "Bubbling along."

"Just bubbling?"

"Yes." She looked aghast. "I'm taking my time, trying to get to know him as much as I can."

"I'm proud of you, after everything that—"

She took a deep breath. "I, erm, okay, something *has* happened. This is the first time, and it scares me."

Jessie looked confused.

Lisa began to fiddle with her fingers nervously, looking around to make sure she couldn't be overheard. "I think, well, no." She shook her head. "When you and Dean first met, how did you feel?"

Jessie frowned. "You know. I was with you the first time I saw him, and again when we met him in the office. I guess I thought he was fit."

"That's what you thought, but how did you feel?"

She curled the side of her lip, rocking her head from side to side. "Warm?"

"See I didn't have that, my feelings for Ethan have

grown from nothing and developed from there."

Jessie still looked confused. "Oh, I didn't fall for him because he was fit, I mean Martyn is fit, but I was never going to take things further with him, obviously."

"Martyn? Which, oh, not Martyn, witty, one leg shorter than the other, lecturer Martyn?"

She looked embarrassed, and nodded her head, her lips pursed. Lisa looked like she had just seen a naked football team. Jessie just laughed as her cheeks turned pink.

"Dean was eye candy, cute, but as I started to get to know him, my feelings started to develop. Even the smell of his aftershave gave me tingles. He made me feel like I was walking on air."

"That's what I was wondering." She took a deep breath. "That's happening, Ethan is affecting me so much. If what you describe is love, then I think I've fallen in love with him. I've never loved anybody before, ever."

Jessie wasn't sure what to say, unsure if this was what Lisa wanted or not. Lisa just stared at her.

Jessie was struggling to make sense of it. "Is it a good feeling, or bad?" She didn't really know what to say.

"It's good, but I don't want to mess it up."

Jessie felt more relaxed. "Well, we need to get back, but bring him along on Friday lunchtime, and just go with the flow."

— ❧ —

The rest of the week felt calmer and the buzz in the office calmed. Jessie felt happy about not rushing into making firm plans about the wedding yet, especially as she had to liaise with her parents over their availability. She also wanted to get her final exams out of the way.

Friday lunchtime was soon upon them, and they walked down to The Red Lion, where most of their colleagues joined them. It was incredibly busy, and being back at the centre of attention was difficult for them. As soon as she could, Jessie sneaked off into a corner with Lisa, pleased to have some breathing space.

Lisa looked around her, lowing her voice. "Ethan has invited me to stay at his tomorrow night."

Jessie looked pensive. "What did you say? I mean, is that what you want?" It took her back to her own feelings about staying with Dean for the first time. A crazy mixture of fear and desire.

Lisa grinned. "Yes. I'm going to be honest and tell him how I feel."

Jessie was about to respond when Ethan returned from the gents, putting an end to their discussion.

"I'll leave you two to talk. I should support Dean over there."

The crowd gradually thinned out as people returned to the office, and soon, only the two of them remained.

"I'm glad we got that over with." Dean slumped onto the bench seat next to Jessie.

She gripped his hand. "Relax, we're off the hook now."

They finished their drinks and got a taxi home.

On Saturday evening, Jessie had been thinking about Lisa, the emotional turmoil of her own blossoming romance still fresh in her mind. Dean joined her on the sofa with a glass of wine ready to watch a movie on iTunes. She hadn't told Dean the full story, but did tell him Ethan had invited her to stay over.

He reassured her she would be fine. "She's a big girl now. She can look after herself." He was right.

"I know."

He pointed at their framed sketch on the wall. "Look what happened with us. That'll happen for Lisa one day too."

Her phone dinged. "Erm, it's from Lisa, I hope she's okay."

Dean rolled his eyes. "You worry too much."

Her mouth dropped open and her eyes filled with tears.

"What?" He looked concerned.

She couldn't speak. She handed him her phone.

"Bloody hell, that's awful." He raised his hand to his mouth. He cuddled her as she sobbed.

It took a while before she managed to speak. "Dead, how could he just die?"

Dean shushed her as he wiped away her tears.

She didn't even know if she was crying for Ethan, or for Lisa. "She was going to tell him she loved him, but now he's gone." She sniffled though streams of tears. She felt sick and ran off to the bathroom.

She returned and collected a glass of milk.

"She called. She wasn't really in much of a state to talk, but she managed to tell me what happened." He put his arm around her and pulled her close. "Were you sick?"

"No. I just had a horrible acid taste. This should help." She took a swig. "What did she say?"

"She's in shock. He was knocked off his bike by a car this afternoon. He wasn't wearing a helmet and hit his head. It probably happened so fast he didn't know anything about it."

"Life is so cruel." She blew her nose. "I didn't know him that well, but Lisa thought the world of him."

"I know." He rubbed her shoulders to calm her.

She sat for a moment, staring into space. A sudden wash of pity hit her. "She's been through so much, and just as things are settling for her, just as she falls in love and—"

He crouched at her feet and held her hands. "I told her to come over tomorrow, the best thing you can do now is sleep, then be there for her and support her."

She sniffled. "Okay."

—  —

Jessie had a restless night, unable to get Ethan and Lisa out of her head. She tossed and turned while Dean slept soundly beside her. She didn't want to wake him, but equally, didn't want to be alone in the dark either. She rubbed his arm gently, then waited. He groaned slightly, but didn't wake. She tried again, and still he slept. She gave up, rolled over and cried herself to sleep.

"Jessie, Jess, it's okay honey." Dean gripped her hand.

She looked around the room, startled, and realised it

was light outside. She looked at him in a daze. Her eyes all puffy and red, and her hair flattened, damp with tears to one side.

"You were shouting in your sleep."

He put his arms around her and pulled her close. He probably knew what was going on inside her head, so he didn't need to ask.

Her phone vibrated on the bedside table, so she picked it up to check her messages. "Lisa, she hasn't slept at all. She said she'll see us at work tomorrow."

He cuddled her again as she lay with a vacant expression. They didn't speak, but there was an air of understanding between them, so they didn't need to. Even when they eventually got up, they were both somewhat subdued.

They went for a walk along the river to get out for some fresh air.

"I didn't know him well, but knowing he's gone, in an instant, just like that, that's hard." She dabbed the corner of her eye.

"I understand." He put his arm around her shoulders. "Only a couple of days ago he celebrated our engagement with us at The Red Lion."

She sniffled. Dean held her tightly, but they continued to walk. They didn't discuss it again for the rest of the day.

— 🍂 —

Returning to work on Monday brought the shock of Ethan's death back to the surface. A general announcement was made, and there was a lot of talk about the tragedy of somebody so young dying so suddenly.

Jessie stepped outside for some fresh air with Lisa. They both struggled to hold themselves together. Lisa didn't speak. She couldn't open up and let her feelings pour out. Just as they went back into the building, they saw Claire being escorted out, clearly distressed and being taken home. She didn't lift her head or acknowledged them at all. Jessie didn't know the full story of what happened with her and Ethan, but they had been going out for a few months, and had remained friends, so it was understandable that she would be deeply affected.

They somehow managed to get through the day, but Lisa still didn't open up, in fact it took until the next weekend before she mentioned Ethan at all. She turned up at The Moorings on Saturday morning. Jessie made coffee. Dean went to the bedroom to give them space. They sat on the sofa, in silence at first.

Lisa took some deep breaths. "It's been a week." A stray tear rolled down her face, her pain clear to see.

Jessie gave her a tissue and put her arm around her.

"I feel like it was my fault, like he died as a punishment for me." She sniffled into the tissue.

Jessie shook her head. "You can't think like that. It was an accident."

"I had just fallen in love with him."

"I know, and I bet he felt the same way about you."

She nodded, evidently too choked up to speak. They sat in silence again while she regained her composure.

"I need to go, have some more time on my own. I have a counselling session on Monday, so I need to think about my feelings and how I plan to move on."

Jessie rubbed her arm. "Okay, well when you want

to talk, or even text, I'm here."

Lisa gave her a hug and Left. Dean returned from the bedroom and she told him what she had said.

"It's going to take time, but I can see why she would blame herself." He shook his head. "She feels like the world is conspiring against her. This is just another negative in a long line."

"I know, but it's not good for her wellbeing to see it like that. I just hope she gets that message through her counselling on Monday." She sat on the sofa.

He sat beside her. "It's got her through all the other stuff, so I'm sure it will help."

She put her arms around him. "You're right, plus it's going to take time."

— 🐛 —

As the weeks went by, Jessie supported Lisa, alongside her counselling. Talking about it helped Jessie to move on from her own shock and get over what happened. It was always going to be much more difficult for Lisa, but as they sailed through June, she had fewer breakdowns, and started to return to normal.

It was halfway through June when Jessie and Lisa were sat in the park at lunchtime, talking about all the things that had changed during their year.

Jessie slouched back on the bench, sunning herself. "It's certainly been a year to remember."

"For many things, all of which have hopefully made us all stronger."

"Hopefully yes." She nervously changed the focus of their conversation. "How are you getting on with your counselling?"

Lisa perked up. "It's good, it's helped me to put a lot of things into perspective. Like blaming myself for Ethan's death, we discussed how self-centred it is to think things like that could happen because of me."

She rubbed her arm. "I never thought it was your fault, but put like that, hopefully you'll be able to move on now you realise it really was just a horrible accident."

Lisa's eyes filled with tears. "He was only twenty, such a waste. It might have been easier to move on if I could have attended his funeral, but I couldn't have gone all the way to Sweden."

Jessie suddenly looked inspired. "How about we have a small gathering, like a memorial?"

Lisa smiled. "I think that would be really nice. I wonder if we could plant a tree in the office grounds?"

"I'll talk to Dean and see if anything like that has ever been done before, find out who we would have to talk to for permission."

Lisa forced a tiny smile. "I really like that idea. I can't imagine them refusing."

"Leave it with me."

She spoke with Dean when they got home, and he confirmed they had done similar things for staff who had died in the past. They normally had statues or ornaments placed in the courtyard outside the canteen. He promised to talk with the facilities department to get the required permission. Lisa was delighted when she found out, and they organised to meet with Brian from facilities to choose the spot for their ornament. Max offered to help because he went to the same university as Ethan, and suggested he ask the Art department of their university to organise the ornament. They came up with a brass bicycle to symbolise Ethan's love of cycling, though Lisa was worried it might have been considered bad taste. Jessie told her it simply meant he died doing something he loved, so not in bad taste at all, just adding to the symbolism. The memorial was organised for the last week of June, followed by drinks at The Red Lion.

Lisa gave Jessie a big hug. "Thank you, this is exactly what I needed, a chance to say goodbye, and somewhere to go when I want to connect with him."

20 THE QUEST FOR CLOSURE

Jessie was preparing breakfast when she realised it was the first day of July, a whole year since she started work at Webber OMC. She began to reflect again on how her life had changed, and how she herself had changed. Recent tragedies aside, her new life was extremely fulfilling. Her engagement to Dean made her smile. It was difficult to believe it had all began with a flash of lightning. Would they really have got together if it hadn't been for the storm? Unlikely. He had been so afraid of rejection, and had only managed to overcome it to rescue her from her own – much bigger – fear.

Her thoughts drifted to her job and her studies, more than aware she was nearing the end of her year-long work placement. She had just remembered she had to write a report on the experience she had gained, when Dean walked in and sat down, shower fresh and smelling incredible. There was nothing in the world more likely to sidetrack her thoughts.

"Just in time." She put two plates of poached egg on toast on the table, and sat down to join him.

"Thank you. The perfect start to a busy day."

"You can treat me tomorrow." She grinned. "I've got to make a start on my placement report at the weekend. I had stupidly forgotten all about it."

"That sounds onerous."

"No, I just have to outline the experience I've gained, how I've used theory in my work, and what skills I've acquired that they couldn't teach in the classroom."

"*All* the experience you've gained?" He raised his

eyebrows.

"No, that might be classed as erotica rather than media studies." She giggled, thinking about her raunchy diary.

He chuckled as he tried to eat. She sat gazing through the window thoughtfully, admiring how lovely and green it was with all the trees in full bloom.

"What are you thinking?" Asked Dean.

"This time last year, I thought this was still abandoned factory land, smashed up derelict buildings, but now, well I can't believe how beautiful it is."

He smiled. "That's how I felt about my personal life this time last year, smashed up and derelict. Then you walked in and changed everything."

"No I didn't. I was sat on a bench. You walked into *my* life." She giggled.

Dean smiled and shook his head. Passion in his eyes.

During the day, the report played on her mind. She felt stupid for forgetting. There was so much to cover, and even though she wanted to put it off, she knew she couldn't. When they arrived home, she went to the spare room to get her study bag, intending to grab her instruction sheet, notepad and pen, but she opened the side pocket and found the letter Mike had sent her earlier in the year.

I had forgotten all about this. She stared at the wall. *I wonder if it'd be a good idea to go and visit him now, make clear where he stands.*

She sighed, shook her head and tucked the letter back into the bag, then carried on with what she was doing. She jotted down a few notes for the report, but kept thinking about the letter. Nothing would please her more than finding closure, a definite end to the hell he caused her. She wanted to ensure he knew not to bother contacting her ever again. She didn't say anything to Dean, but decided to talk with Lisa about it.

After their meal, she sent Lisa a text message to organise a meet up, then tried to put it out of her mind. The next afternoon, she met Lisa in the canteen for a tea break and explained her dilemma.

"No, Jessie, don't do it." Lisa's face was stone cold serious. "I told you to burn that letter. Have you spoken with Dean about it?"

"Of course not, I didn't think he'd be keen."

Lisa shook her head adamantly. "That has to be your answer. If Dean would be against it, it's wrong."

"Maybe if I talk to him and explain my reasoning, he might understand why I need to go."

"Oh Jessie, I've never had to guide you before, but please, tear the letter up. Throw it away and never let that snake into your head again ever."

She became defensive. "You don't understand."

"I do. Please don't do it. He'll just get the wrong idea and that'll cause more problems in the long term."

It didn't matter what Lisa thought. Jessie had decided. The only struggle she had was whether to tell Dean or not. When she got home she couldn't settle. Her mind raged with chaos. She *had* to tell him her plan, but it had to be at the right moment. She struggled every evening, trying to find the right words, but it didn't feel like the right time, so she delayed, hoping the weekend would be better.

They lay in bed cuddling, cosy and naked, on Sunday morning. It felt like a quiet enough time, void of distractions. She took a deep breath, still unsure if she was doing the right thing. "I had forgotten all about it, but I found a letter in my bag from Mike." Her heart thumped hard.

"When did he send that?" He looked disturbed.

"I found it in my post pile when I cleared my room out. I put it in my bag, but forgot all about it until I found it when I was preparing for my report."

Rage invaded his eyes. "You should burn it, that man doesn't deserve any more of your tears."

Ignoring what he was saying, she ploughed on. "He was asking me to go and visit him."

"Idiot, as if you would."

"Well I wouldn't have gone back then, but now, maybe it'd be good to find closure, to tell him once and for all that I've no interest in him."

His face turned to stone. "No! No absolutely not, you are *not* going to visit him."

"But you need to understand the—"

"I don't need to understand anything." His tone was sharp. "You're *not* going."

She just stared at him. She should have expected a negative response, but this was beyond negative. He was dictating what she should or shouldn't do, it was unlike him, and that didn't sit right with her. They lay in silence for a few minutes before she tried again to get her point across.

"I just want to go and tell him face to face never to contact me ever again."

"By doing what he wants, reacting to him?" Fury

returned to his eyes. "No."

"Dean, please don't be like this. I just—"

"I'm not being like anything, I'm protecting you. Visiting him would be a huge mistake and I won't let you do it."

She began to cry. "Please, just listen to—"

"I'm not discussing it any further." He got up and walked out of the room.

She lay on the bed with tears streaming down her face. She had never seen him like that, and she didn't like it. Mike had tried to dictate to her, and he didn't get away with it because she had vowed never to let any man boss her around.

As she lay there, still naked, Dean stormed into the room, put on some clothes and walked out without saying a single word. She heard the apartment door close behind him, and she felt alone, lost, and completely abandoned. Her tears continued to fall and she felt stupid for letting Mike slither his way between them. It was their very first argument, and she couldn't understand how he could be so perfect, but so unreasonable and dominant.

She got up, put some clothes on and waited. He was gone for hours. She became more and more distressed, and tried to call him. All her calls went straight to voicemail and she realised it was over. Everything was ruined. She moved all her belongings into the spare room, resigned to the reality, then left him a voicemail to say she had moved to the spare room until she finds somewhere else to live.

It was a further hour before he finally arrived home. He didn't speak to her, but went straight into the bedroom, closing the door behind him. He didn't come out all evening.

She felt bad. Her proposed plan was crazy, so his reaction was justified. Suddenly, she understood his point of view. What she couldn't cope with was his domination and the anger in his eyes. She had never seen that side of him, and she didn't like it.

A cold and lonely night followed in the spare room, away from the warmth of her soul mate. She tossed and turned for most of the night, and considered speaking with him again, but when she woke up next morning, he had already left for work without her. She followed in her own car, parking next to his, as she always used to. She wasn't going to confront him in the office, but he refused to even make eye contact with her.

Lisa knew there was something wrong and tried to talk with them both, but neither wanted to allow it to flood over into work. The atmosphere reminded Jessie of when Lisa had fallen out with her over Rob and Dan, and it was a very unpleasant feeling.

She walked to the park with Lisa at lunchtime and explained what had happened. Lisa wasn't surprised, but she was sympathetic nonetheless.

She tried hard not to cry. "It's over, he won't even look at me."

"You just need to tell him you've taken his opinion onboard, and changed your mind."

Her voice was cracking. "No, I'm not going to let him think he can control me, that's not going to happen."

Lisa looked angrily at her. "So you're prepared to throw everything away for this, for Mike?"

The air became tense, Lisa was clearly on Dean's

side.

"It's not for Mike."

There was a moment of silence.

"Yes, it is, that's what started it. Look through Dean's eyes for just a moment."

"I sympathise with his opinion, but not his reaction." Her sadness calmed her slightly.

"Do you love him?"

She looked horrified. "Who, Dean?"

Lisa nodded. "Yes."

"With all my heart." She dropped her head into her hands. "We were supposed to have been getting married."

"Then you need to work through it and get over it. I wasn't there, but Dean would only have been looking out for you."

"I'll try to talk with him, but I don't know if I can get over it."

"Just deal with it. Come on, let's get back."

Her mind had been taken over by the chaos of the situation. Every now and then another random thought popped up to ruin her day. The recollection of telling him she would find somewhere else to live was an ugly one. He hadn't even said or done anything to try and stop her from doing it.

This really is the end.

He continued to avoid her all evening, so after another difficult night, she contacted student services to organise alternative accommodation. She avoided talking to Lisa because she felt too delicate to open up about what was happening, and she didn't want any further confrontation.

It was late on Tuesday afternoon when student services finally called back to confirm the availability of a room in one of the old accommodation blocks. She accepted without hesitation, desperate to escape the suffocation she felt. Her room would be ready in one week, so she spent the rest of the week awkwardly trying to pack her things whilst dodging him. She was completely heartbroken, but couldn't change anything even if she wanted to. He wouldn't even look at her, never mind speak with her.

When she arrived at the apartment on Friday evening to find a short note from him to say he was going to spend the weekend with his family. She was distraught and relieved at the same time, because the atmosphere had been overwhelming through the week. Spending the weekend living on eggshells would have been so much worse, but it also gave her time to finalise her packing in the spare room.

When he returned on Sunday night, he didn't speak to her, he just averted her gaze and went straight into his bedroom. She returned to the spare room and sat on the bed to write him a note ready for her departure on Tuesday. Monday was just another frosty day at work, and she realised he had no idea she was moving out on Tuesday, but she hadn't been able to tell him because he wouldn't speak with her.

She had organised to take the day off work on Tuesday, enabling her to move out without the awkwardness of him being there. She finished putting the last of her things in the car, and returned to the apartment for the last time. The place was full of wonderful memories and things she had never wanted to walk away from, but it had gone too far. There was no way to turn back and change what had happened. She placed the note on the breakfast bar along with her engagement ring, played a few notes on the piano, and left.

Dean,

Thank you for all the memories, the time and experiences we shared. I don't blame you for what happened, and hope you can forgive me for ruining what we had. You'll always be the sexy boy from the park who saved me from the storm, and hope you can remember me with fondness too. Lisa will give you the apartment key at work tomorrow.

Jessie

— 🌱 —

The new room was grotty, much worse than the last one, and worlds apart from Dean's perfect apartment. She cried all night – with real sobbing tears – for the first time since that awful Sunday morning.

Lisa was disappointed in her when she turned up at work on Wednesday, but she stood by her and gave Dean the key. Jessie looked up just in time for Dean to make eye contact with her. He didn't look away as he had done all through the previous week, he maintained a gaze, but as gorgeous as they were, his eyes were absent and hollow. He didn't attempt to speak with her at all, but day after day, he met her gaze and just looked at her with an empty expression.

She felt sad, far more than she ever had before. Her happiness had been ripped out and destroyed, and she felt like she was living in darkness. Seeing the absence of joy and love in Dean's eyes was like a bird with no song, it was wrong, and it was all her fault.

Every day ended with another night of painful isolation, and she just cried herself to sleep. Even her pretty purple fluffy things didn't hide how drab her room was, and there was nothing to fill the emptiness in her heart. Many thoughts and regrets ran through her head, but one stark memory haunted her over and over again. Dean holding her warmly on New Year's Eve, saying, "I have a feeling this will be a very special year."

She sighed. *It would have been if I hadn't been so stupid.*

21 LIVING WITH THE CONSEQUENCES

Jessie's last few weeks at Webber OMC Ltd felt awkward, but she had no option other than to cope. She maintained her professionalism to the end, even working with Dean on his projects. They spoke very little, and only when they had to, but the emotionless tone in his voice that matched the emptiness in his eyes was like some torturous, unimaginable pain.

She considered speaking with him to clear the air, but she couldn't do that without caving in and admitting she still loved him. She had no idea how he felt, and even though he hadn't given her any reason to think he hated her, she couldn't help but think he did. It really was too late to turn back time.

Walking in the park became an escape, but the memories taunted her. Dean's confidence issues played on her mind. No matter how he felt, he wasn't going to approach her to talk about it, even more so if he wanted to make a peace offering. His history of rejection was much more of an obstacle than her stubbornness, and as time went on, her ability to make a move to rectify their situation became increasingly unlikely.

Memories were eating away at her, his family, the welcome she received at Christmas, the drama of Angela giving birth and looking after the alien child. Even though she had been adamantly against it at the time, she would give anything now to be in Angela's shoes; a wife and mother, carrying Dean's children, watching him crawling about on the floor building train tracks for his own son. But no matter how much she dwelled on it, she couldn't just delete what had happened. She couldn't bring herself to admit she was wrong. Day after day, her thoughts were haunted by the what-ifs as she suffocated in anguish.

The dread of her job coming to an end filled her with sadness. Her placement had been every bit as fulfilling as she had hoped, but her ongoing emotional suffering left her counting the days until the end. Each day was harder than the last, but she was brave, on the outside, until she reached her very last day, when she really struggled to hold herself together. She had loved working there and would have liked to have had the chance to go back when her degree was finished, but she couldn't envisage doing that with the atmosphere between her and Dean. Leaving the job she loved would be incredibly hard, but the hardest thing of all would be walking away from Dean. She loved him dearly and leaving that job would be their last tie broken.

She spent her final morning gazing at him, he was clearly as broken as she was, but despite her desperate wish to tell him how much she loved him, and how much she wanted to marry him and carry his adorable blonde children, she felt stupid for letting it happen. He met her gaze several times, and as the morning went on, the emptiness in his eyes turned to pain and sorrow. He was clearly dreading the end of the day, and the end of their time together, just as much as she was. She tried so hard to put it out of her mind, but she wanted to hold him. She wanted him to hold her, and she needed to inhale his fresh woodland fragrance. But she didn't, she couldn't. It felt like an invisible wall stood between them, forcing them to accept their eternal separation.

During the afternoon, everybody was saying their final goodbyes, but Jessie was too focused on the fact Dean was nowhere to be seen. He had gone off at lunchtime and not returned, meaning she probably wouldn't even have chance to say goodbye. His computer had been turned off and his desk tidied, just as he would when he was going home, so it wasn't even as though he was in a meeting.

She struggled with herself over what to do, even if she had persuaded herself to make peace, she had missed her chance. He was gone, and she couldn't help but think it was because of her. After a battle with her emotions, just before leaving, she scribbled a very short note on a sheet of paper.

I will always love you.

J xx

She slipped it into an envelope and fed it through the tiny gap above his locked drawer. As she walked away to collect her belongings, she had to fight back her tears. She didn't regret the note, but knowing he would find it on Monday morning left her feeling guilty. Offering him a tiny olive branch like that, delayed until she was gone was cruel, but it had to be said, he needed to know. She walked to her car with Lisa, who had luckily parked in the main car park, and as they walked, her tears came flooding out.

Lisa rubbed her arm. "Are you going to be okay?"

"Yes, I just need to get home and clear my mind. Everything just feels raw at the moment."

Lisa gave her a hug, but she could hardly think straight. She clutched the small pile of cards people in the office had given her and Lisa gave her another envelope. She didn't pay too much attention, because she had a sudden thought. It couldn't have been easy for Lisa to walk away, leaving behind Ethan's memorial.

"What did they say about the memorial?"

"We're welcome to drop by to visit and sit in the garden if we like, but I'm okay, Ethan lives on in my heart." She swallowed hard. "I'm fine, but please call me when you get home, when you've opened that."

Jessie gave her another hug and thanked her for the card. She hadn't even considered getting one for her because they would be going back to uni together, but the sentiment was appreciated.

Lisa held her at arm's length. "Promise me you'll call me if you need me."

"I promise."

They got into their cars ready to leave, but Jessie was distracted, looking at the empty parking space where Dean normally parked. She was overcome with fresh tears. Luckily Lisa didn't notice as she waved and drove away. She kept staring at the empty parking space, willing Dean to pull up and rescue her from her sadness, but he didn't. It really was the end, she knew that, and it took a few more minutes before she could compose herself enough to drive. She sobbed all the way home, especially as she passed the traffic light turning that led to his riverside apartment.

Unable to focus on anything, she lay on her bed, snuggling into one of her fluffy purple cushions, wallowing in her own self pity. She realised she was back to the emotional despair she had before her exams, just over a year ago, and it was an unpleasant realisation. She was distracted from her thoughts by her phone, a text message from Lisa.

"Did you open the envelope yet?"

She didn't quite understand at first, then remembered the white envelope Lisa gave her in the car park. She went through the pile of envelopes and pulled out the small white one Lisa had given her. She hadn't noticed it before, but it wasn't Lisa's handwriting, the J was very distinctive, memorable, this envelope was from Dean.

Jessie,

I couldn't bear to say goodbye, that would be too final. Your sweet lips are still etched all over my body, but my apartment is empty without you in it. There is no laughter, no warmth and my bed is too big and too cold without you. A year ago, you said to call you if I was ever scared of anything, but the only thing that scares me now is facing the rest of my life without you.

I was stupid to let you go and I hope you can forgive me for being so thoughtless. We shared something so special and I want you to know that I'll never forget you.

Dean

She read it over and over, and cried. They had the most amazing thing going on, and she had walked away from it. She was so stupid. If Dean couldn't accept that offer to call her, he really did hate what she had done to him, what she had done to them. Unable to speak, she sent Lisa a text to confirm she had the envelope and would see her back at uni. Suddenly, the phone rang, it was Lisa.

"Hi Lisa."

"What did he say?"

She started to speak, but stopped because she was choking up.

"Do you want me to come over?"

"No, I'm going to take a shower and sleep."

"Okay, but I'm here, so please talk to me when you can."

"Okay, thanks."

She kept thinking about Dean's letter while she had her shower, and when she went to get her pyjamas from her drawer, she pulled out the cow onesie that Lisa had bought her.

"Mooving-in present indeed. She's so funny." She started crying again.

The magical feeling they had on the day when they wore their matching cow onesies for the first time. It was such a fond memory, but tainted with the sadness of their separation. Lots of little things would be guaranteed to set her off, and she wondered if she would ever get over him.

They had a whole week off before starting back at university, and she spent the time alone, isolated and dwelling on what she could have had. She looked at her diary, abandoned since the day of their argument, but couldn't bring herself to open it. Memories of Dean feeding her strawberries, hunting for clues on Valentine's Day, proposing next to the Eiffel Tower, and so many more constantly invaded her thoughts. She relived them, running from the storm together over and over again, sharing his towel and assuming he just wanted to be her friend. Even that was lost, the warm friendship they shared long before he kissed her for the first time.

Time wasn't healing, instead, it drove her crazy. Lisa kept trying to call but she didn't want to talk, she couldn't, her pain was too great. She missed Dean so much and just wanted to run back to him, but she was stubborn, and his words *never forget you* felt final, he would never forgive her for snatching away his happiness. But he had her number and if he couldn't bring himself to call, there's no way he would forgive her.

It was Friday evening, a whole week since leaving her job, a week since she first read Dean's letter. Jessie had just three days before she was due back at university, three days to pull herself together ready to face the world. There was a knock on the door. She froze while various scenarios ran through her head. Dean, her heart leaped, but he didn't know where she had moved to. Mike, but he was, hopefully, in prison, and if he wasn't, that would be very scary. Then she pictured Lisa, the only obvious answer.

Her voice spoke on the other side of the door. "Jessica Samantha Williamson, open—"

She didn't allow her to continue, opening the door in a flash. It felt like déjà vous. Lisa tried to brighten her up and helped her to get ready for uni.

"Do you want me to stay for the weekend?"

She hesitated, sighed, then looked up. "No, I have to stand on my own two feet and do this on my own."

Lisa didn't argue with her, she was good at gauging her. A lot had changed over the year, and Jessie had grown up a lot.

Monday arrived and they returned to uni. The week dragged by, slowly, very very slowly. Even eccentric

Martyn didn't make Jessie smile in his lectures. They sat at the back of the lecture theatre, just where they had sat observing Mike over a year ago. Martyn waffled on about something or another, but Jessie couldn't take in anything he said.

Lisa leaned over. "I can't believe you fancied him all that time and never told me."

She shrugged. She hadn't really considered it. It no longer mattered because she only had eyes for one man and she might never see him again.

"You haven't taken a single note all week." Lisa watched her shrug again. "Please don't let this ruin you." She lowered her voice further. "If you want to talk to someone other than me, I can recommend my counsellor."

Jessie looked at her astounded. She couldn't believe she would even suggest professional help. Lisa obviously had no understanding of the concept of relationship breakdown. She didn't even think the suggestion warranted a response, and blanked it completely. She pretended to focus on what Martyn was saying at the front of the class, but in reality, she was thinking about Dean, the happy, romantic Dean.

Lisa didn't mention counselling again, but didn't allow it to cause a rift between them. She stood firmly at her side and continued to give her moral support. The first week back had been overwhelming, and Jessie longed for Friday so she could go back to her room and drown in self pity once more.

Being back at uni was a distraction, but not enough to dull her ongoing pain. Each day went slower than the last, and Friday was extremely long and emotionally draining. It had been two weeks since she left Webber OMC Ltd, and two weeks since she last saw Dean's gorgeous face.

The pain of walking away, leaving behind her declaration of love, was fresher than ever. She sat through Dead Ed's boring lecture dwelling on the relationship she had ruined. It was the most precious relationship, with the most precious man, and it ended because she was stubborn.

The end of the lecture was greatly welcomed with a big sigh of relief. Jessie gathered her books together and placed them into her bag. Lisa waited for her and suggested they go out at the weekend, but Jessie was just not feeling up to it. They walked slowly across the car park towards Jessie's little blue Ford Ka while Lisa outlined ten or more reasons why she needed to go out instead of isolating herself again. Jessie wasn't really listening, she was completely fixated on the back of the black Mazda RX8 parked next to her Ka.

"Lisa." Her voice anxious. "That's Dean's car. There." She pointed. "Parked next to mine."

"What is..." She froze. "Jessie. He's—"

The car door opened. Dean stepped out and stood between the two cars.

"Here." Jessie's heart pounded. She mirrored his footsteps, getting closer and closer to each other. All her senses aware of his presence, longing to smell him.

He paused within an arms length of her. "I'm so sorry. I've tried so hard not to do this, but I love you. I can't live without you. Please, Jessie, my Sweet Lips, please come back to me."

Tears streamed down his face, pain evident in his

voice. Her eyes filled with tears, so did Lisa's. He held his hands out and opened his mouth, clearly about to speak. Before he could say or do anything, Jessie threw her arms around him, inhaling the spicy overtones of his fresh woody aftershave, sobbing on his crisp white collar.

"I'm sorry for leaving. I've tried so hard to fight it but I actually really love you." Jessie blubbered through her tears.

Dean took a deep breath. "Good because I love you too, and I've decided that I really do want you to be a consequence that I can live with and treasure for a lifetime."

THE END

ABOUT THE AUTHOR

Tess M Garfield was born in the North of England in the 1970s, finally emigrating down south to the land of opportunity, according to her grandmother, after leaving university. Tess now lives in the East of England in the midst of chaotic family life where the only people who listen are the dogs. She is inspired by her children who are avid readers and knows that her grandmother Dorothy would have been proud.

ALSO BY TESS M GARFIELD

Virtually Strangers – A romantic fiction that will have you torn. Reviewed multiple times as a book you don't want to put down.

COMING SOON – SPRING 2016

Lightning Attraction 2: Surviving the storm – Can Jessie and Dean really move on and live happily ever after?

FOLLOW TESS M GARFIELD ONLINE

https://www.facebook.com/TessMGarfieldAuthor

https://twitter.com/TessMGarfield

https://www.goodreads.com/tessmgarfield

https://tessmgarfield.wordpress.com/

Printed in Great Britain
by Amazon